HER BODY SCREAMED IN PROTEST

It had been too long, too lonely, too empty without David. Chris had never known the kind of agony she was enduring now.

Grasping the rail of the deck tightly, she leaned her head back and closed her eyes. She remembered the way it felt to have him stroke her, his hands warm and intimate, the way it felt to have his moist mouth against her breast...the feel of their hot, aroused bodies straining together. A tortured moan was wrung from her.

"What's the matter, Chris?" David was moving toward her. His muscled body, naked except for cutoffs, was silhouetted against the soft light that spilled from the bedroom.

She fought desperately to master her desire, but she was powerless against the urgent need that possessed her, and her battle was lost the moment he framed her face with his hands....

D1013979

ABOUT THE AUTHOR

Life in Judith Duncan's Calgary household—which includes the romance author, her husband, four children and a snooty cat—is hectic at the best of times. Add to this chaos a computer breakdown and a frantic search for parts only days before the deadline of the author's latest book. The result: Judith Duncan's fourth Superromance, a love story that will move readers to tears.

Books by Judith Duncan

HARLEQUIN SUPERROMANCE

51—TENDER RHAPSODY
77—HOLD BACK THE DAWN
114—REACH THE SPLENDOR
143—WHEN MORNING COMES

These books may be available at your local bookseller.

Don't miss any of our special offers. Write to us at the following address for information on our newest releases.

Harlequin Reader Service
P.O. Box 52040, Phoenix, AZ 85072-2040
Canadian address: P.O. Box 2800, Postal Station A,
5170 Yonge St., Willowdale, Ont. M2N 6J3

Judith Duncan

WHEN MORNING COMES

Harlequin Books

TORONTO • NEW YORK • LONDON
AMSTERDAM • PARIS • SYDNEY • HAMBURG
STOCKHOLM • ATHENS • TOKYO • MILAN

Published December 1984

First printing October 1984

ISBN 0-373-70143-8

Printed in Canada

CHAPTER ONE

THE DANK SMELL of seaweed rose from the watery darkness of the Pacific Ocean and a chilling breeze cut through the fabric of her coat, shrinking her skin with its icy fingers. She was standing on the wharf, the blackness of night enveloping her, her mouth dry with fear.

The months of meticulous and secretive planning, the endless nights of barely controlled panic, the never-ending days of grim anxious waiting were inching toward the unknown finale. He was coming home. After four years he was finally coming home—and the gruesome reality was that she didn't even know if he was coming back dead or alive. Nor would she know until the boat docked. Her insides folded into a knot; her unanswered questions grated at her nerves. Was the nightmare nearly over, or was it just beginning?

Chris Spencer shivered and turned up the collar of her heavy jacket, her hair whipping across her face. She stuck her hands in her pockets, her body huddled against the penetrating cold. The eerie slap of the waves against the barnacle-encrusted pilings and the creaks and groans of the weathered pier were the only sounds she could hear above the low ghostly moan of the wind.

With a fixed gaze, she stared out across the inky water, watching for the running lights of a cabin cruiser. It seemed as if she'd been standing here for an eternity in the cold, her body rigid with paralyzing dread. This waiting, this solitary waiting was a subtle yet refined torture, especially when she didn't even know if they had managed to get him out alive.

Those months of agony, of negotiating, the mad scramble for enough money, might all be for nothing. The only thing the telegram said was that the shipment would be delivered tonight, and even though the terseness of the message had been prearranged to safeguard the operation, its lack of information terrified her. For the millionth time her mind cried out a desperate silent plea for his safety. He had to be alive. He had to be. It couldn't end this way. God, it just couldn't.

The pain, the awful apprehension, the horrible sense of failure she had experienced when they split up was nothing compared to this. Nothing. This all seemed like a badly written drama of dark intrigue and gut-twisting suspense. But it was terrifyingly real.

She turned her back to the biting wind and once again fought down the nervous urge to test the powerful battery-powered light that sat at her feet on the splintered boards of the dock. Peter's instructions had been very clear. She was not, under any circumstances, to turn it on until he signaled her from the boat. It was to be the beacon that brought them safely into the sheltered cove, undetected. They could not risk discovery—not now.

The familiar twist of guilt unfolded within her. If it hadn't been for all the bitterness, the resentments, the vicious accusations they had leveled at each other, David would never have gone to Central America in the first place. He wouldn't have been caught in a violent rebellion; he wouldn't have been used as a human pawn in the deadly game of political chess.

And it was a deadly game—a game that had begun several months earlier and was now locked in a grim stalemate in which human beings were ruthlessly exterminated in the quest for unconditional victory. As more and more atrocities were exposed, the situation became even more dangerous and unpredictable.

The opening move in the life-and-death match for power had been an unexpected rebel uprising in the small unstable republic. When the left-wing insurgents had tried to overthrow the existing military regime, the fighting had been bloody and violent. In a play for international intervention, the guerrilla forces had taken thirty-two influential foreign nationals as political hostages and attempted to force their governments into negotiating with them, thereby acknowledging the rebels as a political power to be reckoned with. David Spencer had been one of the thirty-two.

His family was the major shareholder of a Canadian corporation that had developed a vast mining industry in the impoverished country. Because of the immense internal wealth generated by these newly discovered natural resources, the military junta had found new popularity among the people.

As a Canadian, David wouldn't have been a primary target for political abduction, but as David Spencer, director of LaFontaine Minerals International, he was. The success of the mining operation was one of the trump cards the existing government held, and by capturing David, the rebels were trying to force the government of the republic into negotiating with them.

The Spencer family had been anxious to pay a vast ransom for his release, but the left-wing forces refused to deal with them. They needed full control of the mining industry, along with LaFontaine's guarantee of assured cooperation in supporting a leftist takeover. Heavy political pressure had been brought to bear on LM International. World leaders pleaded that the company not give in to the insurgents' demands. An ugly political eruption in the country could create shock waves that would be felt around the world. The left-wing rebel forces had strong links with the Soviet Union, and if they were to attain power in the small republic, a definite threat to Western security would result.

The actual news of the abduction, which had taken place more than nine months ago, was bad enough, but when reports started to filter out about the horrendous conditions the hostages were enduring, Chris had suffered keenly. What had been the final breaking point had been the films.

An Australian reporter who had managed to make contact with the rebel leader had smuggled films of the stronghold and the prisoners out to the free world. When she had seen how appalling the conditions were, Chris simply couldn't endure any more. That night she decided she could no longer sit there like some passive vegetable and do nothing but wait helplessly for the inevitable news that David had died from starvation or abuse.

She had called Dr. Peter Larsen, a close friend of David's whom she hadn't seen since she and David split up. Peter had spent five years in Central America with the World Health Organization and he was familiar with the political system there. He fully understood how remote the chances were of David coming out alive if something didn't happen soon.

The outcome of that renewed contact was an insane rescue plan, and that plan required a crack mercenary commando team to pull if off. All Chris needed was money—a staggering amount of money—and she knew she didn't dare go to the Spencer family for help.

With the exception of maintaining weekly contact with her two young sons, the Spencers had completely severed all association with her since David had left Canada, and she doubted they would even speak to her let alone support her in a highly risky attempt to get him out. The second reason was that she had a strong gut feeling if they knew what she was planning, they would try to prevent her from going ahead, fearing such a wild scheme would put David in even greater danger. One way or another, they had the resources to stop her before she ever got started.

For the very first time, Chris was truly grateful for the generous settlement she had received from David when the marriage collapsed. He had given her full title to their luxurious home and all its contents, plus an income-producing property: a large block of apartments in downtown Vancouver. Unable to unload the pricey properties on such short notice, she had mortgaged everything to the hilt to raise the required money.

The refinancing of the two properties had yielded a fortune in ready cash, and as it turned out, Chris had needed every cent. As an added incentive she had contracted the mercenaries on the basis that if they brought David out alive, they would each receive an additional fifty thousand dollars.

The first meeting with the retired British major who commanded the mercenary force clearly defined that the actual strategy for the rescue was to be left in the hands of the mercenaries, with all final plans to be approved by Peter and Chris.

The one critical decision they had left entirely to

the major was how David was to be snatched from the fortified compound. That detail would be plotted only after the commando leader and some of his men had infiltrated the area and evaluated the security measures of the camp. It was agreed, however, that David's disappearance would appear to be an act of insurrection by a known splinter group within the rebel forces.

Because of the unpredictability of the guerrilla commander it was imperative that the lives of the other prisoners were not jeopardized by a news leak. It had been unanimously agreed that David's return to Vancouver Island must remain a closely guarded secret, and until David was well enough to advise them on how to handle the volatile situation, his return to Canada would be revealed only to a select few.

From the films, both Peter and Chris realized that if they got him back alive he would be in dire need of medical care for some time. Consequently, over the past few weeks Peter had equipped his secluded retreat on the west coast of the island with medical supplies and drugs he thought might be needed, providing David's condition was stable enough to avoid hospitalization—and *if* he survived the trip.

When, after countless hardships, the rescue squad finally reached the southern coast of Mexico, they managed to get word to Peter that David was in extremely critical condition. Since then Peter and

Chris had heard nothing. Chris had been adamant right from the beginning—whether dead or alive, she wanted David brought home. Now she was waiting, fear gnawing at her.

With the back of her hand she wiped away the tears the cold wind had drawn, then she huddled again in the thick wool of her coat. If only they would come and end this never-ending wait.

Peter had left hours ago to travel to a rendezvous point several miles off the Canadian coast. There he would meet with a cargo-carrying Portuguese vessel that had David and two members of the commando squad on board. Chris didn't want to think of the problems they could encounter transferring David from one vessel to another. Even the weather seemed to be working against them. It was uncommonly cold and stormy for July, and the last thing Peter needed to contend with on a pitch-black night was rough seas.

Peter's cabin had been built on the rocky point of a broad, heavily treed peninsula, which swept out from the rugged coastline in a southward direction to form a deep sheltered bay. Below the craggy bluff, the rock formation folded in sharply to create a safe secluded harbor that was usually protected from the pounding tide. But tonight the harbor was fully exposed to the cut of the wind. Chris could have watched for the signal from the bank of windows in the living room of the cabin, but it was as though her body had been relentlessly drawn to the beacon light. Never before could she recall time passing with such agonizing slowness.

As she stood there, her body hunched against the wind and dampness, she tried not to think about what might be transpiring on the cruiser. And she tried not to let her mind wander back in time. It was all too painful. But as the minutes dragged by, it became more and more difficult to remain detached and unthinking.

If she was honest with herself—and she was usually brutally so—her obsession to bring David home was twofold. The obvious reason was to save his life, and that was the main driving force behind the months of unbearable tension. But the second reason was probably more vital to her own well-being: she needed a chance to try to right a terrible wrong.

She desperately wanted to tell David she was sorry—more sorry than he would ever know. She had made so many unforgivable mistakes, had reacted so immaturely and said so many untrue, bitterly unkind things in the past. Something deep inside her needed him to know that she regretted what she had done. It wasn't that she expected forgiveness, what she prayed for instead was just the chance to tell him she had been wrong, so very wrong.

A large wave broke against the end of the dock and sent a spray of salt water into the darkness, dampening her face with a chilling sting. She wiped the wetness away and glanced at the sky. There was no sign of a star. The dense cloud cover was still hanging over the island, and though she couldn't see it, she could sense the thick shroud of fog the stiff breeze was rolling in from the sea.

Peter had hoped that both the cloud cover and the fog would hold for camouflage. Any delay at the rendezvous would mean a risk of encountering one of the many fishing vessels that plied the coast. A responsible seagoer who witnessed a transfer from a foreign ocean-going ship would likely notify the Canadian Coast Guard, and that was the last thing Chris and Peter wanted to have happen.

A feeling of forewarning slithered down her spine, sending a shiver through her, and Chris tried to penetrate the curtain of blackness before her. She could see nothing, but she thought she detected the far-off reverberation of diesel engines. She was instantly alert, her head turned as she listened intently, trying to tune out the intruding sounds of the wind and the tide. The throaty rumble became more distinct, and she let her gaze slowly sweep across the expanse of night. Off to the south she detected a faint glimmer of light. Her muscles tensed and fear drove her stomach down, twisting it into a hard cold lump.

She knelt down by the beacon, her eyes transfixed on the enlarging specks of light that undulated through the darkness. The sound became a steady throb as the craft neared the coastline, and Chris waited, her breathing arrested, her numb fingers on the switch. Waiting. Watching.

Then it came—the two flashes from a blue light. Her body trembling, she flicked on the switch. The brilliant beam slithered across the heaving oily surface of the water in a weird tunnel of light, which only intensified her fear and sense of isolation. She stared at the incoming craft with such unblinking resoluteness that her eyes began to water. At last the shape of the cruiser emerged from the ebony night, and she was able to detect the outline of two men on the bow.

The sound of the powerful engines dropped in pitch as Peter smoothly navigated alongside the wharf, the white hull of the boat brushing against the tires that hung suspended on the structure. The impact echoed with a hollow thump. For a moment Chris was unable to move, then very slowly she stood up, her clenched fists rammed in her pockets, her face a bloodless mask. She waited, a slight solitary figure in the night.

The rumble from the diesels died, leaving in its wake only the slap of waves against the hull. It seemed to take forever as an unfamiliar figure secured the sleek bobbing craft to the pier, and the band of apprehension tightened in Chris's chest, compressing her lungs with a painful weight.

A tall lean man sprang lightly onto the dock, and Chris moved toward him, her muscles stiff with cold and fear. "How is he, Peter?"

Peter Larsen wrapped his arms around her shaking form and held her tight, his voice edged with concern. "He's alive, Chris, but he's in bad shape."

She experienced a nearly paralyzing wave of relief, which was quickly followed by overwhelming alarm, and she was sure her knees would have buckled if Peter hadn't been holding her up. Resting her forehead against his chest, she made herself take several deep breaths in an attempt to discipline her trembling body into some semblance of calmness.

Peter caught her white face in his hands, his touch like ice against her already chilled flesh. "Hang in there, kid," he said quietly, his voice carrying a sober warning. "We've got a long night ahead of us yet."

She took another deep shaky breath and stared up at him, meeting his dark worried look with one of her own. Her jaw clenched in a rigid line, she nodded her head and squared her shoulders. Peter patted her cheek, then turned away.

Two men were bringing the stretcher with David's blanket-wrapped form strapped on it from the cabin below. Their movements were hampered by the pitching of the boat, and Peter strode down the pier to assist in the operation, the light from the lantern casting a long wavering shadow before him. Muted voices drifted toward Chris and she nervously licked her lips, the taste of salty sea air permeating her mouth. She raked her hands through her wind-whipped hair, pulling it back from her face as she watched them lower the stretcher onto the dock. It took all the restraint she possessed to keep from rushing to David. The one thing that held her back was the knowledge that the two men who attended him would not appreciate her coming close enough to see their faces.

Peter's voice broke from the darkness. "Start up the path with the lantern, Chris, but take it slow and give us as much light as you can."

Her hands were so numbed by cold she could barely unclench them, but she picked up the heavy light and started to slowly climb the winding rocky path that led up the rugged escarpment to the natural clearing at the top where the cabin was located. The only sound she was conscious of was the heavy pounding of her heart; her senses were nearly as numb as her body. It was over. The waiting was over. Now the agony of watching over him as he fought to survive would begin—and that was going to be just as difficult to endure.

The progress of the men was slowed by the winding uneven trail, and it seemed to take forever to reach the smooth planked surface of the sun deck that skirted the log structure. Chris opened the patio door that led into the bedroom and switched off the lantern she carried in her hand. The heat radiating from the fireplace stung her cheeks as she set the light on the hearth, then turned around.

The large cozy room had been stripped of the king-size bed to make room for a hospital bed and another single cot. Folding back the covers of the bed, Chris glanced quickly around the room in a final check, then left, closing the door firmly behind her.

She was shaking so badly she could barely undo the zipper of her coat, and she wasn't sure if it was from shock or the penetrating cold she had endured for so long. She seemed to be functioning in a vague nebulous vacuum—nothing was real, nothing registered. It took a conscious effort for her to walk to the fireplace in the living room and add two more logs to the dwindling flames, then with sharp jerky movements, she removed her coat and tossed it on a chair. She folded her arms tightly in front of her and stood before the fire, her eyes fixed in a glassy stare as she watched the flames lick around the white bark of the birch logs.

A dream—it all seemed like such a bizarre disjointed dream.

"Where's the rest of the money, Chris?"

She turned around to find Peter standing in the doorway of the bedroom, his drawn face lined with utter exhaustion. She motioned to a case on the floor by the door. "The money's in that briefcase, and there's a lunch and a thermos of coffee in the hamper. I thought they might want to take something with them."

He nodded as he picked up the two items. "Are the keys in the car?"

"Yes, and the lease papers are in the glove compartment—there are road maps there, too." Her voice sounded strangely artificial to her.

Peter turned to go, then he paused and faced her again. With a heavy sigh he leaned against the closed door, a defeated sag to his body, and stared at her with solemn contemplation. After a moment he wearily rubbed his hand across the back of his neck and said quietly, "There was a bit of bad luck at the compound, Chris. Two of our group were shot by guards when they went in after David. They didn't have a chance."

Chris's face didn't reveal a flicker of emotion, but she was sickened by the grim finality of the life-and-death game they'd played. There was a tense silence as she stared blindly at the dancing flames, struggling to come to terms with the revulsion she felt. She would have sold her soul to prevent that kind of loss. Her voice was uneven when she finally spoke. "Is there some question about their share of the money?"

"Yes."

"Ask the major to make the necessary arrangements for their families to get it."

"Okay." Peter watched her, his eyes dark with compassion. He picked up the briefcase and absently checked the lock as he tried to find the right words to ease her guilt and anguish. "They were well aware of the risks they were taking," he said softly.

Chris turned to face him, her lips colorless, her eyes bleak. "But that doesn't change the fact that they died, Peter." She wrapped her arms tightly around herself. "Tell them that I'm truly sorry."

Soberly, Peter nodded. He placed his hand on the doorknob and his tone became more inflexible. "I don't want you in here until I have a chance to talk to you first, okay?"

She stared at him, her dark hazel eyes assessing his expression, then she tipped her head back and closed her eyes, not wanting to acknowledge the concern she saw in his. "Is he that bad?"

"Chris, it's been...."

She looked at him, her eyes like flint, her voice flat. "Answer me, Peter."

He let out his breath in a harsh rush. "Yes, he's that bad."

Chris turned toward the fire. "I see."

From behind her, his voice was a monotone. "Give me about half an hour. I want to get an IV going so we can get some antibiotics into him."

"He's unconscious then?"

"Yes." There was another pause, then he said with quiet determination, "We'll pull him through, Chris, come hell or high water."

She realized that intractable tone was meant to reassure her, to give her courage. But that reassurance was short-lived. When she finally saw David, the shock was devastating. She wouldn't have believed it was him except for the crescent-shaped scar above his left eyebrow. The man in the bed was unrecognizable. He was an emaciated skeleton, his body covered with ugly festering sores, his bones visible through taut unhealthy skin. His thick dark hair hung in an unkempt tangle to his shoulders, and he was heavily bearded.

For the first time in her life Chris felt hysteria welling up in her, and she clenched her teeth together to keep from crying out. With shaking fingers she reached out and gently brushed his hair back from his deathlike face. He was so hot, so scalding hot, that she nearly jerked her hand away.

The cool touch of her hand against his face must have penetrated his fevered coma. His eyes fluttered open and for a brief second he stared up at her ashen face, his bewilderment registering before his eyelids drifted shut again. Another stab of pain knifed through her as he slowly mouthed, "Christine," and once again she was launched into a new terrifying nightmare.

AND IT WAS a nightmare—a day-and-night vigil beside his bed, watching him fight for his life against a stubborn infection that poisoned his blood, his wasted body offering no resistance to the disease's tenacious hold.

Peter seemed to understand Chris's need to be with David constantly and said nothing, but he watched her, worry embedded in his expression. Every time she bathed the unconscious man in an attempt to cool his fever, some of the abscesses on his body would erupt, filling the room with a nauseous stench. She wouldn't even flinch, but would continue to bathe him, talking to him quietly the entire time.

It wasn't until the fourth day that there was any improvement in his condition, and when the break came, it was dramatic. Chris awoke at dawn and was instantly aware of the change in the man who slept in the bed next to hers. His breathing was less labored and more regular.

Her pulse racing, she slipped off the cot and went to David. She laid her hand on his face. His temperature was finally down. Cradling his ravaged face in her hands, she closed her eyes and bent her head in heartfelt thanksgiving. He was better—so much better. She stood there for a long time, completely motionless, savoring a respite from the fear that had been her constant companion. At last, after drawing the blankets up, she quietly left the room.

Peter was sleeping on the hideaway bed in the living room, his long body sprawled facedown on a tangle of blankets. She touched his shoulder. "Peter?"

He groaned and rolled over slowly, his unshaven face imprinted with the pattern of the quilt he'd been lying on. It took a massive effort for him to get his eyes open, and when he did they were still groggy and unfocused.

For the first time in days Chris managed a smile. "You'd better wake up, Doctor, and tell me I'm not dreaming."

Instantly alert, he sat up, the top of his track suit bunched up around his chest. "What is it?" He shook his head sharply and looked at her with a penetrating stare. He didn't have to ask anything more—the look on her face answered his question. Without another word he bolted off the bed and headed for the bedroom.

Chris's eyes never left Peter's face as he checked David, his expression intent, his attention unwavering. After giving his patient a thorough examination, he tossed his stethoscope on the end of the bed and combed his hands through his tousled hair. Looking across the bed at her, he let out his breath in a rush of relief. "God, I can't believe it. I just can't believe it. He's so much better. That new antibiotic really knocked the hell out of that infection."

The elated relief she had experienced gave way to a feebleness that left her shaking, and Chris sank down on the edge of the cot. Propping her elbows on her thighs, she rested her forehead against her clasped hands and struggled against the overwhelming emotions that encompassed her. God, she had been so scared, so damned scared.

Sensing her distress, Peter came over and sat down beside her, his arm a comforting weight around her trembling shoulders. "What's the matter?" he asked softly.

It took a while for Chris to regain her composure, but when she finally raised her head, she fixed her solemn gaze on David's face. "I've been so scared for so long, anything else but fear seems like a foreign emotion." Her voice grew husky as profound gratitude constricted her throat. "I think I would have gone stark-raving mad long before now if it hadn't been for you."

He withdrew his arm from around her shoulder and took one of her hands in his, a disconcerted frown appearing on his face as he stared unseeingly at their interlaced fingers. "I want to say something, Chris, and I hope like hell it isn't out of line, but it's important that I do say it." He looked at her, his eyes serious. "I was pretty peeved at you when you left David, and without knowing the whole story I laid all the blame on your doorstep. It's taken me a damned long time to sort it out, but whatever caused your breakup was between you two, and I had no right to make biased judgments." His grasp tightened and he looked away, as though he was too ill at ease to hold her gaze. "Over the past few months I've come to realize that I, for one, have treated you very badly, and I feel like a bastard."

Clasping his hand with a firmness that wordlessly absolved him of any fault, Chris readily dismissed the past. "None of that really matters anymore. What does matter is that you were there when I needed you most." She gave him a tired little half smile as he looked at her. "Now where do we go from here?"

Releasing her hand, he stood up and stretched, his attention fixed on David. "If you don't mind being left alone, I think I'll take another blood sample and urine specimen into the lab." He turned and looked at her, his long lean hands resting on his hips. "How long before the boys are back?"

"David's parents wanted them for a month, so I really don't expect them back much before that. They've been gone just a little over a week now."

"Where did they go?"

"Disney World—then they're going to go deep-sea fishing off Florida."

The tone of her usual melodious voice was flat and unemotional. Peter squinted at her. "David's folks cut you off pretty harshly, didn't they?"

Chris tried to keep her voice noncommittal. "There was a lot of bitterness, Peter. People don't get over that very easily." She stood up and began straightening the bedding on the cot, deliberately dodging his penetrating look. She did not want him uncovering those old wounds. "I'd rather not talk about it."

"Yeah...well..." he said with a touch of awkwardness. He moved the blood-pressure equipment away from the bed, rolled up his stethoscope and placed it on the bedside table. "Is there anything you need from town?"

"No. . .unless you want to stop by the house and see if there's any mail."

Peter turned toward her, his face relaxing in a lopsided grin. "Mother is hoping for at least some postcards from her vagabond family, I take it."

"I hope—a month is a long time." That was part of the reason for her anxiety, but the other factor was that the boys weren't really that old. Tim was just ten and Mark was turning eight that summer, and both of them were inclined to get homesick if they were gone too long.

But the length of their absence simply couldn't be helped this time. She had to let them go with their grandparents for the month because of this whole clandestine affair with David. Even under the circumstances, Chris had experienced grave misgivings about it, but she had no alternative. She wanted their father up and well before they saw him—*if* they saw him.

David had made a point of keeping in touch with his sons. They spent a few days of Christmas vacation with him, usually part of the summer holidays, and they always went skiing in Aspen, Colorado, during spring break. They adored him, and it would have been a devastating shock to them to see him in the condition he was in now. She had deliberately played down the hostage drama, telling them just enough to satisfy their questions. She desperately wanted to protect them from the real horror of the situation if she could.

Her face became reflective as she fluffed up the pillow and placed it on the cot. She wished that she felt more comfortable about the boys spending so much time with David's parents, but she had a nagging feeling that since she and David had split, grandpa and grandma made no effort to hide their disapproval of her from the boys.

"You finish up in here, and I'll start breakfast," offered Peter. "I'd like to leave for town fairly soon so I can get to the lab before the morning rush. And I want to phone the States first thing, as well. I'm hoping I'll be able to get the results of the lab work we're having done at the tropical research center. We don't want some new crisis like a tropical disease or some weird fungus cropping up unexpectedly if we can avoid it."

Chris drew her hand across the bed, smoothing the wrinkles in the blanket, then tucked the bedding under the mattress. "In the condition he's in, he couldn't even handle a complication as minor as a slight cold right now."

Peter stared at her for a moment, his eyes clouding with worry as he studied the dark circles under her eyes. He opened his mouth to comment on her own condition, but decided against it. He shook his head and left the room.

With swift efficiency Chris finished tidying up the room, then turned her attention to the man in the bed. His condition had dramatically improved, but his unconsciousness was worrying her—really worrying her. She kept her concern to herself, though. Peter knew what he was doing; he didn't need her fluttering around like some high-strung neurotic.

With infinite gentleness she touched David's face as she gazed down at him. He looked more familiar now. He had been so acutely dehydrated, but the intravenous had alleviated that symptom and given him a slightly fuller appearance. She and Peter had been forced to crop off the beard to treat the abscesses on his face, and even that made him seem less alien. But he was still so gaunt, so hollow looking—and so deathly still.

She smoothed his hair back off his forehead, then drew the sheet up over his inert form. "Don't quit fighting, David," she whispered. "Please don't quit fighting." His eyelids fluttered ever so slightly and his lips parted, but he didn't stir. The coma held him fast.

After breakfast Chris had a quick shower while Peter was busy with David, and then she slipped into a clean pair of blue jeans and a baggy yellow sweater and returned to the sickroom.

Peter had just finished taking a sample of blood from David's arm, and as Chris approached the bed, he released the rubber tourniquet from around his friend's forearm with a little snap. He placed the vials of blood in his medical bag, then looked at Chris. "Do you still remember how to use the marine radio on the boat?"

She gave him a quizzical look and nodded. "I think so. It's pretty straightforward. Why?"

"If something comes up and you need me in a hurry, you'll have to contact me on that. I don't have a phone, remember?"

Chris did remember; she just hadn't had a reason to give it much thought. Peter's log cabin, though very rustic, had all the luxuries of home, everything except a phone—and that had been a deliberate omission. The cabin had been his hideaway for years.

He snapped the bag closed and picked up his jacket. "Do you want to come down to the dock and I'll run you through the procedure for using the radio?"

"No, it won't be necessary. You don't forget things like that." That wasn't exactly the truth, but Chris did not want to go on that cruiser unless she absolutely had to. The boat had been placed in Peter's care when David left Canada, but it was, in fact, David's. That boat held many memories for Chris, memories she'd just as soon hold at bay if she possibly could.

"Okay, I'm off then. I shouldn't be gone more than a few hours. You're sure you don't want anything?"

"Not that I can think of. This is very basic living out here." She followed him out the patio door and stepped onto the veranda, which encircled the cabin. Relishing the feel of the warmth from the early-morning sun on her face, she turned the corner and silently followed Peter along the north end of the cabin. She watched him amble to his car, his long lean body moving with the muscled gracefulness that spoke of a former basketball player; his untidy sandy hair gave him the look of a small boy. She raised her hand in farewell as he climbed into the car, then waited for him to turn the car and drive away before turning back.

The bedroom had a western exposure with a breathtaking view of the rugged coastline and the ocean. She leaned against the railing for a moment, absorbing the incredible panorama spread before her.

She was a child of the sea, tuned to its everchanging moods, its surging and ebbing tides, its foam-crested depths. It was her source of energy, her source of peace, forever calling out to her in an arousing frenzy with its crashing surf, or whispering to her of ethereal mysteries with its gentle ebb. Its spirit was hers, and she knew some vital part of her would die if she ever left it.

Chris tilted her head back and closed her eyes, absorbing the soft murmurings of the wind and water, tasting the freshness of the sea breeze, its soft caress feathering across her face. For the first time in months, an untroubled tranquility seeped through her, pushing aside the grim shadows of doubt that had tormented her for so long. She could feel her tense tired muscles beginning to relax as a soothing lethargy infused her, neutralizing her weariness, easing the stress caused by too many pressures. Peace. The sound of the sea. It was the balm she so desperately needed.

Stretching like a cat, she turned and stepped back into the bedroom, the wind fanning the loose tendrils of hair across her cheek. It took a moment for her eyes to adjust to the dimness of the room, but when they did, she felt as if her insides were being sucked out.

He was awake and watching her, his penetrating blue eyes riveted on her. His look of loathing immobilized her with an odd paralysis, and she stared back at him. Brief segments of old memories flipped through her mind as she stood there, entrapped by his gaze, and suddenly she felt very alone.

CHAPTER TWO

A VOICE HAD PENETRATED through his pain, its golden huskiness luring him to the edge of the drifting semiconsciousness that held him prisoner. It was a familiar haunting voice, and he struggled through the waves of grayness to reach it. It seemed as if he had been swimming for a very long time toward that voice, which kept calling to him, and his exhaustion, like a weight, was holding him back. But finally the fog began to roll away and he became fully aware. The dream was real.

She was standing just outside the door, her profile turned toward him as she gazed at some distant view. Her hair was swept in a soft knot on the top of her head, and loose tendrils feathered around her face. Sunshine glinted in the light brown silken sheen, highlighting the gleam of gold.

He'd always liked her hair best that way, the style exposing a long slim neck and classic jawline. It gave her finely featured face a whimsical fragile appearance that made him think of some mystical free spirit. Even from a distance he could see the long thick sweeping eyelashes, which accentuated eyes that were like a sorceress's: mesmerizing, bewitching, fathomless. Haunting eyes, which had tormented him through countless nights.

Like a ballerina, she stretched, her body arching gracefully and exposing the firm fullness of her breasts beneath a yellow sweater that seemed vaguely familiar. That movement sent a deep pain slicing through him, and that pain kindled an anger he had lived with for four years. He would never forgive her for ripping his world apart. Never.

She turned and stepped into the room, the softly draped cowl neck of her sweater emphasizing her slender neck and delicate face. As he stared at her, bitterness welled up inside him. He licked his dry cracked lips and spoke, "What in hell are you doing here?" He had wanted his words to be hard and cutting, but they came out a hoarse whisper.

He saw it happen. He saw her tense, a guarded look registering in her expressive eyes, and it was only then he knew for certain he wasn't dreaming. Confusion swept in, neutralizing the anger. Where was he? What had happened?

As if sensing his bewilderment, she came toward him, her voice soothing and calm. "You're back in Canada, David. Peter brought you back four days ago, and right now you're in his cabin."

Reality began to register. The open beams of a log cabin he'd helped build, the smell and the sound of the sea, the softness of a bed beneath him—and her. He closed his eyes and swallowed, his mouth dry and parched. Confusion...fragmented images...a sense of lost time...it all pressed in on him, and the grayness began to eddy through his brain. Panic began to rise within him as he felt this dream, this shadowy dream slipping away from him, and he fought to hold on to it.

There was a movement beside him, and her arm slipped beneath his shoulders, the familiar fragrance of her hair permeating his senses. "Would you like a drink?"

Her voice calmed his agitation, and he responded. It took an immense effort for him to open his eyes and assure himself that Chris was indeed supporting him, a glass of water with a straw in it held in her hand. He was barely able to move his head in assent, and her hold on him tightened as he took the straw in his mouth. Water. Clean cold water. A racking thirst had possessed him for so long that he could think of nothing but satisfying that terrible need. But even the simple act of drawing water through the straw sapped what little strength he had, and he could feel beads of perspiration dampening his brow.

He was really sweating. He'd been parched for such a hellish eternity he had forgotten what it felt like to sweat. But the fog swirled in again, clouding his mind. Water. Chris. The smell of her.

"Easy, David," she murmured. "Peter said you could only have a few ounces at a time."

He didn't even have the strength to protest as she

eased him back. His energy spent, he lay there with his eyes closed, loathing her for denying him the satisfaction of quenching his gnawing thirst. Damn her. Damn her control over him.

The sound of running water was like a torture, feeding the rage that was building in him. She was just like those bloody-minded bastards who tormented him with water and then always denied it. A cool draft touched his skin as she drew back the covers, and with a gentle touch that was so distinctly hers, she began to bathe him. The warm moistness was like a balm against his heated flesh. His anger subsided beneath her tender ministrations, and his thoughts drifted into a dreamlike state, unconnected by time or place.

A sharp burst of pain in his shoulder and a vile smell penetrated that odd suspended feeling, and he clenched his teeth. A cold fear cut through him: it was all a dream. The pain, the odor was real. The ugly reality. He had only escaped his living hell in his mind. He was still trapped in that foul pit of a cage, a stinking, lice-infested straw mattress beneath him. The will to survive was strong within him but his strength had been starved away, and he could only twist weakly beneath the hands that held him.

"David—I'm sorry. I know I'm hurting you." The voice was so strained that it reached through his pain and he forced his eyes open. Chris was bending over him, her face pale, her eyes tormented. "Another boil ruptured on your shoulder and I have to clean it. It's going to sting." He touched her hand, and the feeling of relief was so overpowering it was almost sickening. She was real. Warm and real.

He closed his eyes in compliance and fought to hang on to this link with sanity, his awareness focusing on the touch of her hands upon him. He drifted in and out of consciousness as she tended to him, but when she drew up the covers a feeling of panic coursed through him. She was going to leave, and he couldn't let her go. She was his only link.

"Don't go," he whispered, his voice hoarse. Her hands gently framed his face and he looked up at her.

Her eyes were dark with compassion as she softly caressed his brow, her touch cool and soothing. "I have to go wash my hands, then I'll come back and give you another drink. Would you like a glass of milk?"

He nodded his head slightly in assent, his gaze welded on her. As she moved away from him he turned his head, his eyes never leaving her for a second as she moved around the room. When she left him alone to go to the kitchen, fear kept him alert and he waited tensely. It seemed to take an eternity, but finally she returned.

Setting a glass of milk on the table by his bed, she gazed down at him. "I'm going to raise the head of the bed a little so you can drink from the glass. If it's uncomfortable, tell me, David." She touched the controls that were clipped to his pillow, her eyes fixed on his face for any indication of pain. When she had him in a semireclining position, she sat down on the edge of the bed, slipped her arm under his shoulders and placed the glass against his lips.

Never in his life had he tasted anything as good as that sweet cold milk, and he drank it greedily. When he finished, Chris started to ease him back against the pillows, but with a massive effort fueled by desperation, he dragged his arm up and laid it across her back, holding her against him. "Don't go," he said again.

Turning, she set the glass on the table and slipped her arms around him, her breasts pressed against his chest. He felt her take a ragged breath, then she buried her face against his neck, her embrace tight and secure. Closing his eyes, he let her fragrance envelop his senses, and for the first time in many months David Spencer did not seek the refuge of unconsciousness. This was real, too real to let escape.

God, but it felt so good to hold her and smell the clean freshness of her. This was a reality he expected never to know again. But eventually exhaustion did claim him and he slept soundly, his confused and battered mind locked onto a single thought: as long as he had physical contact with her, he would awake in this reality rather than in the horror of his previous hell.

The late-afternoon sun was slanting in through the

patio doors when he awoke again, but Chris was still beside him, her arm draped over the stainless-steel rails of the bed, her hand firmly clasping his. David swallowed with difficulty, loathing the sour taste in his mouth. "Could I have another drink?"

She had been gazing out the window, and she shifted her pose to look down at him, a smile softening the lines of exhaustion around her mouth. "I was beginning to think you were going to sleep all day." Smoothing her hand across his forehead, she combed her fingers through his tangled hair, brushing it back from his damp brow. "Do you want water or milk?" she asked softly.

He tried to smile back at her. "I'd like a tooth-brush—and a cold beer." His voice was so weak it was barely audible.

Chris stared at him blankly for a moment, then the weariness in her eyes gave way to a glimmer of amusement. "The toothbrush I can manage, but Peter would skin me alive if I gave you a beer, David."

He shifted his head against the pillow and sighed. "The toothbrush...will have to do then."

The brief flash of lightness seemed to drain out of her as she touched his shoulder, her voice heavy with distress. "Your mouth is badly ulcerated and your gums are infected. It's going to hurt like hell."

It took him such an effort to answer her. "I'd rather have the pain...than the taste."

Her eyes clouded and she bit her bottom lip in

that expression of concern he remembered so well. She didn't say anything, but squeezed his hand before releasing it. He watched her walk into the bathroom, her shoulders set against the coming ordeal.

He really thought he had enough strength to manage the simple task of brushing his own teeth, but it was simply beyond him, and he experienced a certain resentment having to let her do it. He could taste blood in his mouth, and the bite of the toothpaste scalded the sores, but it was a strangely comforting kind of pain: it was a part of this existence, not part of the one he had endured for nine months. And the toothpaste tasted good.

It took Chris a long time to do a thorough job, and by the time she was finished, her face was pale and drawn. David looked at her, a touch of dry humor surfacing. "Dental hygiene hasn't been a major priority lately."

He saw her swallow hard before she forced a smile. "Shame on you, David." She wiped his mouth and placed a glass of water against his lips. By the time he'd finished drinking it he was so exhausted he could barely move his hands, and he could feel a film of perspiration breaking out on his body. Chris carefully wiped his face and neck with a damp cloth, then grasped the rail of the bed to raise it. It was as though she was closing a trap on him, and anger ignited in him.

"No—don't," he demanded, his voice harsh.

Her eyes flew to his face, then she looked away and a sudden tautness immobilized her expression. She straightened the blankets that covered him, the jerkiness of her movements revealing that his abruptness had startled her. He realized her silence was a defensive screen to give her time to think of some way to defuse his wrath, and knowing that only irritated him more.

When she finally spoke, her voice was passive. "Would you like me to wheel your bed out on the sun deck for a while?"

He was prepared to stubbornly oppose any suggestion she made, but the irresistible lure of warm sunshine and a cool sea breeze against his skin was too powerful a temptation. Without looking at her he answered tersely, "Yes."

He gritted his teeth. Suddenly he was slammed with an intense loathing for his lack of strength, his dependency on her, but most of all he was filled with loathing for the power, the control she had over him. As she set about moving him outside, his growing resentment knotted in his belly. In his weakened mental state he had nearly succumbed to the spell she wove so well, but he must never forget how close she'd come to destroying him. He had depended on her once, believed in her, and she'd let him down. He had vowed he'd never allow her to get close enough to do that to him again. Never.

He stared rigidly ahead, his jaw set, nurturing the bitterness that was swelling in him. But in his weakened condition he could no longer dictate to his emotions with the single-mindedness he once possessed, and when he saw the scene that unfolded before him like an incredible forgotten dream, his control shattered.

The ocean, the ocean he loved so much was rolling in, the sound of surf crashing across the distance, the sun dancing over the heaving cresting water with blinding brilliance. Seagulls cried out as they soared overhead, and the smell of the sea filled his nostrils with an invigorating freshness. And it was real—not some illusive memory that tormented him. It was real, and beautiful, and for the first time David truly comprehended that he was free from his sordid nightmare of brutal beatings and never-ending starvation. He had really escaped the horror.

Gut-twisting emotions clawed through him, rising up in his chest to choke him, and he looked away, fighting for control. But his gaze collided with the vision of Chris. She was leaning against the railing, her head slightly to one side, the angle of the sun laying soft shadows across her face. She stood transfixed, like some marble goddess absorbed by the tranquility of her surroundings.

But she was breathing—alive and breathing—and so damned beautiful and so damned real. An agonizing explosion of relief tore through David with the force of an oncoming train. It was no dream. He was really back. He clenched his eyes shut, and his face was twisted by a tortured grimace as a sob was wrested from him. Thank God, the hellish nightmare was over. It was over. Somehow he had managed to survive.

Warm strong arms encircled him, and his anguish gave him strength. He crushed her against him as one tormented sob after another ripped through his ravaged body, and he hung on to her, desperately needing her—needing her as he never had before. She held him in a secure protective embrace that shielded him from the horror, the pain, the torture that was imprinted in his mind, and the excruciating agony of his emotions came boiling out with a violence that was torture in itself.

The only thing David was aware of was the warmth and strength of her soft body pressed tightly against his as she gave him a safe haven from his inner agony. And like his outward festering sores, his emotional abscesses ruptured, purging his mind and soul of the brutal suffering he had somehow survived.

THE NEXT FEW DAYS were oddly disjointed—long lapses of deep sleep fractured by short periods of lucid wakefulness. But no matter what time of day or night he awoke, Chris was always there beside him. David accepted her constant presence with a fatalistic sense of helplessness. But the sense of helplessness was not entirely connected to his physical dependency on her; once again he found himself drawn to her like a moth to a flame. She was as dangerous to him as she was irresistible, but even knowing this, the old intrigue was still there.

Even during the night he would open his eyes to find her asleep on the small cot next to his bed. Her presence and the soft night-light she always kept on were strangely reassuring for him, and he would often simply lie there, watching her sleep. Other times he would fabricate some need so he had an excuse to summon her. All he had to do was murmur her name and she would be instantly awake and tend to him with that gentleness that was so much a part of her.

Day by day he could feel himself growing stronger, both physically and emotionally, but as his strength returned, so did his wariness. Suspicion infiltrated his thoughts again, and he could not fathom why she was there in the first place, nor could he determine what she hoped to gain by staying. Her ceaseless dedication only made him more distrustful.

He had completely trusted her, depended on her once before in his life, but when things started to go wrong between them, she had withdrawn into a silence that had filled him with frustrated rage. He didn't know what she was thinking, what she was feeling, and her mute retreat had put a distance between them that he had found grimly threatening.

Because he didn't understand, because she refused to talk, he had reacted with anger and viciousness. He hadn't wanted to hurt her, but he could see their life crumbling before his very eyes, and it frightened him. He had tried repeatedly to force her into a confrontation, but she only became more and more withdrawn.

Their day-to-day existence had become trapped in a tension-riddled silence as his barely suppressed rage mounted steadily and a sickening helplessness rankled him. That nerve-grating tension mounted until the first explosive incident of ugly words, and from then on, what had once been so special between them deteriorated into the bitter reality of a shattering illusion. The final fragments of that illusion were swept away the day she moved out, taking the two boys with her.

It had taken him a long time to piece his life back together after that, and he swore that he'd never again fall victim to that kind of total dependency on another human being. Now, here he was, once again totally dependent on her. The old bitterness, the old pain, the old resentments began to reassert themselves. If he was foolish enough to allow himself to be trapped in her spell, he wouldn't survive.

David couldn't stop brooding about the past, and the more he did, the more he resented Chris's presence and his reliance on her. He could feel himself being drawn into her web of enchantment and he hated himself for being so damned weak. Finally it got to the point where he simply could not stand to have her around him, and he made no effort to hide how he felt.

He allowed his growing bitterness to insulate him against the wounded look that appeared in her eyes every time he snapped at her. He couldn't trust her. She had walked out on him once before and she would do it again, and he swore he'd be damned certain he'd never subject himself to that hell again.

But one afternoon it was brought home to him how dangerously fragile his defenses against her really were, and he had to admit that not only could he not trust Chris, he couldn't trust himself.

He had reached the stage of his recovery where he was strong enough to be more self-sufficient, and he was reveling in that freedom. He still tired quickly, but he was no longer constantly tied to that damned bed, nor was he dependent on Chris to provide for all his needs.

He was able to manage showering on his own, and that alone was a luxury. After months of filth and squalor, he silently swore that hot water and soap were simple pleasures he'd never take for granted again.

His hair still wet, he slipped into a comfortable track suit and went out on the sun deck.

Peter was there, relaxing in a deck chair and soaking up the sun. He grinned as David sat down in the chair beside him. "You know, you're beginning to look almost human—except for that wild head of hair. Why don't you get Chris to cut it?"

David stared out to sea, his face set in an enigmatic mask. "It can wait."

His friend's voice was clipped with impatience. "Quit acting like a dolt, David. If nothing else, you owe her the courtesy of being civil."

His expression unrevealing, David looked at him. "And what's that supposed to mean?" he asked, his voice hard.

Peter stared at him then looked away, his own face set in stubborn lines. "When you're really interested enough to want to know, I'll tell you."

David leaned back and closed his eyes. He was too tired to get into a hassle over something as stupid as a haircut. "All right," he said with weary resignation. "Get her to cut my hair."

There was the sound of movement, the sound of the patio door opening, then David could hear indistinct voices from inside the cabin. Only a short time elapsed before Chris appeared, a towel, scissors and comb in her hands. Without speaking she wrapped the towel around his neck and shoulders and silently set to work. Not many moments had passed before David bitterly regretted relenting. Her fragrance invaded his senses, and her touch became a tormenting reminder of the past.

Whenever he'd had a bad tension headache, she used to stand behind him and massage his scalp and knotted neck muscles with slow circular movements, her slim strong fingers soothing the dull ache that encompassed his head. She wouldn't speak, she wouldn't hurry, but slowly and silently she'd ease his pain. Her touch was like a calming drug, and eventually he'd relax, his head resting against her abdomen. Invariably she'd slip her arms around him, one hand lying along his jaw, and continue to quietly hold him.

Now, as she carefully cut his hair, the same weakness was permeating his mind, robbing him of coherent thought. She was a sorceress, weaving a spell that would destroy him, and he had to clench his fists and stiffen his spine to keep from resting his head against her. He was still too susceptible to her magic, and he had to fight against the insane longing to surrender. He knew he couldn't trust her, but it was then he knew he couldn't trust himself to maintain his resistance.

By the time she finished he was damp with sweat; his body stiff with tension. The ordeal had drained him of all strength, but he remained rigid and unmoving beneath her hands as she gave his hair a final combing. Neither of them spoke, and it was with a sense of relief that he watched her leave the deck and move down the twisting path that led to the beach. He continued to watch her as she reached the bottom of the rocky butte and climbed over the tangle of logs swept in by countless tides. She started walking along the beach and stooped to pick up a stick, her body moving with unstudied grace as she threw it into the waves. Her movement triggered an image in his mind.

He wondered where the dog was. Downer always romped alongside her when she walked along the shore, eagerly waiting for her to play a game of fetch with him.

He had given her Downer when she'd lost their first baby three months into her pregnancy. He had been so worried about her after the miscarriage and had brought the golden retriever puppy home, hoping it would help ease her grief. If he lived to be a hundred, he would never forget the look on her face when he had given the dog to her. She had looked up at him, her eyes swimming with tears, and he knew he couldn't have done anything that could have given her more comfort or touched her more deeply.

David closed his eyes and clenched his jaw. He had to get away from her or he'd lose his mind. Too many memories came flooding back when he was around her, and he couldn't handle the emotions that came with them. Not now. Sucking in his breath sharply, he stood up. Not now. Not ever.

He entered the cabin through the sliding doors that led into the living room, his mouth set in a grim line. Peter was sitting at the table, a magazine spread out before him and a glass of milk and a sandwich by his elbow.

David took another shaky breath, then spoke. "I don't want her around me any longer, Peter. Either I have to go, or she does."

Peter clamped his lips tight as he considered David's blunt directive. When he looked up, there was a dejected slump to his shoulders. "Could we talk about this before you give me an ultimatum like that?"

"Not if it means discussing Chris and myself," David answered flatly. "What's finished is finished, and I don't want to discuss it."

Peter got up and walked over to the patio door. Resting his hand against the frame, he stared out. "You aren't being very reasonable with her."

David glared at his back, anger flashing in his eyes. "Just out of curiosity, how come you've changed your tune about her? Have the two of you got something going on the side?"

Peter pivoted, a look of disbelief on his face that was quickly obliterated by disgust. "If you weren't half-dead I'd drop you for that comment, my friend," he snapped. "That was a goddamned foul thing to say, and you know it."

David glared at him, his nostrils flaring. "I think maybe I'd better get the hell out of here."

There was a tense silence as Peter clenched and unclenched his hands, struggling to control his temper. Realizing his old friend was not going to relent, no matter what argument he used, Peter sighed and reluctantly yielded. "You can't leave. I'll tell Chris to go."

David slowly expelled his breath to ease the enormous weight in his chest. Narrowing his eyes thoughtfully, he fixed his cool and assessing attention on Peter. "What do you mean I can't leave?" he asked tautly.

"After you cool off, and after I cool off, I'll tell you about it. But right now I think it would be best if you went to bed and got some sleep. I'll go talk to Chris and send her packing."

For some unexplainable reason David was irritated by Peter's callous phrasing, but he said nothing. She was going, and that was all that mattered. Exhaustion dragged at him and he went into the bedroom and collapsed on the bed, trying desperately to ignore the hollow feeling that had settled in his gut. He forced his mind to go blank as he lay there staring rigidly at the ceiling. He didn't want to think, he didn't want to feel—he just wanted to forget.

That incident and the feelings that accompanied it knocked the strength out of him, and for the next two days he did little else but eat and sleep. But on the third day, during those colorless hours of early morning, he began to mull things over, and for the first time he began to speculate about his return to Canada. He remembered nothing about his release, and the comment Peter made about him not being able to leave sparked a critical question. It was all very strange. As soon as he heard Peter stirring in the other room, David got up and dressed, determined to find out what in hell was going on.

He found his friend in the tiny kitchen making breakfast, his hair rumpled, a stubble of beard darkening his face. Leaning against the cupboard, David looked at him, his face sober. "I owe you an apology for that crack about you and Chris, Peter. I'm sorry."

Peter shrugged and grinned lopsidedly at him. "You always were a testy bastard, but I guess I can overlook that flaw in your character."

David's eyes flashed with wry amusement as he took the glass of juice Peter handed him. "Considering you've been doing that since you were six years old, it shouldn't be too much of a strain."

"Yeah. . . well, some of us never learn."

David watched him stir the scrambled eggs, his voice deceptively quiet as he asked, "What did you mean when you said I couldn't leave?"

He had to tolerate a long strained silence as Peter dished up the food and carried the plates to the table. The doctor slouched down in a chair and laced his hands behind his head, his long legs stretching in front of him. A preoccupied look on his face, he focused his full attention on David. "You don't remember anything about leaving the rebel camp, do you?"

"No. The last thing I can remember was a guard putting the boot to me then throwing me in the pit."

Peter pushed the lumps of slightly scorched eggs around on his plate for a moment before he looked at David. "You weren't released, David. You were rescued by a group of mercenaries."

David leaned forward and rested his arms on the table, vaguely aware that his pulse rate had altered. "What do you mean I was rescued?"

Peter stared at him gravely. "I don't know if you're ready for this yet."

David's voice was intractable. "Spit it out, Peter."

There was another tense silence as Peter scrutinized his friend's face, and finally he began to speak. "The entire operation was kicked off about eight months ago—after that Australian reporter, Doug Kellerman, smuggled out some film of the guerrilla stronghold." Peter watched David's face. "Did you see him while he was there?"

"Yes—briefly."

"Well, the pictures he brought out were pretty damned appalling, to say the least. I got a phone call from Chris, and she sounded like she was coming apart."

"From Chris?" David's features were frozen by absolute incredulity, and his voice was hoarse with shock.

Peter raised his eyebrows in an expression that subtly mocked David for his disbelief. "Yes, from Chris, and she was damned near frantic. She'd seen the film on the late-night news." He paused and shook his head slightly as he stared soberly at his plate, his thoughts caught up in unpleasant memories. "It was rough for her, I can tell you that. The whole mess had turned into such a political can of worms that there didn't seem to be any hope for a break in the hostilities." He glanced at David but looked away quickly when he saw how pale he'd become. "Anyway, I went over to see her. She'd come up with this crazy scheme to hire a commando team to get you out. We knew it would take time and one hell of a big bankroll, but we decided to go for it."

David knew very well what an operation like that would cost, and just the thought of the detailed planning to pull it off staggered him. His face felt paralyzed, and his voice was choked when he was finally able to speak. "Where in hell did she raise that kind of money?"

"She mortgaged that block of apartments in Vancouver, as well as the house. And I think she unloaded most of her jewelry."

David squeezed his eyes shut, trying to suppress the sickening feeling that rose in him. Wearily he rested his elbows on the table and locked his fingers together, his hands shielding his face from view as he struggled to come to terms with this unexpected bit of information. What in hell had possessed her, especially after the way he'd treated her when they split up? What had driven her to do it? He raised his head, his voice as colorless as his complexion. "What possessed her to dump everything on a long shot?"

"That's something you're going to have to ask her, David. We kept the personal stuff out of it. In fact, we kept the planning sessions very businesslike. She always seemed so in control, so damned coolheaded. But I have a sneaking hunch if she had ever admitted to herself what a long shot this whole insane plan was, I doubt very much if she could have endured the pressure. As it was, I don't know how she stood it.''

With a powerful thrust of his body, David stood up, sending his chair crashing over. He strode over to the window and stood staring out, his hands jammed in his pockets. Behind him, Peter's explanation continued in a low drone. ''The reason you can't leave is that nobody knows you're back. Your rescue was deliberately staged so it would appear that a splinter group within the rebel force grabbed you.''

David rested his shoulder against the glass and struggled to marshal his fragmented thoughts. But the only thing he could think of was Chris walking down the beach alone, that hurt look in her expressive eyes, a beaten slump to her slender body. He dragged his hand across his face and turned to Peter. ''God, how in hell did you keep from pounding me in the mouth when I demanded you get her out of here?''

Peter gave him a warped grin. ''If it'll make you feel any better, that's the closest I've ever come to drifting you one.''

''Where is she?''

''In town. I've stopped by every morning to let her know how you're doing.'' With careful precision he arranged all his eating utensils on his plate before glancing at David. ''She looks like hell, David.''

''Take me in to see her.''

Peter shook his head. "I won't take you in. You aren't up to that yet, and besides, it's too big a risk. Somebody might see you. I'll contact her on the marine radio in the cruiser, though—we have a pre-arranged signal."

A chilling dread was pumping through his veins as David sat down at the table. If he were in Chris's place, there would be no damned way he'd come back—not after the way he'd treated her the past few days. He had an ugly premonition that she'd refuse to come. Still, he looked at Peter, his voice ragged with guilt when he spoke. "Go get her, Peter."

Peter studied the cutlery arrangement on his plate for a moment and made a minute adjustment to the knife, obviously stalling for time. After a moment he rocked back in his chair and lifted his eyes to look at David with a determined steadiness. "Before I go get her, I think you'd better tell me who Maria is."

David's head jerked up, his eyes narrowing.

Peter avoided meeting his friend's steely gaze. "You were delirious when I went to pick you up, David. All the while you were on IV here, I was administering a light sedative to keep you quiet." He lifted his head, his deep concern apparent. "What we *don't* need now is some unexpected surprise turning up on the doorstep."

David slumped in his chair, deliberately keeping his face devoid of any readable expression as his thoughts splintered into unrelated segments. "Are you going to tell Chris?"

"Not if you don't want me to."

Pushing his plate away, David slowly stood up. Weariness radiated from him as he walked over to the hideaway bed Peter had been sleeping on. He stretched out on his back, his hands behind his head, and stared pensively at the timbered ceiling. He remained silent for a long time, his eyes haunted by troubled thoughts, his gaunt face enigmatic.

As Peter sat down in the easy chair by the bed, David turned his head and looked at him with tormented eyes. "I think we both need to do some talking," he said quietly. "I need to know all the details of my rescue, and you need to know what's been happening in my life."

Peter tipped his head in acknowledgment. "I think you're right." He clasped his hands across his chest and slouched further down in the chair. "How important a role has she played in your life—Maria, I mean."

"That depends on what you mean. If you're asking me if I owe her a great deal, yes, I do. If it hadn't been for her, I wouldn't be here now. But if you're asking me if I love her, no, I don't. I'm obligated to her, I'd do anything humanly possible for her, but I don't love her."

"You'd better give me the whole story, David."

David gave him a twisted smile that held no shred of amusement. "The story isn't one I'm very proud of, my friend."

"All of us have done things we haven't been too

proud of at one time or another," answered Peter.

With a disgusted snort David shook his head. "I think I've used up my lifetime quota of stupid moves."

Peter's voice was quiet. "Why don't you tell me about her and let me make my own judgment?"

David shrugged, a grim set to his mouth as he fixed his gaze on the ceiling. "I met her about a year and a half ago. She's very beautiful, very intelligent, very much like Chris in a lot of ways. We had a brief affair, until I realized I was simply using her to fill up the emptiness. I was honest with her at least, and she seemed to accept how I felt. But when I was taken hostage, Maria went to pieces. She comes from a very wealthy influential family and she had contacts everywhere. Through some of those contacts she established connections with the rebel hierarchy. Once she had an in with them, she managed to negotiate a deal with that bastard Sanchez—"

"Who's Sanchez?" interjected Peter.

The fury in David's voice was barely contained. "He's one of the little Hitlers in the guerrilla movement, and the son of a bitch who was in charge of the hostages."

"So what did Maria do?"

David sucked in a ragged breath as he tried to quell the nausea in his stomach. "She made a deal that she would be his mistress as long as he kept me alive. Every goddamned day he reminded me of that, and he made damned sure that he kept his end of the deal, but just barely." He took another deep breath. "Frankly, I envied the captives who died. Death was a damned sight better than living in that filthy hell hole and knowing what perverted abuse she was enduring because of me."

There was no disguising the horror Peter felt as he breathed, "Good God!"

David looked at him, his face twisted by the ugly recollections. "So I owe her, Peter. God knows, I owe her. But I don't love her." He placed his arm across his eyes, his body trembling. "I don't think I'm capable of those kinds of feelings anymore, and believe me, I loathe myself for what happened to Maria. And now that I know what Chris has been through, I really am convinced it would have been better for everyone if I'd been one of the ones who had been blasted to bits in the first escape attempt."

The self-reproach in his voice cut through the room with the hollow ring of truth. Peter didn't doubt his friend's sincerity for one moment. David didn't make idle threats—ever. He had meant every word.

CHAPTER THREE

THERE WERE DARK HOLLOWS of exhaustion beneath her eyes and fatigue pressed down on her shoulders with a heaviness Chris couldn't seem to shake. She was so tired, so damned tired, but she just couldn't sleep since she had come back to the city.

The knowledge that David had wanted her to leave had been a crippling blow to what little self-esteem she had left, and she felt as though she didn't have the strength or energy to carry on with her life. If only she'd had a chance to talk to him, to explain, but that one hope had been crushed. She had never felt so beaten in her life.

She wandered aimlessly into the living room and stretched out on the sofa, knowing it was futile to try to sleep. Closing her eyes, she tried to stem the flow of disturbing thoughts that were racing through her mind. But that was like trying to arrest the tide.

If she'd experienced a burst of anger at his rejection of her, or if she had been aroused by a sense of injustice, those feelings would have helped to sustain her now. But she didn't even have those. She had nothing. Nothing except old memories that tempted her with glimpses of happier times, haunting her with their clarity. The memories that tormented her the most were inconsequential fragments of her past, bits and pieces of another time.

There was one crystal-clear image of David and the boys that developed in her mind every time she closed her eyes. It was so real she could almost smell the dusty fragrance of dry grass and feel the heat of warm sunshine.

She could see them so clearly. They were all dressed in blue jeans and plaid shirts, the bright splashes of color adding depth to the scene. They stood on a hill in the middle of an abandoned hay field, their bodies profiled against a cloudless autumn sky. A bright red-and-yellow kite, snapping and fluttering high above them, was suspended in the bright blue dome by a stiff breeze. The mixture of grasses was touched with the russets and bronzes of fall, the nodding heads of fescue and brome grass bending and swaying in the wind.

Suddenly the kite swooped down in a crazy spiraling plunge, its wings crackling. To prevent it from crashing to the ground, David had started running through the sparse grass, one arm outstretched behind him as he pulled the kite along. Elated by the challenge, he fought to maintain the haphazard flight, laughter creasing his rugged face, boyish delight flashing in his eyes.

His two small sons flanked him, their arms

brushing aside the wispy stands of hay as they stumbled over the uneven ground shouting encouragement, their short chubby legs pumping to keep up. Mark tripped and staggered, but before he hit the ground his father, without missing a stride, caught him around his waist and carried him like a sack of grain as they continued their mad dash across the field. There was a loud clap and Timmy shouted, and they all looked skyward. A fresh gust of wind had caught the outstretched wings of the kite and sent it soaring, and it glided aloft like some magnificent bird on an erratic flight.

Chris groaned in protest and sat up, the impact of the recollection leaving her shaken. She leaned her head back and closed her eyes, trying to will her body to relax. She simply could not continue on like this much longer.

The sound of the doorbell cut through the stifling silence of the empty house, and with a weary sigh she got up from the sofa and went to answer it. With unsteady hands she smoothed the upsweep of her hair in an attempt to tidy it, then took a measured breath and opened the door.

Peter was standing on the step with his hands rammed in the back pockets of his jeans, his sunglasses hooked in the breast pocket of his faded red T-shirt. He looked quite solemn.

Her first thought was that something had happened to David, and there was urgency in her voice as she said sharply, "What's wrong?"

Peter shook his head and raised his hands in a placating gesture. "Nothing's wrong, Chris," he reassured her. "I just have to talk to you."

Opening the door wider, she stepped back into the foyer and motioned him in. "What about?"

His warped smile conveyed reluctance rather than amusement. "Well, actually it's David who wants to talk to you. He sent me in to get you."

A puzzled frown appeared on her face. "Why didn't you just call me like we'd planned?"

"I think he was afraid you wouldn't come after the way he acted."

Chris looked away, completely caught off guard by this unexpected turn of events. She wished she didn't feel so vulnerable, so exposed beneath Peter's penetrating stare.

"Will you come?" he said quietly.

There was only a hint of hesitation before she nodded and answered in a barely audible whisper, "Yes, I'll come." She started to turn away. "I'll just get my jacket."

Peter caught her by the shoulder and she glanced up at him questioningly. "You'd better pack a few things and plan on staying for a couple of days," he said. "I think you're both going to need time together to work out some of your problems."

An empty feeling of defeat settled over Chris and she bent her head, her exhaustion accentuated by hopelessness. "I don't think that's possible, Peter. David's feelings toward me aren't going to change."

Grasping her shoulders, Peter turned her to face him, his tone low and comforting. "For what it's worth, I think he's feeling just as uncertain as you are. If you give him a chance and don't let pride get in the way, I think you can talk things out." He gave her a little shake of encouragement. "I'm not saying that you can ever patch up your differences completely, but I *do* think you're going to be able to bury some of the bad feelings."

There was anguish in her eyes when she looked up at him, but for the first time in a very long time there was also a tiny ray of hope. "If we could achieve that kind of understanding, I'd be content." Her voice broke and she turned away. "I'll only be a minute."

THE DRIVE to Peter's retreat followed along a winding coastal highway. The black ribbon of asphalt threaded through dense tracts of coniferous forests, the towering cedar and fir trees stretching up to the clear blue sky with stately splendor. Through the green sweeping boughs overhead, sunlight occasionally punctuated the heavy shadows with elongated yellow shafts, laying patches of brightness across the road.

Then suddenly the twisting road would break from the forested tunnel into brightness, and the Pacific Ocean, with its rugged, tide-swept coastline, would come briefly into view, its green heaving waters undulating off to the horizon until they melded into the intense blue of a cloudless sky. The dancing brilliant sunlight on the tossing waves would abruptly be obscured as the highway was once again swallowed up by the majestic verdant forest.

It was so incredibly beautiful and so awe inspiring, nature in harmony, and it filled Chris with a deep quiet pleasure. This was intrinsic to her; this was where she belonged in the universal scheme of things.

"Chris, David and I had a long talk this morning."

His tone dispelled her feeling of well-being and she looked at Peter with a touch of uncertainty. "About what?"

He glanced at her, his eyes obscured by his sunglasses, and then he refocused his attention on the twisting road. "Mostly about the train of events leading up to his rescue, and what's taken place in his life since he left."

Chris shifted her position in the bucket seat so she was facing him more squarely. The wind from the open window wafted in the clean scents of pine and cedar as it whipped at her hair. She could tell by the tone of his voice and the look on his face that something was bothering him, and whatever it was, it had something to do with David. "What's on your mind?"

She could sense his deep reluctance as he hesitated, the corner of his bottom lip caught between his teeth. Finally he answered her. "I know I don't have any right to pry into your personal affairs, but there's something I need to know."

She stared at his profile, then looked away, suspecting she was not going to like what he was about to ask. "Like what?"

"Like how do you feel about David?"

He had hit on a raw and sensitive nerve, and there was a tense silence before she was able to answer him. "I care enough not to want to see him hurt."

"Do you care enough to forgive him for some stupid mistakes?"

There wasn't even a hesitation. "Yes," she said.

He nodded his head slightly, as though he believed her, but there was a set look around his mouth that protrayed an element of doubt.

Chris reached out and touched his arm in an attempt to reassure him. "I mean that, Peter."

It was the truth. She no longer harbored any ill will toward him, in fact, she hadn't for a very long time, and she truly did want him to find some measure of happiness. Besides, there was no room for foolish pride or rash shortsightedness if she and David were ever going to erase the bitterness caused by their broken marriage.

Above all else she wanted the welfare of their two young sons to be a common priority for both of them. She was mature enough to realize it would be impossible to reconstruct a life together, but they could at least arrive on some neutral ground where they could be civil to each other.

Her disturbing thoughts intensified the awful sense of loss she'd lived with for so long, and her loneliness became more acute, creating a tight band around her chest. She took a deep breath in an attempt to ease the ache before looking at her companion.

He was driving with his elbow propped on the open window, the side of his hand resting across his mouth. His brow was creased with a worried frown, his preoccupied manner warning her of trouble ahead. Uneasiness tightened her insides into a hard ball and she gathered together her courage. "What is it, Peter?"

She saw his jaw tense and his frown deepen. She experienced a sudden unpleasant hollowness and clasped her hands around her unraised knee in a white-knuckled grip, determined to keep her face void of any expression. She knew. Without him saying a word, she knew. Somehow she managed to keep her voice from breaking when she answered her own question. "You're trying to find a tactful way of telling me David's involved with someone, aren't you?"

His startled response confirmed her unspoken fears, and she could feel the color drain from her face. For one awful moment she thought she was going to be sick. Turning her head so he couldn't see her face, she swallowed hard, and in spite of the nearly unbearable pain that twisted through her, she managed to maintain a facade of control. "I had to expect that to happen sometime. I didn't really expect him to go through life alone."

The sound of Peter speaking echoed in her head. "It isn't what you think, Chris."

Slowly she drew a breath past the aching tightness in her throat, trying to quell the churning in her stomach. "You don't have to give me an explanation."

"I think I do, but I'm afraid the explanation isn't very pretty." As though realizing it was a rash and unwise decision, Peter told her about Maria with uncharacteristic abruptness.

By the time he finished, Chris was feeling truly ill, and she was fighting a silent battle to dominate the panic building in her. In spite of how hard the news hit her, her own pain was outweighed by the heart-wrenching compassion she felt for David. Something like that would tear him to shreds.

"Chris?"

With great difficulty she schooled her ashen face into mannequin blankness before looking at Peter.

He recognized her silent response but he hesitated, worry lines crinkling the corners of his eyes. "He made a revealing comment when we were talking about her."

"What did he say?"

"When I asked him how important she was to him, he said he'd do anything for her, and that he owed her, but he didn't love her. He said he wasn't capable of those kinds of feelings anymore.''

Chris felt as though she'd been roughly yanked to a jarring halt. She stared blindly at the landscape that was sliding by the window of the moving car, her mind registering nothing. God, what had she done to him? She must have nearly destroyed him for him to feel that way. In her blind unthinking stupidity, what had she done to him?

Peter reached across the car and took her cold hand in his, his firm grip drawing her numb thoughts back to what he was saying. "Chris, I didn't tell you this to lay a guilt trip on you," he said gently. "I just think you should know that he's so busy hating himself right now, and so loaded down with his own guilt, that he doesn't realize what he's doing to you."

With a weary gesture she brushed loose strands of her windblown hair off her face before laying her head against the headrest. "Does he know you were going to tell me about her?"

"No. In fact, I told him I wouldn't. But after I'd had a chance to think about it, I could see more reasons for telling you than not."

Chris closed her eyes, feeling more and more tired by the minute. "I don't want him to know that you told me, Peter. It would just make everything more awkward."

"I think that might be best," he agreed quietly.

Nothing more was said and Chris kept her eyes

closed, trying to empty her mind. But old memories kept creeping in to torment her with a vividness that was all too real.

By the time they reached the cabin, strain had eaten away at Chris's composure. Her pallor was accentuated by dark circles under her eyes, and there was an unnatural rigidity to her movements as she climbed out of the car. She just didn't know what to expect. She had no idea how David would react to her now, or if he would even listen to what she had to say.

Peter carried her suitcase to the veranda, set it down and turned to go. "I have a few things I want to pick up from Barnie's," he said vaguely. "I'll be back in an hour or so."

Barnie was a retired fisherman who lived about a mile up the coast, and the old gentleman had an island-wide reputation for both his handcrafted fishing lures and his rum toddies. Chris had a hunch Peter was not in the market for more fishing lures. He was using a trip to the fisherman's as a good excuse to leave. "Just out of curiosity, what exactly do you need to get from Barnie's?" she asked, a hint of amusement in her eyes.

Peter had the decency to look a little sheepish as he glanced up at her and grinned. "I thought maybe I could use a little liquid courage," he retorted dryly.

That wormed a smile out of her. "Then you'd better pick some up for me, too. I'm not feeling very lionhearted right now."

His expression sobered as he rammed his hands in his back pockets and tilted his head in a characteristic stance. "Go easy on him, Chris," he said.

"I will."

She watched him drive away, and nervousness settled in her like a lead weight as she picked up her luggage and entered the cabin. Letting the screen door close quietly behind her, Chris set her suitcase down. Tranquility diffused through her as she glanced around the inside of the cabin. The rough natural mix of stone and wood presented a blend of nature that she found soothing. She loved this place. It was like coming home.

From her viewpoint just inside the back door, she savored the colors, the textures, the uncluttered lines of the structure. Waist-high knotty pine cupboards made up the U-shaped kitchen, which separated the back entryway from the dining nook. Although Peter's summer home had all the luxuries, the interior was still that of a log cabin, and the peeled varnished logs had aged to a rich deep gold.

The spacious design was simple and functional. The living room was one enormous area, while at the far end of the cabin, a huge master bedroom and bath, a second bathroom, a large storage closet and the laundry room were located. Along the back half of the cabin a large loft overlooked the main floor.

A massive fieldstone fireplace made up the wall

separating the bedroom from the living area, while along the south and west sides, walls of windows with sliding patio doors left the entire cabin open to the magnificent view of the coastline and the sea.

Chris sighed and leaned her head back, absorbing the mellowness of the place as the far-off song of the sea murmured to her. Rolling her shoulders to relieve the knots of tension, she started toward the sun deck at the front of the house. But she stopped abruptly.

David was asleep on the hideaway bed, his hair slightly damp from a shower, his face cleanly shaven. One arm was draped across his chest, his other hand tucked behind his head. It looked as if he had fallen asleep as he lay there thinking.

Very quietly Chris moved toward him, drawn by her own longing. It had been only three days since she'd seen him, but she couldn't believe how good he looked. He had obviously gained some weight, and though there were still some lesions from the abscesses, his skin had a healthy, lightly tanned appearance.

His breathing remained deep and even as she sat down on the arm of the easy chair, her eyes never leaving him. His head was turned toward her, and his body was completely relaxed, his face peaceful in slumber.

As she drank in every detail of him, a gnawing emptiness grew inside her. This man had so many fascinating contradictions. The soft curl of his dark hair gave him a boyish look, yet it framed a rugged masculine face. His thick sweeping eyelashes should have seemed out of place, but they only accented the deep-set eyes, which had a network of laugh lines radiating out toward his temples. And his mouth—that full sensual mouth added a chiseled dimension to a strong square jaw.

Contradictions. There were so many in his character. The sleek animal grace with which he moved belied the powerful muscular body. Slim, fine-boned hands that could crush could also be incredibly gentle with a newborn baby. A violent, lightning-fast temper was a cover-up for a profoundly sensitive and caring nature. At times he seemed to be a man at odds with himself, but that was David—and she still loved him.

The revelation didn't come as a surprise. In fact, she felt oddly at peace with herself, finally having faced something she'd tried not to acknowledge. For too long she had tried to deny it, to pretend those intense feelings had died, but now she couldn't hide behind her carefully manufactured barricade of indifference. She could never feel indifferent about him. He had been a major part of her life for too long.

She gazed at him, longing to reach out and caress him, longing to reacquaint herself with the texture of his skin, the contours of his face, the silky feel of his thick lustrous hair around her fingers. For all the endless nights she had lain awake, desperately

longing to touch him, to feel his strong body molded against hers, Chris drank in every detail of him
now. How she loved him.

Without a hint that he was waking, he opened his
eyes and looked at her, the blue depths keenly
aware, and she had the sudden uncomfortable feeling that he hadn't been asleep at all.

She felt a breathless flutter in her midriff as she
eased a long measured breath past the tightness in
her throat. "Hello, David," she said.

He didn't say anything but reached out his hand
toward her, his intense somber gaze riveted on her
face. In one fluid movement she slipped over to the
bed and sat down, her hand grasping his. He closed
his eyes and she watched him swallow hard as his
hand tightened around hers in a forceful grip that
was almost painful.

She saw the muscles in his jaw tense and she
could sense his inner conflict. His suffering was
reflected in his eyes when he finally looked at her.
"Thank you for coming back, Chris," he said, his
voice jagged with emotion.

Chris didn't trust herself to speak so she simply
tightened her hold on his hand. He seemed to
understand, and with a ragged sigh he draped his
other arm across his face; for a long time they sat in
silence, their clasped hands their unspoken communication.

Finally David shifted his arm, allowing the back
of his hand to rest on his forehead as he gazed at

her. "Why did you do it, Chris—after the way I treated you when we separated—why did you send a rescue team after me?"

She couldn't maintain the intimacy of eye-to-eye contact with him, and she looked down at their clasped hands, feeling oddly uncertain. Her strained voice betrayed this uncertainty when she finally spoke. "I couldn't just sit there and do nothing, David. No matter what had happened between us in the past, I couldn't ignore the fact that you were in very grave danger." She glanced up at him, her eyes haunted by grim memories. "But there was more to it than that."

His voice was quiet and encouraging when he asked, "Like what?"

Her face became reflective as she sorted through her thoughts, searching for the right words to express her feelings. "I wanted a chance to tell you that it took a lot of time and a lot of soul searching, but I realize that the collapse of our marriage was my fault."

"Chris, that's not—"

She cut him off, her voice unsteady. "Don't, David. Let me say what I need to say while I have the courage." Taking a deep shaky breath, she continued. "Where I was so wrong, so desperately wrong, was that I refused to talk about anything. I could never tell you what was bothering me because I was so confused, so uncertain of myself that I was afraid. I was afraid you wouldn't understand, I was afraid I'd hurt you, I was afraid of my own feelings." She looked at him, her face ashen, her eyes tormented. "I shut you out with my silence, and you can't resolve anything with silence."

David studied her face for a moment, then he stared up at the ceiling, unconsciously stroking the back of her hand with his thumb. "But my retaliation was pretty damned vicious."

"Yes, it was, but you wouldn't have acted that way if I'd given you a chance to talk."

"The problems weren't all your fault." There was an edge of bitterness in his voice that she found very disturbing, and Chris knew this might be the only chance she'd ever have to make him understand.

"David, look at me," she pleaded softly. He hesitated, then turned his head to look at her, his expression unreadable. "I'm not trying to turn myself into a martyr. I know the problems weren't all my fault, but I *was* to blame for the way we ended up dealing with them." Her feelings were so intense and so close to the surface that it was almost impossible for her to speak, but she forced herself to go on. "I didn't know how to communicate, and I'm sorry. I never gave us a chance to try to sort our feelings out."

He looked away again and Chris eased her hold on his hand, sensing that he didn't want her touching him. But his grip remained firm, and for the first time she experienced a glimmer of optimism.

"Chris?" She met his gaze with unflinching openness, waiting for him to continue. "If I were to ask you now what you felt the two most serious problems were, would you give me an answer?"

He was giving her an option she'd never expected, and she grasped the opportunity like a lifeline. "Yes, I'd answer you."

There was just a hint of a smile in his eyes. "What were they?"

Without even having to think about it, she responded, "The yacht club and your mother's enormous dinner parties."

The bewilderment that registered on his face almost made her laugh. "The yacht club and dinner parties?" he asked dumbfoundedly. "What did that have to do with it?"

She gave him a rueful look. "In a way, everything." She paused and looked away, her face becoming serious. "I was so out of my element in the social circles your family moved in, David, but it had nothing to do with feeling inadequate." She sighed, her head tilted to one side, and looked at him with candidness. "It took me a long while to figure myself out. But I finally did."

His eyes were narrowed as he studied her. "And what did you discover?"

"That I'm not a very gregarious person, and that trait has nothing to do with shyness or feeling awkward." Her voice became thoughtful as she continued. "I simply don't feel like myself in a large group of people. I'm very much a loner and I simply don't fit in that kind of environment."

A frown appeared on his face, and maintaining his hold on her hand, he rolled over onto his side and propped his head up on his other hand. "And you suffered through all those boring obligations because you thought it was expected of you—because you were the wife of David Spencer."

Keenly aware of the warmth and strength of his fingers around hers, she met his gaze. "I did, and I hated it, David. All those big social events at the yacht club and those formal dinners at your mother's made me feel so claustrophobic. But it sounded so stupid I didn't know how to adequately explain my feelings. I was so afraid I'd be a big disappointment to you—that you'd resent how I felt. But it just got to the point where I couldn't stand it anymore."

An odd watchful expression appeared on his face, as though he was about to make a discovery and he wasn't sure it was one he wanted to make. "And that's why you bolted?"

Unable to hold his gaze, she bent her head. When she answered him her voice was hushed. "It took me a long while after I left to work through to that bottom line, to reach that conclusion, but yes, that's why I bolted." When she raised her head, her face was pale. "It wasn't because of you. It was because I desperately needed some space. I couldn't stand the never-ending coffee parties, the luncheons, the senseless chatter of a bunch of women who talked about nothing but clothes.''

As if all his energy had just been sapped, David rolled over onto his back and closed his eyes. There was an inflexible set to his mouth, and Chris knew by the way the muscle in his neck tightened that he had his teeth clenched. He was angry and she couldn't really blame him.

His hold on her hand slackened and she reluctantly drew it away. An awful emptiness expanded inside her, leaving her feeling desolated and alone. She desperately wanted to run down to the sea, to the isolated lonely stretch of beach, where she could grieve alone, but she had to finish. This would be her one and only chance. After hearing this, David would send her away and she would likely never see him again. The thought nearly tore her apart.

Her voice was a tormented whisper when she was finally able to speak again. "I said some hateful things to you, David—things I didn't mean. I know it's a weak excuse, but I was scared and so damned confused." She had to fight to restrain the emotions that were ripping her apart, and her voice broke treacherously. "I'm sorry, David. I never meant to hurt you." She stood up, poised for flight, but his hand shot out and caught her wrist.

His voice was tense. "Where are you going?"

She couldn't meet his gaze, and she could hardly speak. "Just down to the beach."

He didn't say anything, but he didn't release her,

either, and she was compelled to look down at him. He was watching her with a penetrating stare that she found very disturbing, and her pulse accelerated. At last he spoke. "You're coming back, aren't you?"

From somewhere deep inside her she found the courage to ask him the obvious question. "Do you want me to?"

His hold on her became less intense and the look on his face softened a little. "Yes, I want you to come back." He let her go, his hand trailing slowly across her arm. "Don't be long." It was one of those quiet requests that she found so hard to resist, but she knew she had to have some time alone to marshal her thoughts. She was too vulnerable, too unprotected, and somehow she had to shore up her defenses.

If he guessed how she really felt about him, it would only make him feel more guilty, more angry with himself, and she didn't want to burden him anymore. She had been the one to walk away from their marriage; not even in her wildest dreams did she ever dare to hope that he would take her back. She had made the biggest mistake in her life, and somehow she was going to have to learn to live with it. An agonizing ache spread through her and she turned away, suddenly unable to bear being so close to him.

LESS THAN AN HOUR had passed when she returned to the cabin, her hair windblown, her bare feet covered with sand. The invigorating sea air and the exercise had put some color back in her face, and for the first time in a very long while her body was not aching with tension.

David was sitting on the deck watching her, his feet propped up on the railing, his hands resting across his chest. There was a solemn reflective look on his face that she found oddly disquieting, and with unexplainable self-consciousness she sat down in the chair beside him.

There was a brief silence before David said, "You don't look right walking along the beach without Downer. Where is he?"

Downer. Chris had truly loved that dog. He had been such a comfort to her, such a loyal friend, and his death had left a painful emptiness in her life. Putting him to sleep was one of the most devastating things she'd ever had to do.

Aware that David was watching her intently, she tried to hide her inconsolable sorrow from him, but her wavering voice betrayed her. "I had to have him put to sleep six months ago," she said through stiff lips. "He disappeared one night, and I finally found him huddled on the beach among the rocks." She breathed in slowly in an attempt to steady her voice, but it didn't help. "He'd...he'd gone away to die...." She simply couldn't go on, and in a defensive movement she stood up and fled into the cabin.

She wished she could have cried then, and she wished she could cry now, but there seemed to be an enormous dam inside her that held everything back, creating a wall of obstructed agonizing emotions. Something had happened to her after she left David, and from then on all her tormented feelings had remained bottled up inside. Even when her father had died, she had remained without tears.

"I'm sorry, Christine." David's voice was right behind her and she moved away, her sense of survival somehow threatened by his closeness. She hunched forward, her arms clasped tightly in front of her, trying to physically suppress the internal pain.

Death seemed to stalk her—her father, her dog—but at least David was alive. She could take comfort in that. But there was still the loss of her father, and somehow she was going to have to find the courage to tell David about that. He and her father had been very close, and it would come as a terrible shock to him, especially when he found out Timothy Randal had suffered a heart attack when he'd heard about David's abduction. There would be more guilt for David to endure, and she simply couldn't do that to him now.

David moved away, as if giving her space, and casually asked, "When will the boys be back?"

He knew and he understood, and Chris was touched by his sensitivity, but she tried not to let her feelings show as she turned to face him. "They should be back the latter part of next week." It was suddenly imperative that she have something to do

with her hands, and she started folding up the news-
papers that were scattered on the coffee table. She
sensed that he wasn't quite sure how to approach the
topic of his sons, and Chris considered the situation,
trying to be as perceptive as he had been. The boys'
return was an issue they were going to have to deal
with now, before the children arrived home. She
could feel his eyes on her and she finally looked at
him.

David's face looked troubled as he sat down in the
easy chair. "I think maybe we'd better talk about
what's going to happen when they get back. How
much do they know about my abduction?"

"Not much. I tried to play it down as much as
possible." She stacked the folded papers on the end
of the table and sat down beside the pile.

"How do you feel about them spending some time
here?"

There was something about the way he said it that
made the question sound like a challenge, and Chris
wondered if he thought she'd be miserable enough to
oppose him about seeing the boys. It was not a pleas-
ant thought. She raised her shoulders in an off-
handed gesture. "Personally, I think it would be the
best thing for them to spend some time with you. But
it's up to you, David. If your being here has to be a
closely guarded secret, I don't think it's wise." She
smiled wryly. "Timmy can keep a secret, but Mark
certainly can't."

He was watching her closely, and she probably
would have felt very uncomfortable if she hadn't felt

a sudden rush of concern for him. He was so tired.

His exhaustion was even apparent in his voice. "You don't think it would be too much of a shock for them to see me now?"

Chris frowned slightly and abstractedly picked at an imperfection in the material of her jeans. "I wouldn't have wanted them to see you when Peter first brought you back. But it wouldn't be so bad now. You're still much too thin, but other than that you look so much better than you did." She looked up at him and shrugged slightly. "And besides, a few more days of lying in the sun and a decent diet will make all the difference in the world."

He closed his eyes, and Chris suspected he was reluctant to let her see the look in his eyes. But there was no way he could disguise how very much he had missed his sons when he said, "I really want to see them—it's been over a year. They'll have grown so much."

It didn't take a mind reader to know he was experiencing a kind of grief for all the time he'd lost with his boys—the days, the weeks, the months he'd never be able to recapture. Guilt turned on Chris with a vengeance. She'd even deprived him of an ordinary relationship with his own sons.

DURING THE NEXT TWO DAYS the beautiful July weather gave way to heavy rains. The angry sea beat against the rocky shoreline, and the wind lashed against the cabin with a desolate moan.

The confinement made David restless and irritable, and his constant pacing became an irritation in itself. Peter tried to distract him with various activities, but David couldn't seem to concentrate on anything. Normally an avid reader, he couldn't focus his attention on a book for more than a few minutes at a time.

For lack of anything better to do, Peter dismantled the hospital bed and cot, then hauled them upstairs to the open loft, announcing to no one in particular that he would be sleeping up there. After he had the master bedroom cleared, he and David set up the king-size bed, both of them swearing heatedly throughout the entire operation.

Chris made a point of staying out of their way. After laundering all the bedding, she started cleaning out cupboards. She simply had to have something to do to keep busy. David's edginess was infecting them all, and the atmosphere soon became strained.

It was the fourth night after her return that Chris lay on the hideaway bed in the living room listening to David tossing and turning in bed. She stared into the darkness, wondering what was going through his mind. She wondered if the rain had awakened some bad memories for him or if it was the feeling of being locked in that was getting to him. Whatever the problem, it was really troubling him, and knowing that he was in that bedroom going through some sort of private hell all alone tormented her.

Turning onto her side, she tried to shut out the

sounds from the other room. It had been a big mistake, her coming back. A very big mistake. Her feelings were rapidly getting out of hand, and there was nothing she could do to curb them. She was falling victim to that overpowering attraction he'd always held for her, only now it was stronger, deeper, more profound.

Four lonely years without him had heightened her awareness of him until every nerve in her body was screaming out with an unsatisfied hunger, and she felt as if she was slowly going out of her mind.

But there was more to it than that. She desperately missed the closeness they'd once shared. There had been a time, long, long ago, when their life together had been so special, so intimate, and she would sell her soul to be able to have that again. But she'd lost it all, and it hurt her more than she wanted to admit. Having him around her constantly only verified the magnitude of her loss. But she couldn't leave, either. An invisible bond held her there.

In desperation she crept out of bed and went to stand before the patio door. The darkness of the night hung like a heavy black blanket before her, stifling her, and the sound of rain on the roof compounded her loneliness.

She was turning to go back to bed when an eerie feeling that something was wrong crept up her spine with icy fingers. There were no longer any sounds coming from the bedroom, and instinctively she knew the ominous feeling was somehow tied to David.

Her pulse racing, she went to him. In the impenetrable blackness of the room it took her a moment to locate the night-light on his bedside table, and with fumbling fingers she turned it on.

His blankets had been thrown off, and for one awful moment she thought he was having a convulsion. His naked body was rigid and soaked with sweat; his hands were knotted into fists and his teeth clenched. She was just about to call for Peter when David jerked his arm across his face in a defensive gesture, and she realized he was in the throes of a terrifying nightmare.

Sitting down on the bed, she slipped her arms around his shoulders and tried to cradle his stiff body against her. She began to talk to him in a soothing voice.

At first he attempted to fight her off, but she held him securely and kept talking to him. "It's all right, David. It's all right. It's only a dream." She kept saying it over and over, and finally the rigidity in his body began to ease and she was able to gather his thin body closer. She raised his shoulders until she held him firmly against her, his damp face pressed against her neck, and she began to rock him as though he were a small frightened child.

Suddenly he sagged against her and drew in a tortured breath. His arms came around her in a crushing desperate embrace. "God—Christine," he whispered raggedly.

The near-frantic relief she heard in his voice sent a spasm of pain through her, and she held him with all the strength she possessed. He began to tremble violently, and for the first time in months, tears scalded her eyes. She had never before experienced such fierce protectiveness. With a groan he molded her tightly against him, his hold on her unrelenting.

Chris had to bite her lip to keep from crying out in an agony of hunger as their bodies fused together like two white-hot pieces of metal. It felt so good to hold him again, to feel his body against hers, and a wild storm of emotions broke loose with a rending force, paralyzing her with its intensity. Clinging to him, she fought for breath, she fought for control, she fought to keep a grasp on reality.

The perspiration on his skin permeated the thin fabric of her nightgown and the heat from his body suffused her. Chris absorbed it: the sweat, the heat. Her starving body was famished for more, and she longed for him to become a part of her, but from somewhere deep within herself she found the strength to deny this driving need.

That real true pleasure had to come from a mutual desire, and she wouldn't want it any other way. Right now David needed somebody to hold, somebody to give him comfort, and she would have to be content with that.

The heavy aching pulse of unsatiated desire

throbbed through her body, and Chris tried to block it out and concentrate on the feel of his body pressed against hers. Eventually she did discover a quiet contentment. But it would only last through the night; it would not be there forever.

CHAPTER FOUR

BY EARLY MORNING it had quit raining and the wind had died down, but the sky was still heavily overcast. A thick bank of fog hung over the ocean, and thin wisps of mist drifted in to land, hovering over the shoreline and settling among the trees like ethereal phantoms.

Chris stood before the wall of windows in the living room, gazing out at the scene before her. All of nature seemed to be cast in various shades of gray, the oppressive leaden clouds draining everything of color. Only the stark white of the sea gulls, wheeling and soaring in the gunmetal gray sky, gave any contrast. In its own haunting way, the scene was very beautiful and very serene. She loved the sea in all its moods.

With uncontrollable persistence her thoughts kept drifting back to David and what had transpired the night before. She wondered if he'd even remember what had happened when he awakened. After lying awake most of the night quietly savoring the chance to hold him, she had reluctantly left him when dawn began to break. It had been so hard to leave, but logic told her it was the wisest thing to do.

The crackle and snap of the brightly burning fire in the fireplace and the muted sounds of the sea were the only intrusions in the silence. That feeling of complete seclusion was a comfort to Chris, a healing balm to her raw nerves.

When Peter had left for the hospital at five o'clock that morning, Chris had gone with him to pick up a few things from the house and to get her car. Although Victoria was the principal city on Vancouver Island, the streets had been hushed and nearly empty when they arrived, yet even with the early-morning stillness, she couldn't get out of the city fast enough. She needed the space, the silence; she needed the feeling of isolation.

Her inward musings were fractured when she sensed she was being watched. Turning slowly, she found David leaning against the bedroom doorway, his arms folded across his chest. His dark hair was slightly untidy, as though he had combed it with his fingers. He had on a pair of faded jeans that hugged his slim hips, the taut fabric straining against the thick muscles of his thighs.

His body was a marvel. As emaciated as he had been, his rugged muscles had not completely wasted away, and as he stood there watching her he looked extremely fit, far more fit than he actually was. The bulk of the steel-blue fisherman-knit sweater he wore exaggerated the broadness of his shoulders yet subtly camouflaged his thinness. The color of the garment accentuated the incredible blue of his darkly lashed eyes—eyes that were watching her with a steady intensity that held her immobile, heightening her awareness of the virility that seemed to radiate from him.

That old familiar feeling of heady anticipation kindled a sexual excitement in her, and suddenly she found it difficult to breathe. That instant, that one mind-shattering instant when their bodies had fused together, became crystal clear in her thoughts, and Chris felt her strength drain away. Her body burned with the remembered feeling of his weight pressed tightly against her.

She had to speak. She had to break the potent magnetic pull of his eyes, a pull that was leaving her weaker by the moment. It took an effort of sheer will, but finally she managed to murmur, "Good morning."

David didn't say anything but continued to watch her. Finally he straightened and came toward her, his body moving with a fluid grace that mesmerized her senses.

She remained transfixed as he stopped in front of her, and her breath caught in a repressed sob as he slowly traced the outline of her jaw with his fingers, his touch sending a shiver down her spine. He let his curled hand rest under her chin, then with a gentle pressure he lifted her face, his thumb caressing her bottom lip with tormenting lightness. A wild fluttering inside her sent her pulses racing, and her breathing became labored as he gazed into her eyes. Then slowly, ever so slowly, he lowered his head.

She tried to brace herself against the explosion of unrestrained desire, but the moment he covered her mouth with his own, a violent convulsion shuddered through her body. Fireworks, detonated by an agony of longing, rocketted off in her, sending a fermenting heat coursing through her. The force of it wrung a soft moan from her, and her lips parted as his mouth moved against hers in a moist searching kiss.

She heard him suck in his breath as he raised his head and suddenly turned away. Chris was so staggered by what had happened that it took her several moments to master the hot weakness that possessed her. When she finally came to her senses, David was standing in front of the fireplace, his hands grasping the mantel, his head bent.

A feeling of helplessness settled over her and she stood there, unconsciously clenching and unclenching her hands, her eyes tormented. She didn't know what to say. She didn't know what to do.

Finally David turned toward her. His expression was fixed, but the battle raging within him was damned near out of control. He told himself he hadn't meant to do that, but he knew he was lying through his teeth. The memory of last night was still too clear in his mind, and it was going to be a memory that would torment him for many nights to come.

He looked at Chris as he fought to regain some

composure, but the light from the window was behind her and he couldn't see her face. He'd felt her respond to him, and that sickened him. He had no right to go within ten feet of her, no right to play senseless games with her, yet he couldn't keep away.

What was he trying to do to her? Bring her to her knees? Get even? But he knew that wasn't the case any longer. He didn't want to hurt her anymore. She'd done her share of suffering. The simple truth was he wanted her—he wanted her like hell—but there was too much wrong in his life to even think about it. He had to keep his hands off her. He had to keep his distance or he'd end up destroying her.

David knew he should get the hell out of the house, but he couldn't leave her knowing what she was feeling right then. He couldn't do that to her. Taking a deep breath, he went to her and took her hand. Her fingers wrapped around his in a tight grip, and David had to fight down the urge to take her in his arms.

His voice had little strength as he said, "I'm sorry, Chris. I had no right to do that." He felt her shiver, and her grip on his hand became even tighter as she gazed up at him, her eyes reminding him of a wounded doe. He couldn't stand it, that hurt lost look in her eyes, and with a muttered oath he gathered her against him.

For a long time he held her, his face pressed against her hair, his arms folded tightly around her. When he realized what little restraint he had was disintegrating rapidly, he released her. Gently he brushed his knuckles along the curve of her jaw, then let his hand rest against her neck. He tried to keep his voice even, devoid of the vehemence of his feelings. "Come for a walk along the beach with me, Chris."

She took a shaky breath and started to speak. "David—"

He placed his fingers across her mouth, knowing she was going to say something about what they had both experienced a moment ago. He couldn't handle it, whatever it was. He wanted her too much to resist if she gave him one iota of encouragement. He needed time to think, he needed time to cool off.

He smiled down at her. "Will you come?"

She squeezed his hand. "Yes, I'll come."

David gritted his teeth together and tried to fortify his resolve. Even the sound of her voice played havoc with his determination. It was soft and throaty and had the richness and sensuality of velvet—and it nearly drove him crazy.

It FELT SO GOOD to be outside again, even if it was gloomy and overcast. The fresh crisp air revitalized David, giving him more energy than he'd had in a long time, and the space, the unrestricted expanse of beach, soothed the restlessness that had plagued him.

Chris had found him a Windbreaker of Peter's to wear and she'd put on a khaki-colored safari jacket, the olive shade turning her hazel eyes to green. Her thick hair was caught loosely on top of her head, accenting her classic profile. Her slender body reminded him much of a willow in the wind: swaying, supple, yielding.

She looked very beautiful—and very young. But perhaps *young* was the wrong word to describe her. David studied her as they walked hand in hand along the storm-washed beach, the light breeze catching at their clothing. Perhaps *ageless* suited her better.

There had always been an aura about her that fascinated him. She was like an untamed sea spirit, at one with her environment. Of all the vivid memories he had of her, not one stood out in his mind in which she was surrounded by other people. This was how he always remembered her, a solitary figure alone on a beach.

His face grew sober. He'd been blind not to see how confining their life had been for her. But he'd been so wrapped up in his work, so immersed in attaining success, he had failed in the thing that mattered the most. He had screwed up his life and hers, and with the nightmare of Maria hanging over his head, he didn't see how he could ever put it right.

"What's the matter, David?" she asked softly. "Are you getting tired?"

He glanced down at her and gave her a warped grin. "You don't know how I hate to admit it, but I guess I am. It's beginning to get to me—this lack of strength."

Her hand tightened around his, her own strength

oddly reassuring. "It'll come. Just don't get impatient and try to do too much."

She paused to pick up a small perfect seashell, and after studying it closely she put it in her pocket. Brushing the loose hair back from her face, she turned with him and started walking back toward the cabin. Their old footprints were still embedded in the wet sand.

The tide was out, and washed-out depressions in the vast expanse of sand formed a network of small pools and shallow channels. At the coastline, where weathered gray spars of timber lay in massive tangled barriers against the carved edge of grass and rock, the fog-shrouded forest crowded down against the shore. Sea gulls perched on the bleached logs, while others soared so high in the dreary sky that they disappeared from view.

A mile or so down the beach the craggy point of land projected out to sea, its rugged mass silhouetted against the sky. A dense stand of trees hid the cabin from view, and Chris and David walked toward it, their shoulders brushing occasionally, the silence they shared natural and unstrained.

The wind was behind them, and Chris reached up and pulled up the turtleneck of David's sweater, then turned up the collar of his jacket. He gave her a dry look, and for the first time since his return he grinned, her eyes dancing. "Ignore me," she said, amusement animating her voice. "The boys have been gone too long and I need someone to mother."

David had to fight the urge to hug her. Tucking her arm under his, he linked his fingers through hers and stuck their joined hands in the pocket of his coat. They ambled back toward the cabin, the muted thunder of the breakers a distant backdrop for their comfortable silence.

The invigorating sea air carried a taste of salt, and David licked his lips as he looked down at her. "You must miss them like hell when they're gone this long."

She took her free hand out of her pocket and pulled back a few strands of hair that were clinging to her moist lips. "I do." She smiled and gave him a sheepish grimace. "But after they're home a few days and start scrapping, I'm ready to pack them off again."

"And I can just imagine what they're like after grandma and grandpa have indulged all their little whims."

Chris shot him such a startled glance that he knew he'd hit on a sore spot. He squeezed her hand. "I know what my mother's like with them, believe me," he said laconically. "When she brought them down to see me the last time, I finally had to tell her to butt out. She was letting them get away with bloody murder." The expression of undisguised doubt on Chris's face made David laugh. He squeezed her hand again, his eyes sparkling. "We'll gang up on them this time, and the poor little devils won't know what hit them."

Chris smiled ruefully and shook her head. "What really drives me crazy is that they expect to be waited on hand and foot when they first come back."

David's face became serious. "Frankly, I don't know why you let them spend so much time there."

The vitality that shone in her eyes faded and she lowered her head, her face solemn. When she spoke, her voice was pensive, almost hesitant, as though she was afraid to be candid with him. "They *are* their grandparents, David. I felt I owed it to them."

His own voice was very quiet when he responded, "Don't let guilt color your judgment, Chris. You don't owe my parents anything." He became introspective, his own expression sober, and they walked a fair distance in silence. Finally he looked at her. "You were afraid I'd think you were being miserable if you didn't let them go to mom and dad's, weren't you?"

She frowned and abstractedly chewed her bottom lip. With a perplexed sigh she met his steady stare. "That's partly true, but I didn't want the boys to feel that they'd lost their grandparents, too."

David stopped walking and faced her. "Look, Chris, your dad is the best influence those boys can have." Her reaction caught him off guard, and he halted when he felt her body stiffen against his. She quickly turned her head so he couldn't see her face, and instinctively he knew something was terribly wrong. She was trying to hide something from him, and his sixth sense told him it was bad news. "What is it, Christine?" he asked.

She tried to pull her hand free from his grasp, but he held fast. A feeling of dread banded his chest as he lifted her face. She'd gone chalk white and her eyes were tormented by grief. He felt the color drain from his own face as he stared at her in disbelief, then he clenched his eyes shut and groaned softly, "God, no—not Timothy, too."

With a murmured protest, she slipped her arms around him and pressed her face against his neck, the warmth of her body barely permeating the sudden chill that encompassed him. "I didn't want to tell you yet, David," she whispered brokenly.

The shock left his mind reeling and he crushed her against him, desperately needing the warmth of a living breathing person, desperately needing the comfort of her. It all seemed part of a bad dream, and his brain was unwilling to absorb the fact that his father-in-law and friend was dead. He began to shiver uncontrollably and Chris eased away from him.

"Come on, David," she said gently, her voice coaxing. "Let's go back to the cabin."

The dampness from the ocean suddenly cut through his warm clothing, and his body was consumed with a numbing cold. Silently he responded to the pressure of her arm around his waist, his mind as numb as his body.

It wasn't until they were back in the cabin and he found himself seated in an easy chair in front of a roaring fire that his mind clicked into gear. Chris was sitting on the arm of the chair, one arm around his shoulders, the other cradling his head against her breast, quietly talking to him. He felt like hell. He should have been the one who was comforting her, but the shock of Timothy's death had been like a kick in the head, completely stunning him.

Leaning his head back, he stared blindly at the ceiling, unable to face the compassion he knew he'd see in her eyes. "How long ago did it happen?"

She withdrew her arms from around him and rose, keeping her back to him as she went to stand before the fire. He shifted his eyes and stared at her rigid form, waiting for her to answer him. But she said nothing. He sensed that she was trying to think of a way to dodge his question. "Look at me, Chris," he commanded in an ominous tone.

He saw her take a deep breath before reluctantly turning to face him. He glared at her, an irrational anger welling up inside him. "Don't try to protect me. I asked you a question, and damn it, I want an answer."

She stuck her hands in the pockets of her jeans and stared at the floor as she straightened the rolled edge of the braided rug with her toe. "He died nine months ago."

He narrowed his eyes and continued to watch her. "When I was taken hostage." It was a flat statement, a statement laced with bitterness.

"Yes."

"What happened?"

She exhaled slowly and looked at him. Their eyes locked in a silent war of wills, and with another heavy sigh she sat down on the hearth, her arms folded across her thighs and her shoulders hunched forward. "He'd been out fishing when I got word that you'd been taken hostage. I went down to the wharf to tell him before he heard it on the radio. But Ben Cooper had already heard the news and he'd already told dad. Ben must have misunderstood because he thought you'd been killed." Chris straightened up, the only sign of emotion her tight grip on the edge of the stone hearth. "Ben was with him and so was Mike Dirkson. They'd just phoned for an ambulance when I got there. He'd had a massive heart attack."

"How long did he live?"

"Not long." Her voice was a monotone, her face lifeless and pale as a death mask. "He was conscious, though. I was able to tell him that you were still alive." She looked at David, a twisted half smile on her face—a smile that was reminiscent, yet spoke of an unbearable pain. "He said to tell you that it was a lousy trick to get out of working on the boat for him this summer, and that he wanted you to have his old sea chest."

David wanted to drive his fist through a wall. It was so damned unjust, such a waste of a fine decent human being. Somehow he managed to keep a tight rein on his burgeoning rage. "Did they get him to the hospital?"

She shook her head, her eyes fixed on the floor.

Her voice was so choked he could barely hear her. "No, and I'm glad. He'd always said he wanted to die on his boat with the sound of the sea in his ears."

"How did the boys take it?"

"It was rough for a while."

Rough. He felt an unreasonable rage toward her. Rage because she could sit there and tell him her father had died without a single sign of emotion showing on her face. Rage because she'd had nine months to deal with her loss. Rage because he hadn't been there when she'd needed him.

Fury impelled him to lash out at someone or something. Because of that seething anger he didn't dare look at her, he didn't dare speak to her. If he did, he knew he'd say something he'd regret later. Feeling as if he was trapped in an airless chamber that was slowly closing in on him, he swiftly stood up and went into the bedroom.

Chris watched him go, the hollowness inside her rendering her passionless. He slammed the door shut behind him with such force that the windows rattled, and the bang echoed through the looming silence.

She closed her eyes and rested her head on her folded arms, her body stiff with apprehension. There was a suspended lull, and she sat, waiting, every nerve and muscle in her body tensed, expecting the explosion of his wrath.

The sound of shattering glass filled the room and Chris went limp, knowing that his anger was fed by his sense of helplessness, knowing that he was assuming the responsibility for her father's death, knowing his fury was directed at himself. An incredible weariness settled over her, deadening her senses, and she huddled there, longing to weep but knowing she couldn't.

THE NEXT MORNING she heard David leave the cabin at dawn. She lay in bed, tensely waiting for the sound of a car departing. But there was only silence. Chris got up and went into the bedroom. The mirror on the dresser had been shattered, and her mind suddenly focused on a picture of David standing before it, staring at himself, despising what he saw. It was as though he had tried to destroy himself by destroying his image.

She closed her eyes and pressed her hands against her temples, her thoughts churning with a despairing sense of futility. God, where was it all going to end?

With an abject sigh she went to the dresser and began picking up the shards of glass and placing them on a discarded newspaper that was lying there. She had most of the loose pieces gathered up when the door flew open and Peter strode into the room.

He stopped short, his face creased by bewilderment as he looked from her to the mirror, then back at her. "What in hell's going on?" he demanded, his voice throttled by shock.

Deliberately she sidestepped his question. "Have you got any tools here? I need a screwdriver to take the mirror off so I can get it fixed."

He crossed the room in two strides, and catching her shoulders, he whirled her around. "What's going on, Chris? You told me last night when I got home that I shouldn't disturb David because he'd had a bad day. So I get up early this morning, worried as hell that he's had a relapse...." Peter released his grip and stared down at her, his face grim. "Damn it, something's going on. He's down at the beach, trying to jog, for God's sake, and I come in here to find this." He gestured at the shattered mirror. His eyes narrowed and his voice was stern. "Now tell me what's going on."

Chris stared up at him, a tenacious set to her chin, a look of warning in her eyes. "Just leave it, Peter."

He stared back at her, his jaw flexing, then he turned away. "Fine," he snapped. "Then I'll go talk to David. He's in no condition to be pushing himself physically, at least not as hard as he is this morning." He started toward the patio door, and Chris bolted after him.

"No!" She caught him by the arm, and he turned to face her. She closed her eyes and tipped her head back in a gesture of exhaustion. When she finally looked at him, she appeared utterly defeated. "Leave him, Peter," she pleaded quietly. "He's upset and angry, and that's his only way of dealing with it right now."

His voice had lost its hardness. "What's going on?"

Chris went to stand in front of the open patio

door, her arms folded tightly in front of her, and in a subdued voice she told Peter what had happened the day before.

When she finished speaking Peter didn't say anything, and Chris heard him leave the room. He returned shortly and began to dismantle the mirror, an oppressive silence hanging in the air. His face was grave as he set the damaged item on the floor, its weight propped against his body. Sticking the screwdriver in the back pocket of his pants, he looked at Chris. "I'll do my rounds at the hospital, but I'll cancel my office hours today. I don't want him left alone—and I think you've nearly reached your limit."

She knew exactly what Peter was thinking, and she gave him a warped smile, her tone gently admonishing. "He isn't *that* self-destructive, Peter. I think it would be best if we didn't make an issue out of this." Her expression became solemn as she twisted the hem of her nightshirt into a tight little ball. "But I think we'd better be prepared. His judgment is going to be affected by the way he's feeling right now, and he's apt to make some rash decisions."

"As rash as his decision to go to Central America in the first place?"

Chris managed to contain the sudden bolt of fear that shot through her, and she had to make a real effort to keep her voice steady. "Even more rash than that."

Her uneasiness didn't diminish as the day progressed. After returning from the beach in a state of complete exhaustion, David shut himself in the bedroom and didn't reappear until early afternoon. When he did emerge, he was brooding and uncommunicative, his face drawn with austere resolution, his eyes glacial. He was so isolated within himself that he barely acknowledged her presence.

His behavior was frightening. Under normal circumstances David was never irrational. He was quick to lose his temper, but with the exception of his decision to leave Canada, he'd always thought things through logically and thoroughly. But after enduring months of horrendous conditions and brutal treatment, his ability to see things in perspective had become distorted. And on top of that, Chris knew he was unconsciously assuming the blame for her father's death.

The tension kept mounting that day and the following one, and Chris was braced for another outburst from him. But when Peter returned from Victoria Tuesday afternoon, he brought with him some news that changed everything.

Chris was in the kitchen preparing dinner when he bounded in, a broad smile on his face, a buoyant sparkle in his eyes. "Do I have some good news for you, Christine Spencer!"

She gave him a skeptical look, then smiled wryly. "I'm beginning to feel there's no such thing as good news."

"Well, this is." Taking a stalk of celery from the

colander of freshly washed vegetables in the sink, Peter took a bite before he continued. "Mrs. Bradley was in to see me about her arthritis today." Mrs. Bradley was the Spencers' capable and somewhat acerbic housekeeper.

Chris glanced up at him, amusement lighting up her eyes. "Am I supposed to be ecstatic because Mrs. Bradley has arthritis, or is the big news that she went to see you?" she asked, her tone dry.

Peter grinned and gave her a light shove. "Nope. The big news is that David's parents will be back tomorrow. I guess Mark and Timmy got really homesick so they're bringing the boys home."

Chris's expression of amazement was followed closely by one of sheer delight. She could feel the tension in her ease and she let out her breath in a rush. "That's exactly what David needs right now—two kids who aren't going to give him one minute of peace and quiet."

"That's exactly what I thought, too." Peter took another stalk of celery. "Where is he?"

Her eyes darkened and her voice lost its animation. "He's down at the boat."

Leaning against the counter, Peter studied her closely. "How's he been today?"

"The same." She lifted a head of lettuce out of a bowl of cold water and let it drain, then glanced at him. "Why don't you go tell him?"

Peter shot her a sharp look. "Don't you want to?"

"No." It was true. She didn't. She felt that she

was back to square one as far as David was concerned. He'd been so cold and remote since he'd found out about her father. In some ways she felt more alienated from him now than she ever had before, and she was having a hard time coping with that feeling.

She closed her mind to the disturbing thoughts chasing around in her head and looked up at Peter. She experienced a wave of discomfort when she realized how intently he'd been scrutinizing her. She quickly turned away, focusing her attention on what she was doing. "Go tell him, Peter."

When the two men returned a short time later, she could detect a definite change in David. He was still aloof with her, but he was far more relaxed with Peter.

Since mealtimes were informal, Chris took her plate onto the deck. At least with her out of the cabin, Peter wouldn't have to keep making an effort to include her in the conversation. Besides, she wasn't hungry, and if she stayed inside she would have had to make some sort of a show of putting food in her mouth or Peter would comment about her lack of appetite.

She set her untouched plate on the patio table and stretched out on one of the adjustable deck chairs, resting her arm across her eyes. A heavy listlessness enveloped her. Maybe it would be best if she went back home once the boys arrived. David was well enough now to manage on his own with them, and maybe if she was away from him, she could come to grips with the changes in her life.

She could never remember feeling as depressed as she had the last couple of days. She felt as if she had depleted all her inner resources—no energy, no hope, no laughter. In fact, she couldn't remember the last time she'd really laughed. The boys coming home would give her a temporary lift, but she knew it would be only temporary. Chris was just too exhausted, too beaten to make an effort to fight her way out of this emotional low.

And now this thing with David was dragging her down even more. If she hadn't gone to him the night he'd had the bad dream, if he hadn't kissed her, if they hadn't shared that hour of companionable closeness on the beach—if, if, if. But it had happened, and she'd let it happen, and now she was going to have to suffer through the consequences— alone. She didn't think she could stand that awful loneliness, the desperate longing to have him there.

"Do you want a coffee?"

His voice startled her, and she realized he was standing very close. Deliberately keeping her arm over her eyes so she wouldn't have to look at him, Chris shook her head.

"You didn't eat anything."

So what do you care, she thought peevishly, then she experienced a small flicker of amusement. She was getting childish in her old age. Aloud, she said, "I'll eat later."

"Do you have a headache?"

She thought about it a minute and said, "Yes." She heard him pick up her plate and go back into the cabin. For a second there had been a touch of lightness in her, but the moment he left she felt more depressed than she had before. Peter was right: she was pushed to her limit.

When she finally went back into the cabin, she did have a headache, and she felt a certain amount of relief to find the kitchen clean and tidy and the dishwasher operating.

David and Peter were still sitting at the table, but they stopped talking when she came in, and she suspected they'd been discussing how David was going to publicly explain his return to Canada. However he decided to do it, it would have to be a flawless explanation. Any good investigative reporter could come up with several awkward questions—like why Chris had elected to heavily mortage a pricey apartment complex when she did. But that was his problem to deal with, she told herself.

Picking up a news magazine from the kitchen counter, she went over to the conversation area and curled up in one of the big easy chairs. She knew she couldn't focus her attention long enough to read anything, but at least, she thought wryly, she could look at the pictures.

Almost immediately the two men followed her. David sat down in a chair facing hers and Peter stretched out on the sofa, his shoulders propped up against the arm, his hands behind his head.

She had always liked Peter. He was so easygoing, so unaffected, and he had such a neat sense of humor. Ellis, his wife, was another story altogether. She was high-strung, slightly self-centered and very caught up in the social whirl of the high society that Chris had found so stifling. Chris didn't dislike her. She just found Ellis hard to take in large doses.

Maybe Peter did, too. For several years they had maintained two homes—one on the island and one on the mainland in North Vancouver. Ellis spent as much time in Vancouver as she did in Victoria with Peter. It was either through good luck or good management, but she had been on the mainland for the past month. Chris didn't know what they would have done if they'd had to contend with Ellis. They wouldn't have dared tell her about bringing David home: it would have been like printing it on the front page of the newspaper.

Chris's contemplation was interrupted when Peter spoke. "I told David that I'd pick the boys up from his folks' tomorrow." He was staring at her so intently that Chris was sure she'd missed part of the conversation, but then she realized that he was trying to get a silent message across to her. He shook his head slightly, and she knew he was cautioning her not to interfere with the plans.

She understood. "That's probably best, but how are you going to explain—" The question was out before she thought, and her words died on her lips. This was *not* the kind of issue to bring up in front of David. She would have to talk to Peter later.

David was watching her through hooded eyes and she could almost feel him tune in on her uneasiness. Just the way he held his head and rested his hands across his chest, she knew very well he hadn't missed the drift of her unfinished query. "How's he going to explain what, Christine?" he asked, his voice dangerously soft.

Without thinking she made a second mistake when she shot Peter a look of alarm. She felt even more unnerved when she saw a spark of annoyance in the doctor's eyes.

"I asked you a question," David said, his tone like ice.

Chris felt the color drain out of her face, and she took a shaky breath. "It's nothing important...."

Peter rose to her defense, his annoyance flushing his face. "What Chris is trying like hell to avoid telling you is that when you took off to Central America, everyone and their dog turned on her. Your parents don't speak to her—they have the boys picked up and delivered by their driver. I could have happily wrung her neck for walking out on you—I wouldn't speak to her." His voice became bitingly sarcastic and tinged with disgust. "Do you know, David, that when her father died, there wasn't one person from our sanctimonious yacht club that even went to the funeral!"

Chris stared up at him, her eyes wide with shock, unable to believe that he was spouting off the way he was. "Shut up, Peter," she cut in sharply, her voice low with anger. "That's old garbage and you know it."

He clamped his mouth shut and stared rigidly at the ceiling, his silence leaving an electric tension in the room. His voice was more controlled when he finally spoke. "It isn't old garbage, Chris. You're still treated like a leper, and you know it." Shifting his position on the sofa, he turned to look at David. "What Chris is worried about is how can we explain why I'm picking the boys up, especially when your folks think I haven't spoken to Chris in four years. Until you make up your mind what you're going to do, we don't want to arouse any suspicions."

David hadn't altered his position. He was still staring at Chris through squinted eyes, his hands clasped across his chest, his head tilted to one side. But his expression didn't seem quite so inflexible. After a taut silence he said, "Is that what you're worried about, Chris—that you don't know how Peter can explain this to my parents?"

She felt totally spent and she shrugged, the gesture eloquently expressing her feeling of defeat. "Yes, that's what I'm worried about."

He stared at her, then suddenly and unexpectedly a flash of humor brightened his eyes. "Why doesn't Peter tell them it's none of their damned business?"

Chris felt a hot-and-cold current tingle through her body, followed by a powerful surge of relief. His fury, like a wild swiftly moving storm, was finally spent.

CHAPTER FIVE

DAVID WAS BACK TO PACING the following morning, but Chris suspected his restlessness was induced by rigidly contained anticipation. She understood how he felt. She was feeling much the same way herself.

The boys might drive her crazy at times, and there were certainly occasions when she wondered if she was cut out to be a mother, but she loved them and missed them very much when they were gone. The house, her life, seemed empty when they weren't around.

She was in the kitchen making chocolate-chip cookies by the dozens, her ears constantly tuned for the sound of Peter's car. But he would be a while yet. She had given him the key to her house to pick up the boys' fishing rods, their life jackets and anything else they might want to bring with them. Knowing them the way she did, she hoped Peter put his foot down. If he didn't, he could end up with the entire contents of their rooms stuffed in his car.

She and Peter had decided that morning not to tell them their father was at the cabin, partly because they would pester the life out of him on the drive back if they knew, and partly because both of them wanted to see the expressions on their faces when they saw David.

She took the last batch of cookies from the oven and placed them on the cooling racks, her face pensive. It had been such a rotten year for them: the news about their father, the death of their grandfather, the loss of Downer. There had been many dark and lonely nights when she had held a sobbing child in her arms, trying to shield a small boy from the awful hurt, the terrible sense of loss that was so bewildering.

She had ached for both of them, but especially ten-year-old Timmy. Even though Mark was two years younger, he was able to come to terms with his grief much better, probably because his emotional makeup was much like his father's. He'd brood about it for a while then explode in a temper and yell about how unfair it was, but he'd always sit down and talk about what he was feeling.

Timmy was different. He bottled everything up inside and refused to talk about it. He'd always been an excellent student in school, but this year he had nearly failed his grade. Chris knew it was a result of the extreme emotional stress he was under.

He was a deeply sensitive child, keenly aware of what other people were feeling, but he was especially tuned in to his mother. His sensitivity to others was a major factor in the way he dealt with his fears, his uncertainties, his hurt. Because he was the eldest, he felt he had to be strong for Chris, and she'd spent many sleepless nights worrying about him. Both boys needed time with their father, but it was Timmy who needed it the most. They all needed time together.

"I presume you don't intend on making cookies again for at least six months," David commented as he leaned against the opposite side of the counter.

He helped himself to a handful and Chris gave him a meaningful look as she set a baking sheet in the sink. She indicated the cookies he held and said pointedly, "Having been a boy once yourself, don't you *know* they'll simply inhale these like air?"

He grinned. "We never inhaled Bradley's cookies, I can tell you that. You had to soak them in a glass of milk for at least an hour before you could get your teeth through them."

Chris suppressed a smile as she sent an amused but somewhat dubious glance at him. "That's a lie, David Spencer, and you know it."

"It isn't," he protested, fond recollection lighting his face. "They were always like bullets. Bradley's Baked Bullets we used to call them, which was eventually shortened to Bradley's B.B.s."

Chris laughed, her face animated with delight. "That's awful."

His expression altered dramatically, and his eyes became intense and compelling. "Do you know that's the first time I've heard you laugh since I've been back," he said softly, his voice provocatively husky.

Chris couldn't tear her eyes away from his, and she felt a weakness invade her body. *Don't look at me like that, David,* she silently pleaded. *You don't know what it does to me when you look at me like that.*

As though drawn against his will, David slowly reached across the counter and cupped her flushed face in his hand, his thumb lightly caressing her cheek. His expression suddenly became inscrutable.

His touch drugged her, and Chris's eyes drifted shut. The only real thing in her spinning world was the warm pressure of his hand against her face. Her breathing became erratic as he drew his thumb slowly across her lips, parting them with a gentle pressure.

"Look at me, Chris," he said softly.

An intoxicating languor sapped her strength, and Chris had to make a real effort to open her eyes. David was watching her with rapt concentration, his eyes smoldering. With tantalizing lightness he began to caress the sensitive flesh of her neck, his touch sending a current of ice and fire down her spine. She trembled as he slid his hand up the back of her neck, his fingers tunneling into her hair, and he continued to caress her, tormenting her with his electrifying touch.

The distant sound of a car horn sliced through the sexually charged silence and Chris felt her legs almost give way beneath her. David swore. He clenched his jaw tightly and closed his eyes, and his fingers spasmodically grasped a handful of her hair. Finally he took a deep breath and looked at her, his eyes dark with regret. Without saying anything he let his hand slip down her neck to her shoulder, and slowly eased it along her arm. Catching her hand in his, he led her around the end of the counter until she was standing before him. Tenderly he combed the hair from her face, his hand lingering briefly on the back of her head.

His voice was low when he spoke, "Let's go see our boys, Chris."

Chris was in such a state she couldn't answer him, and as she looked up, her hand tightened around his. She was unaware how much her eyes revealed. David whispered her name and pressed her face against his shoulder. He held her for a moment, then with a deep sigh of reluctance said, "We'd better go."

When they stepped onto the deck at the back of the cabin, Chris had to squint against the blinding brightness of the sun. Peter's car was just pulling into the clearing, and David's grip on her hand increased when he heard excited shouts from the car. The vehicle hadn't even stopped moving when the passenger door flew open and two boys tumbled out and started sprinting toward them.

"Dad—it's dad! It's really dad!" they kept yelling as they raced across the open space, wild uncontainable joy radiating from their faces. She felt David's body jerk, and she heard him take a faltering breath as he let go of her hand, vaulted over the railing of the deck and ran to meet them. They flung themselves into his outstretched arms with the momentum of two torpedoes. Crouching down, he swept them up in a crushing embrace and squeezed his eyes shut in a grimace of pain.

Chris had never experienced such heartrending feelings before in her life, and she was utterly helpless against them. As she went down the steps and walked toward them, tears were slipping down her face, and she had to choke back the sobs in her aching chest. The three of them huddled together, clinging to one another with a desperation that spoke of diminishing fear. Each of them had known deep within themselves that there had been a real danger David might never come home again. Now that he was back, safe and unharmed, each could admit how truly afraid he had been, and allow tears to wash away the residue of unspoken terror.

Mark was hugging his father so fiercely he was nearly strangling him, and his own eyes were shut tight as he kept repeating, "I knew you'd come home—I knew you would," in a voice so tremulous it was barely understandable.

Timmy, too, had his arms around his dad, but his face was buried in his shoulder. His husky little body heaved with harsh sobs as he gave way to all the awful fear and hurt that had darkened his life for so long.

Brushing away her tears with the back of her hand, Chris knelt before them, the pain in her chest becoming unbearable. But she had to hang on—she had to. She knew if she didn't contain the pressure that was building in her with such tremendous force, she would be ripped apart. She didn't dare let herself go; she didn't dare. Not now. This man needed her now; he needed her strength; he needed her compassion; he needed what comfort she could give him.

With infinite tenderness she wiped away his tears with trembling fingers, then cradled his ashen face in her hands. A violent shudder bolted through David's body as he took a racking breath and looked at her, his eyes so tormented, so filled with remembered pain it nearly tore her apart. It was there in his eyes—the agony for all the times he'd wondered if he'd ever see his sons again.

Overwhelmed by a surge of compassion and immeasurable love, she gathered all three of them against her, her embrace all-encompassing and fiercely protective. Her arm encircled Mark's clinging body as she pressed David's damp drawn face against the curve of her neck and stroked his head, longing to absorb his anguish, to erase the ugliness and horror imprinted on his memory. For a time they were all bonded together by a profound thanksgiving.

Slowly, very slowly she felt David regain control. She pulled his head against her in one last quick embrace, then reluctantly withdrew her arms and stood up, purposely avoiding his gaze. She didn't want either Mark or Tim to have any false hopes about why she was there. They were too apt to start dreaming the impossible dream about their parents getting back together, and if they did, they would only be hurt all over again. Besides, the three of them needed some time alone. But it was so hard to walk away. So very hard.

She found Peter in the cabin, his eyes suspiciously red, but he seemed relatively composed, or at least he did until he gave her a sheepish grin. "No cute comments, Chris. In case you didn't know it, you're looking at a guy who couldn't sit through *Old Yeller*."

A glint of amusement flickered in her eyes as she gave him an unsteady smile. "Don't worry about it. You're looking at a grown woman who still can't sit through *Bambi* without choking up." Taking a slow breath to ease the tightness that still gripped her chest, she went into the kitchen. "If you were worth your salt as a godfather, you'd tell me where I could hide these damned cookies before the boys come in."

Peter sprawled out in one of the easy chairs at the end of the open room, a cunning smile on his face. "Put 'em in the bathtub. I don't know any self-respecting boy who'd ever go near a bathtub."

That coaxed a chuckle out of her, and she gave him a slightly disgruntled look. "You'll have to do better than that, Peter." She paused for a minute, her expression thoughtful, then she opened the bottom cupboard and dug out an old tin bread box she'd found when she'd cleaned out the cupboards. After lining the inside with foil, she placed most of the cookies inside, put the lid back on and placed the container back in the cupboard. With a satisfied nod of her head, she began to stack the remainder of the cookies on a large plate.

"Mothers are such sneaks," said Peter in an amused tone.

The screen door at the back of the cabin opened and David and the two boys came in. Chris cast a quick glance at them. They all looked a little ravaged emotionally, but obviously the worst hurdle was behind them. She let out a quiet sigh of relief, then smiled at the boys. "Well, guys, how was your holiday?" She knew both of them would rather drop dead than hug her in front of two men, so she made no move toward them.

"Hey, chocolate-chip cookies!" enthused Mark, totally ignoring her question as he helped himself to a fistful of cookies.

With a glance of mild rebuke, David neatly extracted two cookies from his son's hand and put them back on the plate. "It would be nice if you at least said, 'Hi, mom, how are you?' before you started stuffing your face."

Mark grinned at his mother, the spattering of freckles across his nose giving him a mischievous air. "Hi, mom. How are you?" he complied willingly, then flashed an engaging smile at his father as his hand inched toward the plate. "She makes such *good* cookies, dad," he said, blatantly trying to charm his father into relenting.

David pursed his lips to keep from grinning and firmly shook his head, ignoring Mark's charm. "Can it, Mark. It won't work."

Timmy slipped unnoticed around the counter and covertly eased his not-quite-clean hand into his mother's, his fingers clasping hers tightly. "Hi, mom," he whispered timorously. His drawn face was unnaturally pale beneath his tan, and Chris's heart went out to him.

With an aching lump swelling in her throat, she knelt down and hugged him against her. "I'm glad you're home, Timmy," she murmured softly. "I've missed you."

Looping his arms around her neck, he pressed his face against her shoulder, and she could feel his body shudder as he tried not to cry. With a maternal gesture she combed her fingers through his tousled hair, her cheek pressed against his head. "Were you really homesick?" she whispered, compassion adding a soft richness to her voice. He nodded his head as he took a breath that bordered on a sob. She tried to inject some lightness into her voice as she teased, "Does this mean you'll make your bed and throw your dirty clothes in the laundry hamper from now on?"

She felt another shudder course through him, but this time it was a mixture of tears and laughter. He pulled away from her and flashed her one of those slightly disgusted looks that always reminded her so much of David. "I wasn't *that* homesick," he said, a wobbly grin crinkling his eyes.

Catching his face in her hands, she grinned back at him. "I didn't think so." She ruffled his hair and stood up. "Why don't you go wash your face and I'll fix some lemonade."

"Okay." With an angelic expression on his face that didn't fool anyone, Timmy glanced up at his dad. Making a very big production out of it, he carefully selected one cookie that was loaded with chocolate chips.

"Cute, Timmy. Really cute," said David, his tone dry.

Timmy grinned up at him. "Aren't you going to have any, dad? They aren't hard like Mrs. Bradley's."

Raising his eyebrows in a superior "I told you so" expression, David grinned at Chris. There was a gleam of humor in her eyes as she shrugged, silently conceding that as much as she hated to admit it, he hadn't been stringing her a line about Mrs. Bradley's Baked Bullets.

Timmy looked from his father to his mother, his small sunburned face lighting up. He bent his head and with small-boy awkwardness mumbled, "It's really nice having both you guys here together." Without looking at either of them, he spun around and ran outside, leaving a taut and uncomfortable silence behind him.

It was Peter who bailed them out of the tense situation. Sauntering over to the kitchen area, he dropped his hand on David's shoulder. "It's time to put you to work, David. Those two kids of yours stuffed my car with everything from baseball gloves to two boxes of comic books. If we start now, we *might* have it all unloaded by midnight."

Feeling as though everything was suddenly closing in on her, Chris slipped out the patio door at the front of the cabin and headed for the beach. She desperately needed some time alone to think.

The wishfulness in Timmy's voice had been revealing and more than a little disquieting. She'd been afraid of this happening, that the boys would see this as a permanent reconciliation between their parents, and as much as she would like it to be so, she couldn't allow that misconception to take root. The boys would end up being hurt all over again, and David would feel more guilty than ever.

The only solution was for her to go back to Victoria and leave the three of them alone, just as she would any other summer. Somehow she would have to find the words to explain to Mark and Timmy that although she and David had put some of their differences behind them, nothing had really changed.

Just the thought of talking to them was more than she could face. The way she was feeling right now, she didn't know where she'd get the strength or the composure to do it. She felt as though her protective shield was a tough armor of scales, and one by one those scales were dropping off, leaving her raw and exposed. Her defenses were nearly gone, and she was scared. She simply couldn't cope with the stress much longer.

Her despair completely insulated her from the world around her, and she drew no comfort from the sound of the sea or the feel of the wind on her face. She walked along the log-strewn beach, her head bent, her hands rammed in her jean pockets and her eyes haunted by disturbing thoughts.

She hadn't even realized that she was walking back toward the cabin until she saw David loping along the beach toward her. His body seemed so small against the vast expanse of sea and sand. If only she had the right to run to meet him; if only she could lose this awful feeling of sorrow in the strong safe harbor of his arms. But that reflection was too painful, too disturbing, and she closed her mind to her own wishful thinking.

His face was slightly flushed and his breathing a little labored as he approached her, but for a man who was near death three weeks ago, he was in surprisingly good condition. Two more weeks of rest and decent food and he would be fully recovered.

And he would leave again. Just the thought was more than she could handle.

He fell into step with her, and they walked a short distance in silence. When he finally did speak, his tone was sharp, almost blunt. "What's the matter, Chris?"

She was about to invent some sort of evasive response, but she changed her mind. If she wanted to build any kind of association with him for the sake of the boys, she was going to have to learn to be open with him. Squinting against the glare of the sun, she glanced up at him, then looked away, unable to hold his gaze. "I think it might be a good idea if I left."

"Why?"

She shrugged uncertainly. She was feeling too inept and inexperienced to answer his question with frankness. "I'm afraid the boys are going to read more into my being here than they should."

There was an inflection of harshness in his voice as he said, "And what's that supposed to mean?"

She caught a loose pebble with the toe of her shoe and started kicking it in front of her, its path leaving an indistinct trail in the wet compacted sand. She was stalling, trying to give herself some time to sort out her muddled thoughts.

Keenly aware of the tension that had sprung up between them, she wanted to clam up, to say nothing, but she forced herself to try to explain. "You may not realize it, but this is very hard for me,

David," she said, her voice shaking slightly. "I've never learned how to talk about the things that are bothering me. I suppose part of it is because I'm so afraid I'm going to say something that's going to either offend or hurt someone. And because of that, I feel very unsure of myself."

His voice was less intense, a little kinder. "Is it that, or is it a lack of trust?"

She stopped walking and looked up at him with complete candor, her troubled eyes silently betraying her inner anguish. "It isn't a lack of trust," she said, her voice strengthened by her surety. "I've always trusted you, David. The big problem is me—how I think, how I feel." Her hands still stuck in her pockets, she looked down at the space of sand that separated their feet. Sunlight glinted off the gold chain she wore around her neck. "I'm so afraid that I might say something wrong—that I might express my thoughts badly. I want to be able to communicate with you, and I don't know how."

More of her protective armor fell away as David hooked his knuckles under her chin and lightly applied pressure. She didn't want to look at him, but his touch compelled her to meet his unwavering gaze.

The sea breeze was parting his hair with invisible fingers, and the angle of the sun accentuated the masculine contours of his face, giving him an aura of invincibility. But once again there was a contradiction. That aura of invincibility surrounded him, but an unguarded warmth in his eyes revealed his vulnerability. Chris knew that her confession had touched him deeply.

His voice was charged with emotion when he spoke. "Do you know that in the past few days you've been more open with me than you were the entire time we were living together?" Strands of hair were blowing across her face, and he carefully tucked them behind her ear, his hand lingering on her neck as his gaze searched her. "But why now, Chris?" he asked, his voice oddly tormented. "Why are you telling me this now?"

Her eyes never left his as she swallowed, struggling to suppress all the emotions that were threatening to break loose. "Because I don't want any more bad feelings between us, David." Her voice faltered. "I...I don't want any more misunderstandings, I don't want any more bitterness."

He stared at her for a moment and then looked away, his eyes fixed on the distant horizon, his expression inscrutable. "Then why do you want to leave?"

She lowered her head and began pushing the wet sand into ridges with the side of her shoe, deliberately avoiding his gaze. "If I stay, the boys are going to start thinking this arrangement is forever." She shrugged self-consciously and looked up at him, her eyes distressed. "I don't know what your plans are, and that's none of my business, but it's fairly safe to say you aren't going to stay in Victoria." She looked down again, methodically flattening the ridges of sand she'd formed, her voice uneven. "I'm going to have to explain to them that this is just like any other summer—that it isn't going to last forever."

"Do you really trust me, Chris?"

She glanced back up at him and experienced a peculiar sinking sensation in her stomach when she saw how intently he was regarding her. "Yes, I really trust you."

He stared at her for a long time, as if he was weighing her answer. Then slowly he held out his hand, and Chris's heart started racing. She stared at him, unable to believe what he was really holding out to her. It was his way of offering his forgiveness. She wanted to throw herself into his arms and weep, but instead she placed her hand in his, her fingers curling tightly around his firm grip.

"Will you do me a favor?" he asked.

Not trusting herself to speak, she nodded her head, unable to drag her eyes away from his.

"Will you stay for a few more days, and we'll talk to the boys together."

Chris knew she was making the second-biggest mistake of her life, but a few torturous days with him were better than an empty lifetime alone. "If you want me to stay, I'll stay."

DAVID LAY IN HIS BED, listening to the nighttime sounds that drifted in through the open window, trying not to think about the woman who was sleeping in the other room. But try as he might, he could not eradicate her from his thoughts, and he felt as if he was being torn in two.

He wanted her; he wanted her more than anything. He'd been trying to fight that gnawing hunger for four years and had never succeeded. It was not anything new.

What was new was the change in her. In all the years they'd lived together, he could never remember her being as candid as she was now. At first he had been suspicious about what was motivating her, but he couldn't overlook one basic fact—Chris had never lied in her life. She might have kept things from him, she might not have been open, but she didn't lie. He believed her; he believed everything she'd told him since he'd come back. Her confessions had answered many questions, but that didn't alter his own doubts.

When he dug through all the old debris in his mind, he discovered he was quite capable of forgiving her for what had happened, but he also discovered he couldn't trust her. As much as he wanted to, he could not trust her. That was the one thing she'd destroyed forever when she had walked out on him, and it was the one thing he had to have—that kind of deep-in-the-gut certainty that she'd stick with him no matter what.

He would rather have died in that hellhole than have to go through the agony of learning to survive without her again. Yet here he was, setting himself up for a replay. She said she was leaving and he'd asked her to stay. He was leaving himself wide open and it scared him like hell.

But the way she was looking scared him like hell, too. Her spirit, her zest for life seemed to be shriveling up inside her. What bothered him the most was the look in her eyes. God, but it haunted him. She'd look at him, and he wanted to gather her against him so damned much, to protect her from whatever was tormenting her so.

David cursed softly and rolled over onto his stomach, trying to ignore the awful emptiness that was twisting his insides into knots. Night after night he had been plagued by memories—memories of how good it felt to make love to her, how soft, how warm, how giving her body was as she moved beneath him, what it felt like to have her hands on his body.

But he wanted her for much more than just sexual gratification. Some of the most poignant memories he had of her had nothing to do with sex. Memories of her nestled against him at night, her body swollen with his child, memories of the way she'd tease him and make him laugh when he was in a temper, memories of the way she'd guard their privacy with a vengeance when she knew he was under a lot of stress at work.

The memories were driving him crazy, warping his mind. It was insane, but he'd experienced a slicing jealousy that morning when Chris had comforted Timmy. Jealous of his own son—jealous because Timmy had been able to nestle his head against her shoulder and let her comfort him.

He knew why he'd felt the way he had. He'd desperately needed some comforting himself, but not the kind of soothing comfort Chris had given Timmy. David had needed the kind of comfort that only she could give him—the kind of comfort that could be found only when all the pain and anguish had been incinerated in a holocaust of passion, leaving behind the embers of a contentment so pure, so satiated, that it obliterated all else.

But Chris had always had that power over him. The power to arouse, to inflame, to give him a degree of satisfaction he'd never known with any other woman. For a long time he'd hated her for it, but now it made him want her all the more. What it all boiled down to was that he missed her, he missed having her care about him, and he missed her like hell at night. The thought of her sleeping beside him, her naked body pressed against his, made him grit his teeth against the agony of wanting her. Knowing she was just beyond the door, in bed, only made it worse.

But Chris wasn't in bed. She was standing on the deck, frantically hoping that the chilly night air would cool her fevered body. She was trying vainly to fight down the hungry longing that had been tormenting her for days.

But her desire had broken through the thin bond of restraint and was raging out-of-bounds. It had been too long, too lonely, too empty without David, and her body was screaming in protest against months and months of denial. She had never known the kind of agony she was enduring now. Her loins were engorged with a heavy throbbing ache that sensitized her flesh until she felt as if a current of electricity was coursing through her. She couldn't stand it. She just couldn't stand it.

Grasping the rail tightly, she leaned her head back and closed her eyes, unable to block out the thoughts rampaging through her mind. Thoughts of the way it felt to have him stroke her, his hands warm and intimate upon her body; the way it felt to have his moist mouth against her breast; the way it felt to have him enter her, his hips flexing against hers, their hot aroused bodies straining together. A deep tortured moan was wrung from her as waves of scorching desire pounded through her, annihilating her rationality, her awareness.

"What's the matter, Chris?" His voice was so soft that the sound of it barely penetrated her tormented senses. It took the last of her strength to turn her head and look at him. He was moving toward her. His muscled body, naked except for a pair of cutoffs, was silhouetted against the rectangle of soft light that spilled from the bedroom.

Her grip on the rail became her crucial support as he approached her, and she swayed weakly, her throbbing body unable to endure the pressure that was mounting inside her. She fought desperately to master her desire, but she was powerless against the urgent need that possessed her. Her battle was lost the moment he framed her face with his hands, his touch wresting another agonized moan from her.

"Christie, baby—what's wrong?" His voice was ragged, and she twisted her head, but not in denial. It was a frantic gesture that explained more eloquently than words what an impassioned storm was raging inside her. Hoarsely whispering her name, he crushed her against him in a near-savage embrace that severed her last touch with reality.

Whatever his intentions had been, they were shot to hell the moment David gathered her into his arms and felt the soft flesh of her body fused against his. His own unleashed desire came crashing in on him, and he possessed her mouth with a ruthless hunger that demanded sustenance. He nearly went wild when her mouth slackened beneath his assault, completely surrendering the moist hot recesses to his probing tongue.

But a single shred of sanity pierced through his crazed state when he felt how violently she was shaking. He dragged his mouth away from hers, fighting to stay rational, realizing that if he released her, she would crumple to the ground. Breathing as if he had just run five miles, he tried to soothe her, to calm her, but her trembling only became more intense. Finally he comprehended what was happening to her.

Chris had been pushed beyond her limit, her

body could tolerate no more, and she had slipped into a delirium of passion over which she had not one ounce of control. Right then her need was far greater than his, and knowing that gave him the willpower to harness the bombardment within himself.

Supporting her securely with one arm, he reached down and grasped the thick mattress from one of the lounges and tossed it onto the deck. Then, with infinite care, he lowered her onto it. He stretched beside her and cradled her gently in one arm as he undid the buttons on her housecoat, fighting to suppress a driving desire to caress her naked skin. She twisted beneath his touch, and he had all he could do to contain the blaze of passion her frantic movement aroused in him. He could barely breathe as he eased his hand between her thighs. She stiffened against him and cried out, then caught his hand and tried to pull it away.

He tightened his arm around her and pressed his face against hers. "Trust me, baby. Just trust me," he whispered hoarsely against her hair.

"David—God, David—" It was such tremulous plea it was barely audible, but for some reason the helplessness he heard in it gave him strength.

"Hang on to me, baby. Hang on and don't let go," he murmured, his voice choked, and he found her mouth with a soft searching kiss as he began to stroke her. Her arms tightened convulsively around his chest, her trembling body tensing and arching toward his touch, pushing feverishly against his hand. He could feel the tempest cresting in her as her mouth became searing, insistent beneath his, then she jerked violently, as though a powerful voltage had bolted through her body. David pressed the heel of his hand hard against her when he felt the spasms of release shudder through her, leaving her writhing against him.

Pulling his mouth away from hers, he fought for breath and for discipline. His own burgeoning need was so great that he thought he was going to explode, but he disregarded it as he gathered her beneath him in an all-encompassing embrace. Her heart pounded wildly against his naked chest as he waited for the storm in her to subside.

It seemed to take an eternity before her body relaxed and her hold on him eased. Her hands spread out against his back and she began to caress him, her touch galvanizing his senses. With excruciating slowness, her fingers moved up his back until she reached his shoulders, then she caught his head in her hands and found his mouth with a soft pliant kiss.

But David had been pushed to the extremes of his restraint, and the moistness of her mouth as it moved against his drove him beyond his limitations. His response was untamed, uncontrolled and nearly brutal. He knew what he was doing but he simply could not stop himself. When she answered his onslaught with a blistering passion, he realized that her release had only temporarily vented the unbearable pressure of a long-denied and fermenting need.

He withdrew his mouth, his breathing tortured. "Easy, Christie," he whispered huskily against her lips. "Not here—the boys may get up."

She, too, was fighting for breath, fighting to restrain a flaming passion, but she seemed powerless against it. Without releasing his hold on her he rose to his knees, and with shaking hands he stripped her housecoat from her, then stood up and drew her to her feet. He felt her knees buckle beneath her, and he swept her up in his arms and carried her into the bedroom.

As he laid her on the bed and stared down at the physical perfection of her, he felt his own knees weaken. He had forgotten how damned beautiful she was. He slid his shorts over his hips, and she watched him with eyes heavily glazed by desire. As he came toward her, she lifted her arms to receive him.

There was so much longing, such repressed sexuality in the one small gesture that it overwhelmed him, and he collapsed on top of her, unable to stand any longer. He wanted to please her, to arouse her, to give her the most pleasure he could, and he eased down to capture her breast with his mouth.

He had barely touched her when she caught his head and jerked it away. "No, David," she moaned, "I can't stand any more."

David could feel beads of perspiration on his

brow as he framed her face with his hands, his eyes searching hers. "Tell me what you want, Chris." His hold on her face tightened. "Tell me."

She closed her eyes briefly and drew in an uneven breath, then she looked at him and whispered brokenly, "I want to feel you inside me." She slid her hand down his side, and reached for him. Clenching his eyes shut in a wrenching grimace, David eased himself away slightly as she guided him into her. Shock waves slammed through them both, and David had to force himself not to move against her.

But the feel of her hot wetness surrounding him was almost more than he could stand, and he had to grit his teeth to choke back a groan. The gentleness of her hands on his face penetrated the heat that licked through him, and he opened his eyes and gazed down at her, feeling as if he was drowning in the inflamed passion he saw there.

He couldn't endure much more, but his need to please her was more powerful than his need for release, and with immeasurable tenderness he caressed her face. "Talk to me, baby," he murmured hoarsely. "Tell me what you want."

Her eyes fluttered shut and her arms tightened around him. "I want you to hold me as tight as you can. I want you to love me—and I don't want you to be gentle." She moved beneath him, her voice breaking. "Love me David...God, I need you to love me."

Her anguished plea severed the last of his resistance, and David crushed her against him in a savage embrace as he moved his body against hers, straining to give her pleasure, struggling to hold back his own release.

Agonizing moments passed that stretched his control to the limit before she cried out his name and arched her back, silently begging him to satisfy her. His body wet with sweat, he shifted his hold and clasped her hips, welding them against his own. A driving tempo possessed him, and their bodies ground together with a primal craving that demanded fulfillment. Just when he thought he could stand no more, he felt her climax, and his groan ripped the air as release was torn from him with a rendering force. They clung together, their hot bodies fusing into one.

The overwhelming intensity of what they'd shared drained them both, and it was a long time before David could find the strength to move.

Her arms tightened around him as he started to ease off her, and he whispered against her ear, "I'm too heavy, Chris. Let me hold you like I used to." Bracing his elbows against the bed, he slowly withdrew from her, and with a deep sigh gathered her against him and rolled over onto his back. Nestling her head on his shoulder, he tucked her knee between his, then reached down and drew the sheet over them.

A deep contentment he hadn't experienced for a

very long time suffused his body, and he folded his arms around her and began to stroke her hair. For a long while he lay there, savoring the feel of her, the soft warmth of her breasts against his chest, the weight of her arm across his torso, the smoothness of her skin.

As he breathed in the fragrance of her hair, a revelation dawned on him. Because she had been afraid for him, because she couldn't stand knowing about the horror, the filth, the torture he had been subjected to, she had brought him home—brought him back to the sweetest, most-profound pleasure he had ever known. And he realized that he would endure the months of agony all over again if he knew he had a night like this waiting for him.

CHAPTER SIX

CHRIS AWOKE AS THE NIGHT SKY was just beginning to lighten, her senses engulfed by the arousing warmth of David's body against hers. He held her with one arm cradling her back, his other hand resting on her neck, and his fingers buried in her hair. Memories did fade with time, she realized. She had forgotten how marvelous it felt to wake up in his arms, so secure, so contented.

The light beside the bed filled the room with a soft amber glow. She longed to shift her head so she could look at him, but she knew if she moved he would waken. It was strange, but even after the intimacy they'd shared last night, or maybe because of it, she found the thought of facing him a little daunting. She had no idea how he would react, and if she had any sense, the smartest thing she could do would be to leave while he was still asleep.

The weight of his hand shifted slightly as he spanned her chin and tipped her head back. He didn't say anything as he gazed at her, his eyes smoky and slumberous, mesmerizing her with a seductive intensity.

He gathered her tightly against him, and Chris's eyes drifted shut. Her lips parted as he covered her mouth in a languid kiss that set her pulse racing and kindled a breathless excitement in her. How he could prime her body with a single kiss.

That kiss intensified as he moved his lips against hers with a thoroughness that drained her of strength and left her as pliable as warm putty beneath his touch. With the weight of his body he pressed her back until she was lying flat on the bed, his arms like bands of steel around her, his broad chest crushed against the full swell of her breasts.

With tormenting slowness he explored her mouth, his tongue stroking, searching, the moist invasion stirring the fire of desire building in her. She responded with provocative counterstrokes meant to ignite his desire, and David's kiss became almost bruising as he lost the reins to his tightly leashed passion.

Roughly whispering her name, he dragged his mouth away and buried his face against the curve of her neck. His breath rasped against her ear as he fought for control. She could drive him out of his mind with the slightest response, but he had to hang on. He wanted to reacquaint himself with every inch of her beautiful yielding body. He wanted to discover the taste of her, the fragrance of her, the feel of her, all over again.

Last night they had been caught in a driving hunger that greedily demanded immediate fulfillment. But now he wanted time, time to slowly savor this sensuous banquet, and above all he wanted to give her pleasure.

Finally he raised his head and kissed her with infinite tenderness, acutely aware of how tightly she was clinging to him, her soft body molded against his. He slipped his hand around her slender neck, his fingers lightly caressing as he murmured against her lips, "Don't rush it, baby. We have time to enjoy."

Her arms gripped his shoulders and he felt her shudder beneath him as she whispered, "I want you so badly. It's been so long."

There was something about the helplessness of her admission that penetrated the rational depths of David's mind, and his body tensed as suspicion tore through him. So long since when? Since who? His self-disgust gnawed at his conscience. He had no right to feel the way he did, but he was unable to stand the thought of her in another man's arms, and he was filled with a silent rage.

David tensed his muscles to roll away from her, but the recollection of her wild frenzy of desire the night before penetrated his jealousy. She had acted like a starving woman who had been denied sustenance for a long time. A very long time.

His insides were in a hard knot as he took her face in his hands and gazed down at her, hesitant about asking, afraid of the answer.

She touched his cheek with trembling fingers, unaware of the battle that was raging in him. Her voice was unsteady and weak when she whispered, "You touch me and I can't think—I go out of my mind. It's been so long, David. So long."

Relief. Immobilizing relief. Without a shadow of a doubt, he knew there had been no other man in her life since him. No other man had ever possessed her, no other man had ever tasted the intoxicating passion that drove him wild. A fierce protectiveness he'd never known before gripped him, and he folded his arms around her in a crushing embrace. A new strength rose up, reinforcing his control. Regardless of how desperately he wanted her, he would give her pleasure like none she'd ever known. He would carry her to new heights that would leave her without strength, without conscious thought.

David's mouth moved against hers in a kiss that made her melt beneath him. His voice made rough by emotion, he whispered against her lips, telling her how he was going to make love to her, the intimate explicitness of his words arousing her until she was trembling and struggling for breath. Sensing how fragile she was, how raw her feelings were, he eased onto his side and pulled her against him in an infinitely tender hold.

As he had done the night before, he set about assuaging the fever within her, his hand stroking her until she was writhing against him. Passion possessed her until finally she cried out his name and arched against him, her body shuddering with racking spasms.

She lay trembling in his arms and he caressed her back with long gentle strokes, soothing her with his touch and softly spoken words until she calmed and lay peacefully beside him.

But that was only the beginning. The darkened sky faded into the gray mist of dawn and the rising sun tinted the clouds with a blaze of color, and still David held back. Over and over again he brought her to the tempestuous climax of a need that had been denied repletion for too long. Finally he could no longer resist her husky pleadings or her arousing caresses and he took her, struggling to be tender. But the fire in his blood seared through his last tie with conscious thought and he thrust his body roughly against hers, the culmination of his own desire wringing passion-laden groans from him.

His strength totally consumed, he slumped against her, and their sweat-dampened bodies melted together like hot wax. They had both come through a storm unlike any they had ever experienced before, and they were both shaking and fighting for breath, their hearts pounding wildly as they clung to each other. It had been so wild, so incredible.

It took a long time for lucid thoughts to surface, and from some inner source David finally dredged up enough energy to move. Gritting his teeth against the throbbing tenderness of nearly bruised flesh, he slowly withdrew from her and sagged onto his back. With a sigh of utter contentment he gathered her against him and nestled her head on his shoulder, holding her as though she were the most precious thing in the world.

After a long mellow silence, Chris shifted her head and looked up at him, her eyes soft and misty, her throaty voice tremulous and tinged with reluctance. "I'd better get up, David. The boys will be down for breakfast soon."

Closing his eyes, David kissed her, his lips lingering against hers as he slowly savored the intoxicating moistness of her mouth. He did not want to let her go—not yet. He wanted to hang on to this golden moment for as long as he could. With her in his arms and her soft sensual mouth yielding to his, his world was complete.

His eyes were smoky as he induced her to stay with a seductive smile. "Don't go. Not yet. We'll hear them arguing long before they get downstairs." He brushed back the hair that was clinging damply to her face, and cradling her more firmly against him, he laughed softly. "Besides, I doubt if you have the strength to roll over, let alone get out of bed."

He felt her smile, her long eyelashes tickling his skin as she blinked. "I think you're right," she whispered, sounding as though she'd been heavily sedated. With deliberate slow and steady strokes, David massaged her naked back until she finally dropped off into a deep sleep. He held her with tenderness, his jaw resting against the top of her head, his face reflective.

He had just spent the most incredible night of his life, and he had discovered a depth of satisfaction and contentment he had never experienced before, but he also knew it had been the worst mistake he'd ever made. It was all a mirage. There would always be his barrier of mistrust separating them, even if he was at liberty to consider building a new life with Chris.

But he wasn't at liberty; there was still the matter of Maria. He could not abandon her to such a horrendous fate. He was deeply and morally indebted to her. Sometime within the next few days he was going to have to make a decision about what he was going to do about her, and that decision would mean ultimately turning his back on whatever life he might have had here. Maria was the cold hard reality. Chris was the unattainable dream.

His grim thoughts were interrupted by the boys. He recognized Tim's voice as he bossed his younger brother down the ladder from the loft.

With a sigh of reluctance he slowly eased her out of his embrace, taking care not to disturb her as he sat up. Stirring slightly, she turned onto her side and her thick glossy hair spilled across the pillow in a golden-brown tumble. Last night was the first time he'd seen it loose since he'd come back, and he combed his fingers through it, gently drawing it back from her face and neck.

Her hair had always fascinated him, and he was enchanted by the feel of it as he let it sift slowly

through his fingers. It was like strands of silk
threaded with the purest gold. He lightly touched
her jaw, tracing the perfection of her profile. So
finely sculpted, so delicate. Her skin was soft
beneath his touch as he outlined the graceful arch of
her brows, and bracing his arm beside her, he
leaned over and lightly kissed her, his lips lingering
against hers.

She stirred again, and he drew away, his expression strained. He rose from the bed and stood for a
long time gazing down at her, his eyes dark and
solemn, then he eased the covers over her naked
form and carefully tucked them around her. She
looked so damned fragile, so helpless—and David
despised himself.

WHEN CHRIS AWOKE AGAIN she was astounded to
find that it was early afternoon. Her exhaustion was
less pronounced, but her despondency still weighed
her down, and as she stared at the timbered ceiling
of the bedroom, her mood became more and more
melancholic. She had no illusions about what had
happened between her and David. That electric sexual attraction was still there between them and
probably always would be. They satisfied each
other too completely to deny it. But intuitively she
knew he was going to back away from any further
entanglements with her. He could try to rationalize
that last night had happened simply because they
were two people who had been driven together by a

very basic and overwhelming need, but that wasn't David's style; it wasn't in him to callously dismiss it that way. He would withdraw instead, and she didn't know if she could endure his leaving.

She didn't know if she could endure much more of anything. She wanted desperately to let herself believe that David still felt something for her, but if she allowed herself that fantasy, she would be leaving herself wide open to the shattering pain of a reality she would eventually have to face. And the reality was that it could never be. She had hurt him too deeply in the past for him to ever take her back, especially when she knew he didn't trust her. She couldn't blame him for that; she had no one to blame but herself.

Now she was going to have to dredge up enough courage to face him and pretend that nothing had happened. But it had happened, and their night together had destroyed the last of her armor, leaving her frighteningly close to complete and total devastation. She was on the brink of her personal breaking point, and she knew it. That frightened her even more.

Her face was pale and drawn and her nerves vibrating with dread as she climbed out of bed and slipped into her scarlet housecoat, which was lying on the foot of the bed. David had obviously collected it from the deck while she was sleeping, and for some indefinable reason that made her feel all the more vulnerable. Her fingers were stiff and awkward as she did up the buttons, as though they, too, were rebelling against the ordeal that lay ahead. She swept her tousled hair off her face and squared her shoulders, trying vainly to prepare herself for the confrontation.

David and Peter were both in the cabin. David was loading the dishwasher, and he cast a quick glance in her direction when he heard the bedroom door open, then abruptly focused his attention on his task, his face taut, his expression shuttered. His silent rejection was as obvious as a slap in the face, and Chris knew her dread had not been misplaced. An odd numbness spread through her and it took a massive effort to make herself move.

Peter was seated at the table doing a crossword puzzle, and he raised his head to look at her. He glanced across to David and back to Chris, his face creased with a concerned frown. He opened his mouth to speak, then obviously changed his mind.

Her back rigid, Chris went to the closet to get some clothes. The strain of the tense silence was eroding the thin veneer of her composure. There was no doubt in her mind: she was going to have to leave, and leave as quickly as humanly possible.

The nerve-grating tension was interrupted when Timmy came bounding into the cabin, his hot flushed face streaked with dirt. He did look so much like his father. Dark untidy hair that refused to stay parted as it curled softly around his face, and blue eyes fringed with thick lashes—eyes that were now bright with excitement. "Hey, Uncle Peter, can me and Mark build a fort in the bunch of trees by that little spring?"

Peter grinned at him and nodded his head. "Yes, you can build a fort, but don't drive any nails into the trees, okay?"

"Okay." Timmy got a drink of water from the tap and drank thirstily, then turned to look at his father. "There're two big rocks we can't move. Will you help us, dad?"

A reminiscent grin broke across Peter's face as he went to the kitchen and poured himself another cup of coffee. "Your father's an old fort builder from way back, Tim. You should have seen the one we had when we were kids."

Tim looked at his father with some skepticism. "Was that the big one you built on that steep bank by grandma's—the one that caved in and grandma was so mad?"

David laughed and ruffled his son's hair. "That's the one. We both got paddled over that."

Timmy slanted a curious look at his dad, and Chris knew exactly what he was thinking. The thought of someone spanking his father, especially grandma, was just a little too much to be believed. There was a hint of a smile in her eyes when Timmy turned to her. "Can we take a lunch, mom?"

"I guess you can, but don't leave any garbage lying around out there, Timmy," she warned quietly.

David started toward the door. "Let's go, kid-do."

"Can I get the lunch first?" Timmy asked.

David nodded and left by the patio door at the front of the cabin. Chris set about making a lunch for the boys, her thoughts focused on one concern. She knew she had to get out of there immediately, but how could she do it without creating a scene? As far as Timmy and Mark were concerned, she'd have to have an ironclad reason for going, and her brain was so dazed she couldn't come up with one good excuse. The way Peter was watching her didn't help her edginess, either. She strongly suspected he had stayed behind with the sole purpose of talking to her, and she wanted to avoid that at all costs. She just couldn't handle anyone probing her thoughts, her feelings, no matter how well-intentioned the intrusion was.

Feeling more and more trapped by the minute, she packed a stack of sandwiches in a large paper bag and looked at her son. "Timmy, there're small cans of juice in the bottom cupboard. Do you want to get some out for me, please?" She glanced down at his feet and sighed in mild exasperation. "And tie up your shoelaces—they're so ratty and dog-eared from you walking on them, they're almost past salvaging."

Timmy grinned at her, then knelt down to do as he was told. "Will you put some apples and stuff in, too? And cookies?" he added hopefully.

"Ah, cookies," said Peter as he came over to the counter. "Do dig out the cache of cookies."

"She hid 'em in the old bread box," came Timmy's muffled voice from inside the cupboard. "Mom always hides a bunch somewhere."

Peter laughed at the look on Chris's face. "You can't win, Chris. Boys will be boys."

"Yes, boys will be boys," came a cold, cutting female voice from the back door. Peter and Chris whirled around, both of them stunned speechless as Ellis yanked open the screen door and swept in, her body trembling, her face twisted by rage. She stood before them looking very much like a furious model who had just stepped off the cover of *Vogue* to throw a temper tantrum. Her streaked hair was styled with careless perfection, and she raked her hand through it, her long red nails slicing into it like daggers.

"This is a very sweet cozy little scene," she seethed through gritted teeth. "But I hope the two of you didn't believe for one moment you could really get away with this little seaside romp."

Peter stared at his wife as if he'd never seen her before, his expression a mixture of anger and revulsion. Shaking his head in disgust he walked away. "You don't know what in hell you're shooting your mouth off about, Ellis," he said with infinite weariness.

Ellis tossed her expensive leather shoulder bag onto the counter and came a step closer, her face menacing. "Oh, don't I?" she sneered. "When I put two and two together, I *do* come up with four, Peter, darling," she spat out, her voice laced with sarcasm.

Chris glanced at Timmy, who was still kneeling on the floor, his pose frozen by awe, his face white. An ugly scene like this in front of one of the boys made her feel sick, and Chris knew that somehow she had to defuse Ellis's anger before she did something irrational.

The muscles in her body seemed abnormally stiff and unresponsive as she moved around the counter. Deliberately keeping her voice low and calm, she said quietly, "It's not what you think, Ellis."

Ellis whirled to face her, fury radiating from her, her cold voice quavering. "Do you know what you are, Christine Spencer? You're a piece of filth. You walk out on your own husband so you can get your claws into mine. You're nothing but a slut." With unexpected agility and speed she lashed out, catching Chris across the face with a vicious backhand and driving her against the counter. Peter's anger exploded and he pivoted, his face a mask of wrath as he came toward his wife.

But Timmy beat him to her. The small boy threw himself against Ellis, catching her around the hips and shoving her away from his mother. "Don't you hit my mother," he yelled. "Don't you dare hit my mother!"

David had seen Ellis arrive, and instinctively

knowing there was going to be trouble, he took the steps at the front of the cabin three at a time. But he was stopped dead in his tracks, his face twisted in disgust, when he heard what she was saying to Chris. His eyes flashed like blue steel and he charged into the room just as Ellis viciously backhanded Chris across the face, but before he could cover the distance, Timmy had thrown himself against his mother's attacker.

David clenched his hands, his anger flaming into rage. If she were a man, he'd have decked Ellis for instigating this ugly little scene. His eyes were cold and ruthless as he glared at her, his nostrils flaring. "What in hell's going on here?"

"David—oh my God..." whispered Ellis, stunned. All the color drained out of her face, her pallor highlighting the bright patches of rouge on her cheeks. She looked as if she was about to collapse as she stared at him, her eyes wide with incredulity.

Timmy turned to his father, his mouth trembling. "She hit my mom...."

"Somebody had better bloody well tell me what this is all about," David demanded, his voice dangerously taut.

Timmy came over to his father, tears leaving streaks of grime on his white face. "She hit mom. She came in here all mad and she hit her and made her face bleed."

David grasped his son's shoulder and pulled the boy against him, pressing his head against the soft fabric of his shirt. "I saw what happened, son," he said quietly as he massaged Timmy's bony shoulder in an attempt to reassure the boy. "Everything's going to be okay." He glanced at Chris and winced, his anger rekindled when he saw the ugly red abrasion across her chalk-white face. Ellis must have caught her with that monstrosity of a ring she always wore.

But Chris was oblivious to his concern. Like a woman in a trance, she numbly watched the unfocused drama unfolding before her, her ears still ringing from the force of the blow. Her arm seemed unnaturally heavy as she raised her hand to touch her smarting cheek. Her skin was moist and sticky beneath her touch and she stared dazedly at her fingers. They were smeared with blood.

Turning away from the distorted commotion of voices, she picked up her clothes, which were lying on one of the chairs, and walked into the bedroom with robotlike movements. Softly she closed the door behind her and locked it. As she sagged against it she began to shake violently.

She remained like that until the numbness started wearing off, leaving her with a deep raw pain that seared through her chest. She had to get out—now. Escape was suddenly crucially important, and her panicky desperation gave her the power to move. She yanked on her clothes, and like a terrified animal fled from the room through the patio doors.

David had watched Chris pick up her clothes

from the chair and walk into the bedroom, her back unnaturally stiff. For a split second he considered following her, but he turned to face Ellis instead. It took an iron will to hold on to his temper as he snapped, "I think you owe us an explanation, Ellis."

She appeared absolutely stricken, and her eyes sought Peter for some kind of support. But he turned away without so much as glancing at his wife and walked to the wall of windows. Bracing his arm against a wooden frame, he stood staring out, his perennially youthful face looking suddenly haggard and old.

She turned from her husband to David and swallowed hard. "I didn't know you were back, David. Your mother never said—"

"My mother never said anything about me being back because she doesn't *know* I'm back. I take it she's been meddling in other people's business," he said, his voice heavy with sarcasm and barely contained anger.

Ellis started toward him, then stopped, her uncertainty plainly visible. "No—no. It wasn't your mother's fault. I jumped to conclusions." Clasping her hands tightly in front of her, she took a deep breath, then continued, "I heard your parents were back so I phoned her, and she casually mentioned that Peter had picked the boys up, and I got suspicious."

"So you came tearing over here to check it out."

Her voice was strained as she answered weakly, "Yes."

David opened his mouth to let her have it, but he checked himself as he looked down at Tim. It was obvious that Timmy had heard too much as it was. Kneeling down, he took his son's distraught face in his hands. David was deeply disturbed by the mix of emotions he saw in that small drawn face—anger, resentment, bitterness, wariness—but most of all the look of bewildered pain, not unlike a puppy who'd just been beaten. It hurt like hell just to look at his son.

Tim stared at his father with tormented eyes, no longer able to blink back the tears. "Why doesn't anybody like mom, dad?" he asked, his anxious voice riddled with confusion. "Grandma doesn't like her—" He looked at Ellis. "*She* doesn't like her, you don't like her—"

"No!" Without realizing how ashen his own face had become, David stared at Timmy, shocked and sickened by what the boy had said. His hands tightened around his son's face as though he was physically willing him to understand. "That's not true, Timmy," he said vehemently.

Timmy stared at his dad, his eyes sullen and unwavering. There was no doubting the accusation in his voice when he spoke. "What *you* say isn't true, daddy. We could never talk about her when we went to visit you. You always acted like you hated her."

Closing his eyes, David swore softly and rested his forehead against Tim's. Never had he loathed himself more than he did right then. He drew in his breath sharply and looked at his son, frantically searching for words to explain. "I was hurt by what had happened, Tim. And when you're hurt, you sometimes lash out at—"

Timmy acted as if he hadn't heard his father, his small dirty face twisted by an inner anguish. "Mom has nobody but me and Mark." His mouth was dragged down by his valiant struggle not to cry, and his chin was quivering as he roughly wiped away his tears with the back of his hand.

"Mom has nobody. She had nobody to hold her like she holds me and Mark when we were so scared when you were gone so long, or when we felt so bad when grandpa died, and when Downer died. She even held Downer all night when he was sick. She sat on the kitchen floor with his head in her lap and she kept petting him and telling him everything was going to be okay. And Mr. Cooper said that she held grandpa like that when he got sick, and that made grandpa happy."

Uncontrollable tears were streaming down Timmy's face and his voice was choked with restrained sobs as he finally gave voice to the pain he felt for his mother. "Everybody hates her and she doesn't have nobody to hold her and tell her everything's going to be okay when she really hurts inside."

His face crumpled and a loud sob was ripped

from him as he buried his face against his father. "She feeds the birds and she never yells when we bring home a stray cat to feed. . .and she never says mean things to people. Why are people so mean to her, dad?"

Tim was crying in earnest, his whole body heaving with the force of his sorrow, and he wound his arms tightly around his father's neck. David gathered his son securely against him, but he had no words to comfort him. He was fighting his own battle, the emotional pressure in his chest nearly strangling him.

Easing a deep breath past the tightness in his throat, he whispered unevenly against Timmy's ear, "Would you feel better if I looked after mom?"

Timmy nodded his head then twisted his face against his dad's shirt in an attempt to wipe away his tears. David hugged him closer, waiting for the trembling to subside, then he eased his hold slightly. "Can I go talk to her now, or do you want me to stay with you for a little while?"

Sniffling loudly, Timmy pulled away from David and looked at him, his voice wobbly. "You go now, dad."

David smiled at him with tenderness as he wiped away one large tear that hung suspended in his son's lashes. Just then both of them heard a car start, and Timmy's eyes widened in fear as he stared at his dad. They both knew. "Don't let her go, dad. Don't let her—"

David gripped his son's shoulder as he bolted to his feet. "I won't," he said with far more confidence than he felt, and he raced out of the cabin.

Chris's avenue of escape seemed to be through a strange tunnel of indistinct images, and she stumbled over a patch of uneven ground as she ran blindly toward the clearing. Yanking open the car door, she flung herself into the vehicle, slammed the door and wildly fished for the keys, which were in the ashtray. A cold clammy sweat dampened her body as she pressed the switch for the automatic door lock, then tried to insert the key in the ignition. Her hand was shaking badly, but finally she managed to slip in the key and the motor came to life.

By the time David got outside, Chris had already backed the car away from the cabin. Alarm shot through him. If she turned the car around before he got to her, he wouldn't have a hope in hell of stopping her. He reacted instantaneously. Vaulting over the railing of the deck, he hit the ground at a dead run, a nameless fear pumping adrenaline through him.

He reached the vehicle just as Chris made the final maneuver and pulled onto the trail leading from the cabin. One quick glance at her waxen face told him all he needed to know: she wouldn't stop no matter what. He was going to *have* to stop her. Somehow.

He yanked on the handle of the passenger door

but nothing happened. It was locked. He had enough time to test the back door before she began to accelerate, his fear becoming near panic when he found that it, too, was locked.

He had no choice. With lightning-fast reflexes, he drove his fist through the window, the force sending a jarring pain through his arm into his shoulder. Trying to keep pace with the increasing speed of the car, he fumbled with the lock, then in one last desperate attempt yanked open the door and made a dive for the back seat. The car lurched and the door slammed shut, sending a shower of splintered glass over his body. But David didn't even notice as he scrambled to his knees.

Encircling her torso with one arm so she couldn't interfere, he stretched forward over the seat, switched off the engine and yanked the keys out of the ignition. He grasped the steering wheel with both hands, fighting the stiffness caused by the instant lack of power steering, and slowly the vehicle rolled to a stop. For a brief moment he rested his head against the headrest behind Chris as a cold sweat dampened his skin and sapped his strength. God, it had been too close for comfort.

He climbed into the passenger seat and looked at Chris. Her arms were folded across the top of the wheel, her face pressed against them, her body limp. She looked as lifeless as a rag doll.

A shudder quivered through her body, and she spoke in a voice that was a dull monotone. "Just let me go, David. I'll give you full custody of the boys, I'll leave Victoria—I'll do whatever you want me to do, but just let me go.''

Right then David quit playing games with himself. Each had inflicted the worst kind of pain on the other, and he had tried like hell to put her out of his mind, but there was no getting away from one fact he had refused to face until now. He still loved her.

Raising the armrest that divided the seat, he gently eased her from behind the wheel and gathered her against him, holding her with a profound compelling tenderness, a tenderness that healed old wounds and erased old scars.

The game was over, and Timmy was right. She needed someone to hold her. He tightened his arms around her as he whispered against her hair, ''I'm not letting you go, Christine. Ever.'' But there was no response from her. Nothing. Chilling needles of apprehension crept up his spine. She had been pushed too far. Right now she was as fragile as fine crystal, and she could shatter just as easily.

His extreme concern for Chris was penetrated by the memory of a small boy with an ashen face and frightened eyes, and he knew for Timmy's sake he had to get back to the cabin. He located the keys on the floor by his feet, then he climbed over Chris and slid into the driver's seat. He started the car, wishing like hell she would do something, say something, but she just sat there with that frighteningly numb look on her face.

When he parked behind the cabin, Timmy was coming down the steps, anxiety etched into his face. The boy came toward his father, but kept glancing nervously at his mother as she slowly climbed out the passenger side of the vehicle. "Is she all right?" he asked in a hushed voice.

David slammed the car door and draped his arm around the boy as he squatted down in front of him. "She's upset, Tim, and I need to talk to her. So do you think you could do me a big favor?"

Timmy nodded, his eyes still red and puffy as he stared solemnly at his dad.

David's eyes were equally solemn. "Do you think that you could keep Mark busy for a while so your mom and I can have some time alone?"

Timmy nodded, scuffing his foot through the loose pine needles on the ground. Then he looked at his dad. "You aren't going to let her go, are you, dad?" There was no mistaking the unspoken fears in that one single question.

"No, I'm not going to let her go," he answered with quiet assurance. He released Timmy and stood up. "Are Uncle Peter and Ellis still in the cabin?"

"Uncle Peter went down to the boat and *she* followed him."

There was the barest glimmer of amusement in David's eyes as he looped his arm around Timmy's shoulders and started walking toward the steps. "Why don't you pick up your lunch and go back to the fort with Mark for a while?" He grasped the boy's shoulder and gave him a reassuring little shake. "And don't worry, Tim. Everything's going to be okay."

Timmy looked up at his dad, his relief relaxing the drawn expression on his tanned face. "I'm really glad you're here," he said.

"I'm glad I'm here, too."

The two of them entered the cabin, and David had to pause for a moment to let his eyes adjust to the dimness after the brilliance of the bright sun. Chris was in the kitchen, her face completely expressionless as she finished packing lunch for the boys. He remembered one other time, many years ago, when she'd been like this. She had withdrawn into the same shell of silence when she'd lost the baby—only this time she was much worse. He watched her like a hawk, his concern mounting steadily. How he was going to handle this trauma was his biggest concern. He didn't have room for a single mistake.

Finally she handed Tim the bag, and the boy glanced at his dad, looking for another sign of reassurance. David smiled and Tim smiled back, then left the cabin.

Without saying a word David went to Chris and caught her hand in a firm clasp and led her into the bedroom. He locked the door and watched her as she sat down on the edge of the bed, her hands gripped tightly together, her head bent. With a weary gesture he drew his hand down his face and went to stand before the patio door, his hands rammed into his back pockets. What could he say that would penetrate that shell?

Uncertainty gnawed at him as he began to speak, his voice low. "You've been honest with me, Christine, and I think it's time I was honest with you. You've assumed most of the blame for our marriage going sour, but I was just as much to blame." He paused and frowned as he tried to organize his thoughts.

"It's taken me a while to see it, but the truth is, I neglected you badly. I was married to the damned corporation—I felt I had to prove myself, that I had to be a brilliant success. It was expected of a Spencer. I became a first-class workaholic, and everything, including you and the boys, came second to LaFontaine." He turned toward her, his face lined with tension. He couldn't stand her isolated silence any longer and he went to her. Crouching down, he pried her hands apart and clasped them in his, his eyes dark and earnest as he watched her. "I was hurt and bitter when you walked out on me, Christie, and I let my bitterness blind me."

Chris started to tremble and David longed to gather her into his arms, but he fought down the urge. Now was not the time to rush her. "Look at me, Chris," he said softly. For a moment he thought she was going to ignore him, but finally she lifted her face. A mixture of compassion and hope swept through him. There were tears in her tormented eyes, and the expressionless mask was gone, revealing a terrible anguish.

He inhaled slowly, trying to subdue the swell of intense feelings that were building in him. "I love you, Christine. I fought like hell to put you out of my mind, to convince myself that I hated you. But after last night...." His voice caved in from the intensity of what he was experiencing, and he rested his head against her knees. His hands gripped hers. "I can't stop loving you, Chris—it would be like trying to stop breathing."

He felt her shudder and he raised his head, the pain in her eyes tearing him apart. Tears were streaming down her face and a choked sob broke from her as her facade cracked. "Don't tell me that. God, don't tell me that...."

But David understood; he understood her fear of believing him. Tenderly he wiped away her tears with his thumbs, his own voice shaking as he said, "I'm telling you this because I mean it. I don't want to live one more day of my life without you being a part of it. I need you, Christie." He swallowed hard, his voice hoarse with emotion. "God, please don't shut me out again."

She stared at him, her eyes searching his, and another sob was torn from her as she encircled his neck with her arms, her embrace desperate.

With a groan, David crushed her against him and pulled her down on the bed beside him, their bodies welded together as all the doubts, all the old painful barriers came crashing down.

His hand was buried deep in her hair and he cradled her head firmly against his shoulder, holding her in an enveloping embrace. At last she wept, releasing her pent-up despair and misery and grief. His own voice was choked as he whispered, "We'll work it out, Chris. I'll never leave you again. Never."

And he knew it was a lie even as he said it.

CHAPTER SEVEN

THE LIGHT SUMMER BREEZE eddying in through the open patio door carried with it the fresh scent of the sea, the forest and warm sunshine as it wafted across David's naked chest, cooling his heated skin. He stroked Chris's nude back with idle laziness and listened to the far-off sound of the surf.

Chris stirred weakly against him and instantly he focused his full attention on her. He nestled her head more comfortably on his shoulder and kissed her softly on the forehead. His expression became grave as she heaved a tremulous sigh that was the aftermath of her stormy weeping.

He had never felt so helpless in his entire life when she finally broke under the terrible strain, and her grief, her loneliness, her guilt—all the misery she had contained for so long—came boiling out. He had never seen her break apart like that, and there was nothing he could do but hold her. It was like watching a massive dam burst, the once-contained pressure erupting after months and months of stress.

It had not been his intention to make love to her,

but nothing he said penetrated her personal anguish, and in an act of desperation he attempted to reach her with a kiss. Her wild response had staggered him, drawing him mindless and unresisting into the eye of the storm, and only his aroused passion seemed to neutralize her pain.

With immeasurable affection he combed his fingers through the tangle of her hair, then tilted her head back so he could see her face, his solemn eyes darkening with concern.

She looked completely ravaged, the long ugly scratch standing out starkly against the pallor of her delicate skin. But what heightened his concern more than anything was the wary guarded look in her eyes. She was so vulnerable, and so damned frightened. Drawing her head closer to his, he gave her a soft kiss that was meant to reassure her, to comfort her. But her arms tightened around him and he could feel her pulse accelerating beneath his touch as she turned in his arms, molding herself against him. So soft, so warm, so giving.

His breathing was erratic as he slowly trailed his moist mouth across her face and down her neck, acutely aware of the tantalizing fullness of her breasts pressed against his chest. He closed his eyes and drew her even closer, murmuring against the soft curve of her shoulder, "I love you, Christine."

He felt her body stiffen, and sensing her distress, he eased her onto her back and kissed her again, his mouth light and undemanding. He savored the taste of her lips, then braced himself up on one elbow, leaning over her.

Her lips were trembling and her eyes, shadowed by doubt, glistened with unshed tears as she stared up at him. David brushed his lips against hers and softly caressed her face with his fingertips. "Don't doubt how I feel about you."

"I can't believe you could ever forgive me—"

He pressed his fingers against her mouth, gently silencing her. "You weren't the only one to blame. We both made some damned foolish mistakes."

Tears slipped down her temples as she moved her hands up his shoulders, drawing him against her. Her voice was a tortured whisper. "God, David, I missed you so much, and I was so scared."

Sensing despair was about to claim her in its devastating grip, David groped for some way to defuse it. He realized Chris was in the midst of a severe emotional crisis; she needed to cry it all out, to purge herself. But he also knew that right now it was much more important for her to have his calm steadying assurance that what he'd said was the absolute truth. Trying to provide her with the physical security she so urgently needed, he held her tightly and prayed she wouldn't fall victim to the soul-wrenching weeping she had earlier. He didn't think he could endure seeing her suffer like that again.

When he finally spoke, the depths of his emotion made his voice unsteady. "Don't think my feelings for you are only sexual, Christine. These last four years have been hell without you." He slowly stroked her cheek with his hand, his eyes welded to hers, willing her to understand. "I need you to give my life some meaning again."

Her breath caught on a sob as she gazed up at him, her eyes pained. "Oh, David, if only I could erase the hurt I've inflicted on you—"

Again he pressed his thumb against her lips to silence her. "You can. All you have to do is tell me you love me."

Her eyes filled with tears and her mouth began to tremble as she whispered brokenly, "I do. Oh, David, I do...so much."

Unable to resist her unspoken appeal, David gathered her against him and closed his eyes as she slipped her arms around his neck and held him fast. He wanted so badly to give in to the intoxicating excitement she was arousing in him, but he held back. Above all else she needed comforting, a sense of security. For the first time in a very long while he felt at peace with himself, and he longed to infuse her with the same profound feeling. God, but he loved her so.

There was a new strength, a new surety in his voice as he murmured against her hair, "Both of us are emotionally raw right now, Chris. And we need time to do some rebuilding, time to get our confidence back." He firmly caressed her back, trying to reassure her by physical contact, trying to give her some measure of consolation. "We all need time to function as a family again. It's been hell, and there's been too much bitterness, but if we can put all that behind us we can come out of this with a relationship that will withstand anything."

Her face was damp against his neck. "I'm so scared that something will happen to rip everything apart again."

"If we really want to make a go of it," he said with quiet certainty, "we can. If that's what we really want."

She raised her head and looked at him, her pale anxious face revealing how very afraid she was to anchor her hopes on his words. "But is that what you really want, David?"

He caressed her ear and his expression softened into a tender smile, his eyes warm and loving. "That's what I want, Christine. Believe me, above all else, that's what I want."

She stared at him, searching for signs of uncertainty yet afraid of finding one, but his gaze never left hers. At last belief kindled a light in her eyes and she accepted what he was telling her as the absolute truth. Whispering his name, she buried her face against his neck and clung to him with a savage strength. He sensed her struggling for control as he closed his eyes and held her in a viselike embrace; he was almost overpowered by the poignancy of the feelings he was experiencing. At last the anguish caused by their separation was behind them, and a whole new life stretched out before them. This was their new beginning; this was paradise.

An image of Maria suddenly appeared in his mind, but he ruthlessly blocked it out and buried his face in the fragrant tumble of Chris's hair. He would allow no shadow to fall across this very special moment; he would allow nothing to taint this incredible feeling of harmony that bound them together. This was their time—his and Chris's.

She slowly slipped her hand along his neck until her fingers surrounded the back of his head, and she exerted a slight pressure. Her lips were moist and lingering as she trailed tantalizing kisses across his jaw, her caresses tempting him beyond belief. David shifted his head and captured her mouth with a kiss that left them both breathless and longing for more.

His pulse was pounding as he reluctantly raised his head and gazed down at her, his hand curving around her slender neck. "I'd like nothing better than to spend the rest of the day right here," he said huskily, "but we'd better get up before the boys come looking for us." The last thing David wanted to do was let her go, but he knew he had to back off. This vibrating sexual tension had to be tempered. It was too electric, too overwhelming for her, and she was too emotionally raw to handle it right now. If they stayed in bed, he'd never be able to hold back.

He felt her take a deep breath as she touched his

lips with her fingertips and sighed, "Yes, I guess
we'd better." Closing his eyes, he caught her hand
and kissed each of her fingers before he rolled away.

David pulled on his jeans and went into the
bathroom. When he reappeared a short time later he
had a basin of warm water and a cloth in his hand.
Chris was lying with her eyes closed, the sheet draped
across her hips. Sitting down on the edge of the bed
beside her, he began to gently wipe her face, taking
great care to thoroughly clean the deep scratch that
marred her cheek. He was keenly aware she had
opened her eyes and was watching him with a dark
unfathomable gaze as he slowly sponged away the
film of perspiration on her neck and between her
breasts. He had to fight against his own heated reaction when her nipples hardened beneath his tender
ministrations, but through sheer will he managed to
maintain his composure as he continued to bathe
her.

She remained passive beneath his touch until he
drew back the sheet and began to wipe the insides of
her thighs, then she raised up on one elbow and
caught his hand. "David," she whispered, her
throaty voice weak.

David tossed the cloth in the basin and pulled her
into his arms. His own voice was thick as he whispered, "Damn it, Christie, it's so hard for me to keep
from touching you." He sat holding her, her soft
body molded against his naked chest, her head resting on his shoulder.

Knowing that she, too, was aroused, that she wanted him, made it all the more difficult for him not to say to hell with his resolve. But the vibrating sexual tension had to be tempered; it was too electric, too overwhelming for her to cope with now. She needed soothing, she needed comforting—she needed time. For her sake he had to put on the brakes, no matter how much he wanted to give in.

Without relaxing his hold on her, he leaned down and picked up her clothes from the floor, then gently grasped her by the shoulders and eased her away from him. "Come on, love," he murmured. "Let's get you dressed."

She looked so damned delicate, so fragile, and David inwardly winced when he saw how badly her hands were trembling when she pulled her hair back from her face. Spanning her jaw with his hand, he raised her face to his and kissed her once more, forcibly curbing the desire to let his mouth linger.

Stroking his shoulder, Chris whispered, "Are you sure checking on the boys is more important than this?"

The way she said it made it plain she was questioning his sanity, and David laughed softly as he hugged her soundly. "Nothing is more important than this."

She gazed up at him, her eyes warm and misty with such tenderness that it made David's chest ache to look at her. He hadn't seen that look for so many years that he had forgotten how intoxicating it was. It created a fire in his blood. His voice was husky as he slowly massaged her back. "If we don't get the hell out of this bedroom, our kids will be reporting us to child welfare for neglect."

She gave him that low throaty laugh that had such a devastating effect on him, and he had to steel himself not to respond. "I'm willing to run that risk if you are," she murmured.

David groaned, his voice rippling with laughter when he answered her. "Are you trying to vamp me, Christine Spencer?"

"Yes."

"Well stop it, for God's sake. I'm having a hard enough time as it is." He reached for her sun top and with resolute determination pulled it over her head. "You are going to get dressed before I change my mind, woman."

As he pulled the top down, his hands brushed against her breasts and her breath caught. Closing her eyes, she weakly rested her head against him, her body trembling as David tied the shoulder straps with unwilling fingers. They were caught in a heady silence as he finished helping her dress. David gazed down at her, his expression made sober by strain, and pulled her to her feet.

Chris slipped her arm around his waist and leaned against him. "We aren't coping with this very well, are we?" she whispered unevenly.

His expression softened as he smiled at her, his eyes gleaming with humor. "Not when you keep stoking the fire, Christine,'' he said, his tone provocative. He pulled her closer to him as he guided her out through the patio door, shutting the screen behind them. "But then I always did like the heat."

She cast a pithy look up at him. "Yes, I know."

David laughed and brushed his lips against her forehead. "Good. I'd hate to think you'd forgotten."

They were crossing the small clearing beside the cabin, their arms around each other, when Peter appeared at the top of the steep winding trail that led down to the dock. David wished they could bypass the next few minutes, and he tightened his protective hold on Chris's shoulder as they waited for their friend to cover the distance with his long-legged stride. Peter would feel compelled to apologize for his wife's behavior, and it would create an awkward moment for Chris—and more pressure was exactly what she didn't need right now.

Peter's regret was plainly visible as he stopped in front of them, his troubled gaze fixed on Christine. His voice was taut when he said, "I'm sorry, Chris. What happened was inexcusable." Inhaling slowly, he bent his head and jammed his hands in the back pockets of his jeans, his shoulders sagging. "I hope you believe me when I say I would've given anything to prevent that ugly little scene."

Chris placed her hand on his arm, her voice soft and forgiving. "I know that, Peter. It was a stupid misunderstanding—don't make a big deal out of it.''

He straightened up and gave her a warped smile. ''Some misunderstanding.'' Obviously anxious to drop the subject of his wife's behavior, he looked at David. ''I'm going back to Victoria, so I'll take Chris's car and get that window fixed. The keys for mine are on top of the fridge.''

David nodded his head in assent and looked at him with a penetrating directness. ''Don't stay away because of what happened, Peter.''

Peter stared at him for a moment, then a genuine grin appeared on his craggy face. ''I won't. I'll be back in a couple of days with a load of groceries and a fresh supply of comic books for the boys.'' He clapped David on the shoulder before he turned to go. ''If you two need anything, give me a shout.''

''We will.'' David watched him until he disappeared around the corner of the cabin, then he glanced down at Chris. She had grown so pale, and her eyes were brimming with tears. He pressed his cheek against the top of her head. She felt everybody's pain, and right now she was hurting for Peter. He gave her a few moments to get a grip on herself and murmured against her hair, ''Do you want to go back inside?''

Easing away from him, she wiped away her tears and slanted a pointed look up at him. ''I didn't want to leave in the first place.''

David laughed and shook her lightly. ''Nice try,

lady, but it won't work." He grasped her hand and resolutely led her toward the trees. "And to think you used to be such an innocent," he muttered as he caught her firmly around the shoulders and guided her beneath the low-hanging branch of a fir tree.

It wasn't hard to find the boys; one had only to follow the sounds of an argument. They were bickering loudly about where the door of the fort should be located when David and Chris arrived on the scene.

Mark was standing with his hands on his hips, his jaw thrust out in a mutinous set, and Chris was struck by the likeness between him and her father. The same stocky build, the same rust-colored hair, the same high forehead and square jaw: he was a miniature of his maternal grandfather, except he, like Timmy, had his father's intense blue eyes. And they were snapping with annoyance as he glared at his brother.

He looked up, his obstinate expression changing to one of surprise when he saw his parents wending their way through the dense stand of evergreens. He dropped the huge branch he was holding, and wiping his hands on his blue T-shirt, he bounded toward them, his freckled face split with a broad grin. "Are you guys coming to help?"

David grinned back at his youngest son. "I brought your mother to help. I'm going to watch."

"Ah, dad—"

"'Ah, dad,'" mimicked David teasingly as he

ruffled Mark's hair. He dropped his hand on his son's shoulder and looked down at the boy's up-turned face. "I was only teasing you, Mark. If you need some help, I'll give you a hand."

Dapples of sunlight danced across the ground as the three of them walked toward the space the boys had laboriously cleared. David's expression grew solemn when he saw Tim watching them from the shadows, a pinched worried look on his face. Just then Chris stumbled over an exposed root, and in an attempt to steady her, David automatically clasped her closer. Her arm tightened around his waist and she smiled up at him and briefly rested her head against his shoulder.

That one insignificant byplay seemed to speak volumes to Timmy, and his eyes lit up with an almost blinding voltage of happiness. He turned away abruptly, and his father saw him drag his hand across his eyes before he bent over and made a pretense of trying to lift an uprooted stump.

David glanced down at Mark. "Why don't you show your mom the fort's floor plan you and Tim sketched in the sand, and I'll go give your brother a hand."

His tongue going a mile a minute, Mark led his mother across the clearing, and David went over to his eldest son and crouched down beside him. "Do you need some help?" he asked.

The boy was motionless for a minute, then he looked at his father, his eyes darkened by some unspoken fear. "Are you just being nice to her for a little while?" he asked, his voice quavering.

"No, I'm not just being nice to her for a little while, Timmy," David responded soberly. "I've missed your mom a lot—she's very important to me."

Timmy dragged his hand across his face again, his words so choked his father could barely hear him. "Are you coming back to live with us?"

David's own voice was oddly gruff when he asked, "Do you want me to come back?"

Tim's eyes were riveted on his father, and his chin was trembling uncontrollably as he whispered, "Yes, daddy—more than anything."

Tim launched himself into his dad's arms, sobs shuddering through his body. A hard knot bunched in David's throat as he hugged his son in a fierce embrace. He had to swallow hard and take a deep breath before he could manage to speak. "I've missed all of you so much, Timmy, especially your mom. I love her more than I can say. And nothing would make me happier than for all of us to be a family again."

Closing his eyes, David clasped his son against him and silently tried to cope with all he was experiencing. The shattered pieces of his existence seemed to be knitting together into a perfect whole, and suddenly life had never been sweeter than it was right then.

Timmy finally grew quiet and his father eased

him away from him and caught his tear-stained face in his hands. "I know we need to talk about a lot of things, Tim, and I know I have to explain what went wrong between your mother and me, but could it wait for a while?"

His son gazed at him with a directness that caught David a little off guard. "Because of mom, you mean?"

It was then that the father saw beyond the child to the maturity and deep understanding his son possessed. He nodded slowly, unaware that his face was creased with concern. "Yes, because of your mom. She's been under a lot of strain, and she really needs a few days of peace and quiet."

"Don't worry, dad. We'll look after her." He wiped his face on the tail of his shirt to remove all traces of tears, and his eyes began to glint with mischief as he grinned down at his dad, who was still squatting in front of him. "And I won't even thump Mark when she's around."

"It might be nice," David retorted dryly, "if you quit thumping Mark altogether." He stood up and brushed the dried leaves and pine needles off his jeans. "Now, where do you want that to go?" he asked, pointing to the stump.

"It's going to be part of our doorway. Can you put it over there?"

When Chris and Mark returned, they all worked on the construction of the fort, which was really nothing more than a large and elaborate lean-to, for nearly an hour. It didn't require a strenuous effort, but David discovered even though he was rapidly gaining weight, his strength and endurance were definitely not up to par.

Feeling the effects of his labors, he sprawled on the ground beneath an immense Douglas fir, his back braced against a weathered tree stump that had been worn smooth by the elements. Chris was kneeling at one end of the lean-to, and he watched her as she rearranged some of the boughs to strengthen part of the structure. She had on a sunsuit that left her arms and shoulders almost bare. The soft pink color contrasted with her deep tan and the brief shorts accentuated the length of her shapely legs. She looked wholesome and appealing and very, very sexy. Obviously satisfied with her handiwork, she brushed the dried leaves and pine needles from her hands and glanced at him. With a lazy smile he held out his hand toward her, and she smiled back as she stood up.

A broad shaft of sunlight penetrated the dense green canopy of forest, and the cluster of golden rays focused through the overhead boughs like an ethereal spotlight. For an instant it captured Chris in its halo as she came across the clearing toward him, the yellow beams setting her shining hair alight with sun-kissed brilliance and touching her bronzed skin with a patina of gold. There was something about the way she moved—a certain grace, a certain ease—that hinted of the fleetness he knew she possessed. She seemed to be a part of it all—a child of nature, yet a woman of the universe. This was one of the brief instances of time that would be forever imprinted on his mind.

She was going to sit beside him, but he spread his legs and pulled her down between them. Flexing one knee, he drew her back against him. Without speaking, he slipped his arms around her midriff and rested his jaw against her temple. A cool breeze sighed through the heavily laden branches, and the distant roar of the sea was muted to a hypnotizing murmur. The serenity was like a powerful sedative, and he could feel the tension easing from her as he held her. The silence, this quiet closeness, had an indescribable richness to it, and he savored every second.

David had nearly been lulled to sleep when Chris stirred slightly, and he felt her smile. He nestled her closer and asked softly, "And what do you find so amusing?"

She shifted her head so her cheek was pressed against his, and she idly caressed the back of his hand, which was resting beneath her breast. "I was just thinking about the boys when they were small. Do you remember the time your parents had the going-away dinner for the Tompsons? Tim came walking into the dining room with his little dump truck filled with earthworms and plunked it on the table beside your mother."

David laughed and tightened his arms around

her. "I could have killed the kid. How old was he—about three?"

"About that. And your mother never blinked an eye. She patted him on the head and said, 'Why thank you, darling. That's just what I need for my rose garden.'" The recollection had put a buoyancy in her voice, but it didn't mask the tenor of respect when she said, "Your mother definitely has a lot of class."

David's expression altered as his anger kindled. It was one of the basic inconsistencies of life: he may have treated Chris like dirt, but heaven help anyone else who did, and he was not pleased about the way his family had treated her since their breakup. Somewhere along the line they were definitely going to be told exactly how he felt.

Slipping her arm behind his back, Chris turned in his embrace and laid her hand against his rigid face, her eyes grave. "Don't judge them too harshly, David," she said. "Your mother and father were completely in the dark about what went wrong between us, and all they saw was how much I'd hurt you."

He didn't want to discuss it—not now. He wanted a few more days with Chris before they started hauling out the unpleasantness from the past. This was just too special to spoil. They *needed* this time.

"I know you don't want to talk about it," she continued, "but it's not something we can keep putting off."

He shot her a terse look. It had always caught him off-balance when she tuned into his thoughts with such perceptiveness. If only he had been able to do the same with her. Chris tried to sit up, but he held her fast and sighed heavily in resignation. "Okay, Christine—let's have it."

She managed to suppress a smile, but there was no mistaking the gleam in her eyes as she softly caressed his neck. "Don't get huffy, David Spencer," she admonished softly.

He grinned lopsidedly and narrowed his eyes. "Then don't be aggravating, Christine Spencer."

Her expression became serious as she gazed up at him. "You're likely planning on giving them both hell for how they've acted, and I don't think that's very fair."

Her unexpected point of view caught him by surprise, and he stared at her. "Why not?"

"Because they don't deserve it, David. Your mother and I may have had different priorities in life, but she was always very good to me, until I left." David opened his mouth to respond, but Chris didn't give him the opportunity to speak. "They didn't even realize there was any trouble between us. Just imagine how they must've felt when I left without a single explanation. All they saw was how my leaving affected you. And quite frankly, if either Mark or Tim ended up in the same situation you did, I'd probably react the same way your mother did."

"Damn it, Chris, they shouldn't have turned their back on you the way they did."

"Why not?" she challenged. "For all they knew I could have had sixteen lovers and run a bawdy house in my spare time."

The impossibility of her rebuttal delighted David, and he burst into unrestrained laughter. When he was finally able to speak, he gazed down at her, his eyes dancing. "All right, Chris. You've made your point."

"I'm not finished."

"God," he groaned as he raised his eyes heavenward in an age-old plea for patience.

This time Chris laughed and patted his cheek firmly. "There's one other thing you have to remember."

"And what's that?"

She grinned, and as though she was explaining something to a very dull child, she said, "You have to remember that both your mother and father spoiled the boys rotten from the time they were born. It's not a new phenomenon."

"Is there anything else I should know?" he said, his tone dry.

Her expression softened, and she gazed at him with such adoration shining in her eyes that it was suddenly difficult for him to breathe. "I want you to know how very much I love you, David," she whispered huskily. "Having you back is like an incredible dream. And I quite believe it's true."

He sucked in his breath sharply and crushed her against him. "Believe it, Chris. Believe it," he murmured roughly.

"Hey, dad, can we sleep in the fort tonight?" Timmy called out from within the lean-to.

Both David and Chris stiffened, and David muttered through gritted teeth. "I should have killed him over the earthworm episode. His sense of timing is atrocious."

Chris laughed and turned her face to kiss his jaw before she pulled away from him. There was a meaningful look in her eyes that could not be misconstrued as she murmured, "Perhaps his timing is very...timely."

David grinned at her. "You could be right."

"Can we, dad? Can we?" Timmy persisted.

David let his breath out in a rush then looked directly at his son. "No."

"Aw, why not?" wheedled Mark, for once agreeing with one of his big brother's suggestions.

"Because you can't sleep out here alone," answered David firmly.

"You could sleep out here with us," offered Tim hopefully.

"Not a chance, kiddo. I'm sleeping in a nice comfortable bed." And in a murmur just loud enough for Chris to hear, he added, "With your mother."

"But that's no fun. It'll be cool out here. You don't want to sleep in the cabin. That's so boring. Why is mom laughing?"

"Because," answered David in a voice well seasoned with tartness, "your mother has a warped sense of humor."

"Oh." Mark's brow knotted and he frowned in confusion for a moment, then he took up the crusade again. "But it won't be hot out here, dad, and you can hear the ocean real good. We can tell ghost stories, and we could bring out one of the mattresses from the loft so you'll be comfortable."

"Believe me, there are different degrees of comfort," was David's laconic response.

Chris sat up abruptly, valiantly trying to school her face into an expression of blankness. She made the mistake of taking one look at David's face, and her shoulders started shaking again.

"What's so funny?" demanded Tim.

"Your father," sighed Chris, wiping away her tears of mirth.

"Parents," muttered Mark as he turned away, kicking the ground in disgust. "They never give a guy a straight answer."

With an unholy gleam in his eyes, David grinned broadly at Chris as he hauled her to her feet, then he looped his arm around his son's shoulder. "Tell you what, Mark. If you and Tim fix up the fire pit with more rocks, you can have a wiener roast tonight."

Mark looked up at him skeptically. "For sure?"

"For sure."

That seemed to be a fair trade as far as the boys were concerned, and they went tearing off in the direction of the cabin. Chris looked up at him, her face animated by laughter. "They nearly had you trapped that time."

"Not a chance." He drew her against him and smiled a provocative lazy smile as he slowly smoothed his hands across her hips. "They couldn't blast me out of your bed with a cannon."

Her lips parted as she stared at him with those dark beguiling eyes, and there was no way he could resist the smoldering invitation he saw in their green depths. She slipped her arms around his neck, and pulling his head down, she covered his mouth in a searing kiss.

DAVID WAS ALREADY lying in bed, staring absently at the ceiling, when Chris came out of the master-bedroom bath. She felt oddly disconcerted by his unexpected presence. When she'd gone for her shower he had been playing a game of Chinese checkers with the boys, and she didn't think he could have possibly finished the game and put their sons to bed in the short time since she'd left them. Obviously she had taken longer than she thought.

Chris could feel his eyes upon her as she dropped her clothes on a chair and finished drying her freshly shampooed hair. The whine from the blow dryer was particularly abrasive in the heavy silence that hung in the room, but she was sure if it wasn't for the noise, David would be able to hear her frantic heartbeat loud and clear. What made it worse was that she didn't even know why she was feeling so nervous and so ridiculously shy.

Going to bed with him without passion ruling her mind was the first conscious step to splicing together the threads of their life—a life that had been severed when she'd left him. Maybe that was why she was feeling the way she was. But whatever the root of her apprehension, walking over to that bed was going to be the longest psychological distance she'd ever traveled.

Her hands were trembling slightly as she switched off the dryer and laid the brush on the dresser. It was going to be so hard to face him. . . .

"What's the matter, Chris?" he asked quietly. She swallowed against the nervous tightness in her throat as she slowly turned. He was propped up on one elbow, watching her intently. The sheet had slipped, leaving his chest uncovered, and the heavy muscles across his shoulders rippled and tautened as he reached out his hand toward her. His eyes held an intimate appeal that was irresistible. "Come here, love."

The gentleness in his voice drew her to him like a powerful magnet, and suddenly the distance that separated them was no longer threatening. The moment she grasped his hand, Chris was infused with a steadying reassurance, and she sank down on the bed beside him, her fingers curling securely around his. He stroked her arm, his eyes locked on her face. "Tell me what's wrong."

She tightened her grip on his hand. "Nothing's wrong—not now." She looked at him, trying to find the words to explain the confusing feelings that had made her hesitant. He seemed to understand her silence, and he slipped his hand up to her shoulder. With a questioning look, he let his fingers linger at the top of the bath towel she had wrapped around herself, silently waiting for her permission to undo it. It was as though he sensed her uncertainty and shyness. Chris lightly caressed the back of his hand, and as though unwrapping something fragile, he eased the towel from her.

He stared at her with such intentness that she felt as if he were absorbing her with his heated gaze. The charge mounted between them until Chris felt her nerves vibrating like high-tension wires, and she swayed toward him. Whispering her name, he caught the back of her head and pulled it down until her mouth met his in a kiss that started her pulse racing. Her whole body was trembling, and she melted against him.

Enfolding her in a secure embrace, David lifted her on top of him, his arms like bands of steel around her, his breath warm against her skin. "I need to feel you, Christie," he urged huskily.

Chris shivered as anticipation pumped through her, leaving her breathless and weak. Closing her eyes against the sensations his words had aroused in her, she straddled him, her knees drawn beside his hips, and she gripped his shoulders tightly as he entered her. A ragged sob was wrung from her as he settled her hips firmly against his and wrapped his arms around her. The gap created by her reticence had been bridged with such tenderness that she hadn't even realized it was happening.

A warm glow blossomed within her and she held him with a new strength. They were an integral part of each other when they lay together like this; this kind of sharing was like no other, and it was so overwhelming.

"Tell me why you were frightened just now, Chris," he murmured against her ear.

She drew in an unsteady breath before answering. "It seemed like the distance between us was so great right then. I felt as if I had to move through so much time to reach you." She raised her head and looked down at him, confusion clouding her expression. "I've gone to bed with you countless times, but tonight it seemed as though it was the very first time for me."

He trailed his thumb lightly across her bottom lip, his fingers curled beneath her chin. "And you felt a little shy?"

She raised her shoulders in a gesture of disconcertment. "Yes."

As if completely entranced by the texture of her skin, he caressed her face, the line of her jaw, the softness of her mouth. Gradually the laugh lines around his eyes crinkled, and a wicked smile broke across his lips. "As I remember, you weren't the least bit shy the first time." His touch became more intimate, and the seductive tone of his voice left her weak as he murmured, "And I most definitely do remember."

So did Chris. Every minute detail.

Chance. As in so many love stories, their meeting had been one of those chance occurrences that give a special meaning to the word kismet.

Spring had been in the air, and Chris was suffering from an acute case of spring fever. The thought of staying home to study for the last of her university exams was too grim, so she had gone with her father on his early-morning fishing run in his trawler, *The Bonnie B*.

It was one of those glorious mornings when a light mist was suspended over the rocky shore, the oranges, pinks and golds of dawn touching the sea with vivid streaks of undulating color. In no particular hurry to get to the fishing grounds, they chugged along the western coastline, silently soaking up the smell and taste of the fresh sea breeze. They rounded a craggy point that marked the inlet to a secluded bay, and just beyond they spotted a sleek sailing craft riding out the swell with the grace of a gull, its snapped mast trailing in the water like a broken wing.

Timothy Randal brought his trawler alongside, the diesel engines idling to counteract the drift of the tide. He hailed the damaged vessel, and almost immediately a dark head appeared from the hold.

Donald Jackson, one of the men who crewed for Timothy, took over the controls of the fishing boat as Chris's father boarded the sloop. Her feet widely braced against the roll of the deck, Chris leaned against the rail, mildly interested in what was happening.

From her vantage point she had only indistinct glimpses of the owner of the expensive craft, but she developed a vague picture of a muscular rugged individual who moved with uncommon agility. But she was not prepared for the overwhelming masculinity or the sudden unexplainable magnetism she felt when he climbed aboard *The Bonnie B*.

He wore rugged cutoffs and a grubby cream-colored sweater that had holes in both elbows. His dark hair was windblown into a mass of untidy curls, and he definitely needed a shower and a shave. But in spite of all that, there was something about him that instantly fascinated her, and a charge of electric anticipation tingled through her when he turned toward her. Her gaze collided with the bluest, most sensually compelling eyes she'd ever encountered, and she felt as if her bones were suddenly dissolving.

Time was suspended as they stared at each other, immobilized by some strange current that had sprung between them. Chris had to fight to steady her spiraling senses when he finally broke the spell and moved toward her, smiling that engaging smile that did crazy things to her pulse. She was lost.

She'd come face-to-face with a living dream.

The dream lasted for two incredible weeks—until he told her he was leaving for Australia on a long-term assignment with LaFontaine. She had tried to be rational about her association with David Spencer. She was only nineteen; he was twenty-six and years ahead of her in sophistication and experience. His social status was definitely out of her league, and he was not the type to fall for some naive innocent—and he was going away for an indefinite period of time. She didn't think she could endure the pain when she said goodbye to him for the last time.

He'd left on Friday, and by Sunday Chris had looked a wreck. She hadn't slept, and her face was so drawn her father was certain there was something terribly wrong with her. Once again Timothy Randal had experienced that helpless feeling of being alone—a feeling he had come to know well since the death of his wife. She had died of cancer when Chris was barely eleven, and raising a daughter alone had not been easy for him, especially knowing how much someone like his daughter needed a woman around. With obvious misgivings he had taken the boat out that morning, but only after Chris insisted he go.

Shortly after her father had left for the wharf the doorbell rang, and Chris went to answer it, expecting to find one of her friends on the doorstep. But instead, David stood there, looking even more haggard, more miserable than she. There was an instant in which they simply stared at each other, then he hauled her into his arms, crushing her body against his, holding her as if he wouldn't ever let her go. Chris couldn't remember them saying one word to each other. There was no time for talking. Not then. He'd covered her mouth in a kiss that obliterated any conscious thought. And despite how desperately he'd wanted her, he had been so careful, so gentle with her. It had been special, beautiful.

Even now, after all those years, after all the pain and bitterness that had separated them, Chris could still remember every single detail about that first time with him.

David had been watching her face, knowing that she was remembering. As on the day so long ago, their eyes locked together in a feverish message, then he crushed her against him and covered her mouth in a kiss that obliterated all conscious thought.

CHAPTER EIGHT

THE MUSCLES IN HIS THIGHS were burning and his breathing was harshly labored as David ran up the back stairs of the cabin. Perspiration darkened the front of his gray sweat suit and glistened on his face as he bent over to relieve the cramp in his side, his eyes closed. The run had burned off some of the frenzied edginess that had been building in him since the early hours of morning, but the claustrophobic feeling of being caught in a trap had not lessened. Both his body and his mind were poised and tense, waiting for something to happen.

Wearily he straightened and dragged his sleeve across his forehead, wiping away the beads of sweat. David's physical condition still left a great deal to be desired, and he found that frustrating. He'd run a little more than a mile but it felt like five. Exhaling sharply, he rested his hands on his hips and rolled his head back, concentrating on making his body relax, but the tension that encased him could not be disengaged. He leaned against one of the massive rough-hewn beams that supported the overhang of the roof and stared unseeingly across the clearing at the back of the cabin. Trapped. Trapped in a situation that was far more terrifying and far more inescapable than the fetid pit that had held him captive for months. But now the prison was his regret, his self-condemnation, his guilt.

How in hell could he ever level with Chris about Maria, knowing how it would hurt her? And how could he ever adequately explain his need to fulfill his moral obligation to this woman, who had made a supreme sacrifice to save his life, without giving Chris a damned good reason to hate him? She would have every right to walk out of his life for good. Her anger, her pain, her complete rejection of him would be justified—and knowing that terrified him as nothing ever before had.

He couldn't blame her if she did walk out on him again. In the light of cold reality, he knew had their positions been reversed, his male ego could not withstand the feeling of absolute betrayal if she told him she felt responsible for the well-being of an ex-lover. He wasn't even sure he could have handled the existence of an ex-lover. Just the thought of her with another man aroused a bitter jealousy in him.

He had undergone a sweeping unsettling change since he'd returned. It was strange, but looking back, he could even identify when the startling metamorphosis had begun. Maybe it had been because of the acute shock he had received when he broke through the nightmare barrier of his semiconsciousness and realized where he was; maybe it was because of the equally wrenching shock he had experienced when it finally sank in that the months of mind-destroying horror were indeed behind him; or maybe it was because he finally realized how very close he'd come to losing everything, including his life. Whatever had triggered it, something indescribable had happened the morning Chris had taken him out on the sun deck for the first time. It was as though some hard inner shell had been cracked, exposing a sensitivity that was totally foreign to him.

To his dying day he would never forget how helpless he had felt that morning when emotional barriers came crashing down, freeing him from his nightmare. Nor would he ever forget the profound comfort he had found in Chris's arms, or how very much he needed her then. From that time on, pieces of the shell continued to break away until his deepest feelings had been laid bare—feelings so overwhelming they defied description. And even though he had tried to deny it, tried to prevent it from happening, he now had to face a new unalterable fact. Chris had become his obsession. Life without her was unthinkable, unendurable. He had loved and needed her before, but never as much as he loved and needed her now. During this short time with her, he had discovered a kind of peace, a rare contentment he had never known before, and the thought of losing all that left him feeling sick, cold and bleakly empty.

Bracing his arm against the rough wood, David rested his chin on his wrist, his gaze fixed on some distant object. His face was carved by tension and his mouth set in a harsh unyielding line. Only his eyes revealed his personal torment.

He would rather rot to death in that sweltering stinking hellhole than inflict any hurt on Chris, but there was one other bitter reality he had to face. He could not turn his back on Maria. If it hadn't been for her, he would have died weeks ago. He owed her. He owed her for every breath, for every thought, but most of all he owed her for giving him this special time with Chris, and that was a debt that could never be measured. He had come to value Chris above life itself. If he lost her, nothing or no one could ever come remotely close to filling the void her absence would create in him.

He rubbed the back of his neck in a weary gesture, then straightened up and walked toward the door. He knew his time of grace was running out. Within a matter of days he would have to make a decision, the toughest, most-vital decision he would ever be forced to make.

He entered the cabin quietly, checking the spring-loaded swing of the screen door so it closed soundlessly behind him. Instinctively he sensed that everyone was still asleep. The only noise that marred the gray silence of early morning was the electric hum of the clock on the back of the stove.

Stripping off his sweater, David headed toward the small bathroom beside the laundry room, his expression one of inflexible determination. One discipline he'd been forced to master during his months of captivity was the ability to relentlessly control each and every thought, and now he blocked out all thoughts concerning the stark choice that lay before him. It would be several days before he would be physically capable of following through on any plans concerning Maria. Until then, the remaining time he had left with Chris would be inviolate. After all, the next few days might have to last him a lifetime.

There was still no sound in the cabin when David came out of the bathroom some time later, but the duskiness had lightened, heralding the impending sunrise. He had put on a clean sweat shirt and a pair of cutoffs, and as he walked into the kitchen, he shoved the sleeves of the navy sweater up his arms. He turned on the coffee maker, then took a large frosty pitcher from the fridge and poured himself a tall glass of orange juice. He had intended on going out onto the sun deck to watch the magnificent spectacle as the first fiery rays of sunlight kissed the tossing sea, but he was drawn instead to the door of the bedroom.

The harsh lines of his face softened dramatically as he leaned against the doorframe, his gaze locked on the woman who lay sleeping in his bed. She was lying on her side with one arm curled under her head, her silken hair spread out like a disheveled halo around her face. The sheet was draped loosely across her naked form, exposing only her shoulders, but the light fabric barely veiled the enticing curves of her body.

There was something so defenseless, so virginal about her, and it spurred a deep feeling of possessiveness in him. For the longest time he stood quietly watching her sleep, his body responding to the picture of innocent unguarded sensuality she presented. He wanted her. He wanted her very much. Not with the driving unrelenting hunger that demanded consummation, but with a need that went far beyond the physical.

He ached to hold her, to feel her against him. He needed to have the awareness, to savor the softness, the warmth, the fragrance of her; he needed to have the clear-headed consciousness that raging passion completely destroyed. But he made no move to go to her. This too, was something to savor. He'd never taken the time before to absorb the special touching intimacy of a moment like this, and he wanted to hold on to every second.

As if sensing his presence she stirred, her lips parting in a soft sigh. For some unexplainable reason, it was imperative that she not wake up thinking she was alone. Quickly and quietly he moved to the bed, and setting his glass on the bedside table, he crouched beside her. With the gentlest of touches he took her face in his hands. She awoke without a murmur, and for a fleeting instant that old wounded look appeared in her eyes, but she gave him a drowsy smile and the wounded look was gone.

"Good morning." Her voice was husky with sleep and as sensual as velvet.

He smiled at her as he caressed her ears with his

thumbs. Tightening his hold on her face, he leaned over and covered her mouth with his own. "Good morning," he murmured against the fullness of her lips. With a soft sigh, Chris slipped her arms around his neck, wordlessly urging him to lie beside her. As he stretched out next to her, her mouth slackened invitingly beneath his, and she responded to him with uninhibited warmth.

A deep driving hunger welded David's body against hers. A charge of desire surged through him, knocking the breath from him with an emotional explosion that was devastating. Dragging his mouth away, he clenched his jaw, and his expression twisted in a grimace as he drew her face into the curve of his shoulder.

He couldn't even come close to describing what was happening right then, nor could he explain his feelings. All he knew was that he wanted to hang on to this moment for as long as he could. He didn't want to satisfy the primitive passion that was throbbing through his body. He wanted only to hold her.

She started to lift her face and his hand shifted in her hair, holding her head immobile. "No, Chris. God, just let me hold you."

Her arms tightened around his shoulders and he could feel her heart pounding against his chest. "What's wrong, David?" she asked.

The quiver of anxiety he heard in her voice aroused an overwhelming surge of tenderness in him. Closing his eyes, he sucked in his breath sharply, then he looked at her. His voice was unsteady when he finally said, "Nothing's wrong, Chris."

She watched him, her solemn expression speaking of her mute uncertainty.

Searching for the right words to tell her what he was feeling, David slowly trailed his thumb across her cheek, his intenseness trapping them both in an unbreachable spell. Finally he spoke, his words strained and uneven. "I don't want to lose this moment, Chris. I want to stretch it out, to hang on to it, to make it last. Making love to you . . . attaining that peak of physical gratification is so explosive it consumes all my senses."

He hesitated, his face reflecting his frustration at his inability to fluently express his deepest feelings, but he felt compelled to make her understand. "I know it sounds insane, but I want to do nothing more than hold you, to take time to really savor how damned alive you make me feel. Wanting you is as exciting—as fantastic—as making love to you." His voice broke and his eyes flamed with blue fire. "And I do want you. God, Christine, how I do want you." He tried to smother back a groan as he gathered her roughly against him, an urgency in his embrace.

Chris felt as if her world had been blasted out of orbit, and she clung to him with all the strength she possessed. His confession had touched her to a staggering depth. It was indescribable. And beautiful, so very beautiful.

His hold on her was protective and powerful, and

she closed her eyes, relishing the incredible vitality, the feeling of oneness that cemented them together. She was so filled with her love for him she could hardly speak, but somehow she managed to whisper tremulously against his ear, "I can't quite believe this is real, David." Her lips enticed him with a trail of moist kisses down his neck. "You don't know how I longed to have you take me back...and now that you have, it doesn't seem real." She tunneled her long fingers into his hair, her touch soft and provocative as her lips moved against his skin. "I wish this moment could last forever."

David buried his face in her hair and his arms tightened convulsively around her. "It's real, and it is going to last forever." His voice dropped in pitch as he said hoarsely, "I love you, Christie. You'll never know how much."

The first gray of dawn flamed into a magnificent sunrise, and sunrise mellowed into the golden sunshine of morning as they explored a timeless world of sensual discovery—a world in which physical passion was tightly curbed, but where their desire was savored to the fullest.

Chris was mindless to all things except David. His mouth moved against hers with an unquenchable thirst, and his hands stroked her body with a seductive intimacy that telegraphed his own heated arousal, but his restraint never wavered. A throbbing ache swelled within her and cried out for fulfillment, but the spell he was weaving held too much magic for her to break. Her heart was pounding so frantically in her chest she could barely breathe when he dragged his mouth away from hers.

He too was fighting for air as he gazed down at her, his eyes sultry with restrained desire. "Chris... baby." He took a deep shaky breath and eased his hand along her bare shoulder. "I hear the boys moving around in the loft, and I left the bedroom door open."

There was no question about the intense regret he was experiencing, and Chris softly caressed his flushed face then lightly touched his bruised sensual mouth. "If I asked you to lock the bedroom door and come back to bed—" her voice faltered as a current of sexual heat coursed through her, robbing her of strength "—and if I asked you to make love to me, would you?"

A spasm of desire shuddered through him and he rested his forehead weakly against hers, his hand gripping her shoulder. His response seemed to be torn from him. "Yes, if that's what you want. Yes. God, yes."

She took his head in her hands and kissed him, her mouth moving gently against his, trying to soothe the storm that was ripping through them both. Her eyes glistened with unshed tears when she finally lifted his head and gazed up at him, revealing how deeply he had touched her. "David, it's never been easy for me to say what I feel—" she whispered, her love for him shining through her tears "—but this morning has been something so very special that I have to try.''

She caressed his jaw with the back of her hand, then traced the outline of his ear and swallowed hard. ''You gave me back part of my youth. You made me feel like I was nineteen again... when we were just discovering each other. That time in my life was so incredible, so special, and you've made it happen all over again.'' Her mouth trembled and her voice broke beneath the pressure of her deepest emotions. ''But what makes it even more special is that I know you feel it, too. It wasn't just a gesture to please me. It was a mutual sharing, a discovery for both of us.'' Her breath caught on a sob, and she buried her face against his shoulder, hugging him tightly. ''God, David, I don't want to let you go—I don't want to give up this incredible feeling.''

Her admission couldn't have had a more devastating effect on David, and he experienced an overwhelming longing to absorb her—the warmth, the softness, the gentleness of her—into his own being. But oddly enough, it also gave him the strength to withstand the agony of wanting her. Crushing her beneath him, he waited for the assault on their senses to ease.

A sound from above penetrated the thunder of his own heartbeat, and with a massive effort he lifted his head. ''The boys are coming downstairs.'' He closed his eyes as she caressed his neck, letting her fingers rest on the wildly beating pulse in his throat. ''I don't want to let go of this, either," he said huskily.

"Then we won't, love," she murmured, and her eyes were filled with an unspoken promise as he gazed down at her.

They exchanged a long galvanizing look, and he smiled at her slowly, a provocative sparkle growing in his eyes. "This could be one hell of a test, you know."

She laughed and ran her fingers up the back of his head with tormenting lightness. "As I recall, you used to be rather...resourceful about seducing me."

For a moment they were locked in their own private world as he covered her mouth with his own, but the sound of the boys' voices interrupted the interlude. With a heavy sigh David eased away from her and rolled to his feet. For a spellbinding moment he stood by the bed, staring down at her. There was such a leashed animal sexuality emanating from him that it left Chris's senses reeling, and as he slowly trailed his fingers across her breast, she clenched her teeth to keep from crying out. With a muttered oath, he turned and moved toward the door. Leaning against the frame, he looked across the room at her, and their eyes locked for a breathless moment, then he left, quietly closing the door behind him.

Chris rolled over onto her stomach and buried her face in the pillow, struggling to steady her erratic heartbeat. It seemed to take forever for the heady excitement to ease, but even then, she felt she had bare-

ly enough strength to move. At last she sat up and
tilted her head back, focusing her attention on the
sound of her sons' voices in the kitchen. But her
body still throbbed from David's crushing embrace,
and with a soft groan she slid from the bed and headed toward the bathroom. The time had come to find
out if there was any truth to the merits of cold
showers.

When she finally joined the rest of her family, she
still felt like a walking bomb that was about to be
detonated, but she was able to greet Tim and Mark
with a degree of normalcy that surprised her. They
were seated at the table, plowing through a stack of
steaming pancakes.

"Hi, mom," mumbled Mark around an enormous mouthful. "We thought you were going to stay
in bed all day."

She gave her son a pointed look that sailed right
over his innocent head as she responded dryly, "If
only."

A husky laugh came from the kitchen and she
turned to face David. He was leaning against the
cupboard by the stove, his feet braced in front of
him, his arms folded across his chest. A wicked
twinkle lit up his eyes, but there was more than
amusement reflected in them.

She went to him, and slipping her arm around his
waist, kissed him lightly. He draped his arm around
her shoulder and murmured softly against her hair.
"Are you all right, love?"

Chris inhaled slowly and gave him an eloquent look. "I will be if you just keep holding me up."

He laughed as he slipped his hand down her back. "Believe me, I'm not going to get any farther away from you than I absolutely have to." His arm tightened around her, and she willingly yielded to the pressure. His eyes darkened as he lowered his head, and Chris felt an intoxicating weakness sweep through her as he kissed her with breathtaking thoroughness.

"Hey, dad, you're burning up the pancakes," interjected Tim from the table, his voice sharp with reproach. "Look at all the smoke."

Chris felt David stiffen as though he'd just been doused with cold water, and with a muffled groan of frustration he dragged his mouth away from hers. Chris's eyes flew open as she was jolted back to reality. A dense curl of smoke was indeed rising from the griddle on the stove, filling the cabin with an acrid blue haze. Twisting slightly in David's embrace, she reached out to turn off the heat and switch on the fan above the range. She felt as if she'd just climbed off one of those crazy spinning rides at the fair, and she rested her head briefly against his broad chest, waiting for the light-headed sensation to pass, keenly aware of his closeness.

"Thank God it was only the pancakes burning," he said just loud enough for her to hear. "For a minute, I thought it was me."

Looping her arms around his waist, Chris laughed

and looked up at him, her eyes sparkling. "I thought you said you liked the heat."

He gave her a lazy grin. "I do," he said softly. "But I think you're going to burn out my thermostat today."

Christine threw her head back and laughed again, exposing the long slim column of her throat. Gently catching a handful of her hair, David held her head back and pressed his mouth against her silky skin. His tongue traced a tingling path along her neck.

"Kissing," snorted Mark with disgust as he came into the alcove and set his empty plate on the cupboard. "Yuk."

With a sigh of resignation, David raised his head and looked down at his son, his expression one of solemn consideration. Finally he said gravely, "It's like eating spinach and liver, Mark. You have to develop a taste for it." Mark made a face of revulsion and looked at his father with a good deal of skepticism.

Tim placed his plate beside his brother's and looked up at his father, his expression poker-faced but the mischief in his eyes a duplicate of David's. "I like spinach and liver," he said, challenging his dad to get out of that one.

David gave his son a long-suffering look. "You would."

Timmy grinned as he thumped his dad's hip with a playful punch. "Good old dad." He looked around his parents at the scorched pancakes that lay shriveling on the griddle. "Are you going to make some more?" he asked hopefully.

Chris made a move to pull away but David held her against him as he slouched against the cupboard. Shifting her arms from around his waist, she unobstrusively tucked her hands in the back pockets of his cutoffs. David gave her a long hooded look that left her a little breathless, and her voice was slightly unsteady as she spoke to her son. "Just out of curiosity, how many have you already eaten?"

Tim looked up at her somewhat sheepishly. "Six."

"Six," she responded without one shred of sympathy. "I doubt if you'll starve to death by lunch."

"Dad doesn't make his pancakes as big as yours."

Chris was completely unmoved. "Have a banana."

Tim screwed his face into what he hoped was an irresistible expression of waiflike begging. "Couldn't we have some cookies instead?"

"Go brush your teeth," said his mother, firmly closing the door on any further negotiations.

Mark rested his arm on top of the cupboard and propped up his freckled sunburned face with his hand. "If you aren't going to make any more pancakes, what are you and dad going to have for breakfast?"

"Your mother and I," said David with a grin, "are going to share a goblet of ambrosia."

Mark wrinkled his nose in absolute distaste. "Ambrosia! That sounds like some yukky awful health food—like yogurt. Ambrosia and kissing. Yuk!''

David chuckled and ruffled his son's hair. "You're definitely safe for a few years yet, Mark.''

Mark looked up at his dad, his eyes squinted in a dubious look. "What do you mean?''

Still grinning, David used the same dodge Chris had. "Go brush your teeth.''

The boy shook his head in disgusted confusion then turned away and mumbled, "Parents. A guy *never* knows what they're talking about!''

They watched him stomp into the bathroom, then exchanged an amused glance. David kissed Chris lightly on the nose before he nestled her head against the curve of his shoulder and drew her firmly against him, his jaw resting on top of her head. They remained silent and unmoving until a loud argument broke out in the bathroom over who should put the cap back on the toothpaste. Chris made a move to go, but David tightened his hold on her. "Don't bother. You know damned well they've probably lost the top down the drain by now anyway.''

Chris kissed him and grinned. "You're probably right.''

Nothing more was said, and the only noise that eventually penetrated the quiet was the sound of the back screen door slamming behind the two boys. With a murmur of reluctance, she raised her head and looked at him. "What would you like for breakfast?''

David's eyes crinkled as he gave her a slow captivating smile. "Ambrosia, of course," he said, his deep voice seducing her.

An exquisite weakness invaded her body and she melted against him, her breasts crushed against his chest. He slipped his hand up her back, positioning her more snugly against him as he straightened up, and with infinite gentleness he kissed the corner of her mouth.

"David...dear God, you don't know what you do to me," she breathed, her pulse accelerating wildly.

He moved against her provocatively and his arms tightened around her in a nearly savage embrace. "I want you so damned badly, Christie," he murmured raggedly.

Her voice caught on a breathless sob. "David, please—I—"

"Shh," he whispered as he claimed her mouth in a fluid kiss that drove all reason from her mind.

THE HEAT OF THE SUN on her back had lulled Chris into a state of languid semiconsciousness that was perforated by the distant cries of the wheeling sea gulls. The smell of the sun-warmed earth and the pine-laden breeze cast a torpid spell that weighed upon her like a cozy blanket.

She and David were stretched on an old sleeping bag in front of the cabin, soaking up the early afternoon sunshine, both of them too drugged by the warmth to even talk. Something light brushed against her face, and with a drowsy reluctance she shifted her head on her folded arms and slowly opened her eyes. For a moment, miniature sun dogs danced before her line of vision, and she squinted against their blinding brightness.

David was braced on one elbow, his head propped in his hand. His eyes were riveted on her as he idly dragged a foxtail of grass along her cheek and down her neck. The laugh lines around his eyes and mouth were pronounced by the slant of the sun as he gave her an engaging grin. "Do you know you aren't worth a damn after we've made love?" he said, as though it was a significant discovery. "And they talk about men rolling over and going to sleep afterward."

Trapping the hand that was tormenting her, Chris laughed and laced her fingers through his. "Poor David."

"Next time I won't give in to you so easily."

"You do that."

David watched her with an unwavering absorption that seemed to deepen the blue of his eyes, making them even more penetrating, more sensual. Instinctively she knew he was thinking about what had happened between them after breakfast. The boys had gone back to their fort leaving their parents alone in the cabin, and it had only taken a few brief moments of privacy to annihilate any misguided ideas either David or Chris had about continued restraint.

Their lovemaking had been so wild, so turbulent. But the unbelievable pleasure they had tasted had been just as overwhelming. Chris was so completely spent and satiated after experiencing such an explosion of emotions she hardly had the strength to get dressed, let alone follow David outside.

With a knowing little smile playing around his mouth, he reached out and traced the outline of her ear with the grass, the touch sending a shiver of pleasure down her neck. With tormenting lightness he trailed a finger across her shoulders, and his tone was husky and unquestionably suggestive when he said, "How would you like to go back inside?"

Chris heard a tremor that sounded suspiciously like suppressed laughter, and she gave him a caustic look. "Don't push your luck, David Spencer."

He laughed out loud and gave her a playful push. "Well then how would you like a cold beer?"

She grinned at him and sleepily nodded her head in assent. "I think I might be able to handle that."

Still grinning, David slapped her smartly on the bottom before he rolled to his feet. With a lazy smile on her face, Chris watched him spring onto the edge of the sun deck and neatly vault the railing in one fluid move. He was as bad as the boys—avoiding the easy way at all costs.

Chris idly watched the grasses bending in the breeze, her thoughts drifting like the sea. Through the heat-induced drowsiness that blurred her mind, the recollection of the morning Peter had brought her back to the cabin swam to the surface. A sudden chill swept through her, as though a shadow of ill omen had been cast over her. And there was a shadow. There was still Maria. For an instant a flicker of panic stirred in her, but she forced it down. Not now. She couldn't deal with that reality now. She would put off facing her nemesis for as long as she could.

Willing herself to relax, Chris blocked out that disturbing thought and focused on David. His loving her was like a miracle, filling up the emptiness that had haunted her for the last four years. Her eyes drifted shut as the warmth of the sun and her inner peacefulness sedated her. Her awareness sharpened for a moment when she thought she heard a car approaching, but the muted thunder of the surf superimposed itself on all sounds, and Chris let herself be lulled by it.

But the slamming of a car door dispelled her lethargy, and Chris rolled over onto her back. As she dreamily watched the clouds billow and furl she absently wondered why Peter had come back so soon. When David didn't appear, she came to the conclusion that if she wanted a cold beer, she was going to have to go get it herself. She arched her back and stretched, then picked up the sleeping bag and headed toward the deck. Shaking out the blanket, she hung it over the rail, then turned toward the patio door.

Her eyes, used to the brilliance of sunshine, took a

moment to adjust to the dimness of the cabin, but the minute she stepped through the door she sensed an electric tension. When her vision finally penetrated the dusk, she was stunned. David's parents were standing just inside the back door.

Chris had an eerie uncomfortable feeling she had just been thrown back in time. After four years, nothing had changed. They still looked the same. It was hard to believe that David's mother was in her early sixties. Catherine Spencer was still the epitome of elegance. Tall and well proportioned, she wore her deep mauve silk slack suit with a refined ease. Her subtle makeup, right down to the soft mauve eye shadow, coordinated perfectly with her ensemble. Her beautiful silver hair was drawn back in its customary French roll, and her exquisitely crafted silver jewelry added just the right touch of adornment. Yes, Catherine definitely had class.

Matthew, on the other hand, didn't possess quite the same type of elegant style. He had on a pair of dark tan slacks and wore a matching tan shirt under a cream-colored V-neck sweater. He looked as though he'd just stepped off the golf course. He still radiated that same personal magnetism, that same vitality he had passed on to his son. In fact he had passed on more than that to David. They looked very much alike. David's face was a little slimmer and he was taller, and he wasn't quite as stocky or as heavily built as his father, but other than that, there was no mistaking them as father and son. You only had to take one look at the eyes. Matthew's face was a little more wrinkled, his thick hair a little grayer, and he looked as if he might have gained a little weight, but he showed very little evidence of the passing years.

It took only a second for these silent observations to register, but during that time Chris was keenly aware of the mounting tension. No one had uttered a single word since she'd entered. Glancing from one to another with uneasy perplexity, she felt her stomach shrink with alarm when she saw the flash of anger in David's gaze. The silence grew more taut as all eyes focused on her. His father's face was unreadable, but his mother's expression was far more revealing. What Chris identified in the older woman's eyes was hostile accusation and a nearly unbearable hurt.

If she hadn't been so rooted by shock, Chris probably would have bolted instantly. She wasn't ready for this strained confrontation just yet, and to make matters even worse, she had a strong hunch that neither were the senior Spencers. They were not thrilled about her presence. That was plain to see. They saw her as a traitor, and they made no attempt to disguise their distrust of her. Reality—bleak, unrelenting reality—had just shattered the illusion she had been living, and now she was faced with the real world. Without saying a word she turned to go, suddenly feeling very much like an intruder, and very alone.

"Christine." David's voice was quiet, but there

was a hardness in it that she found disturbing. Turning slowly, she looked at him, her eyes again dark and haunted, her face drawn.

He stared at her, his unblinking eyes like cold steel, a quality of ruthlessness in his stance. "I'd like you to stay, if you don't mind."

He was obviously angry, and Chris watched with edgy trepidation as he went to the windows, rested his hand at shoulder level on the frame, and braced his weight on his outstretched arm. Silently he stared out the window. The senior Spencers exchanged a taut glance as Catherine sat down on the sofa and Matthew went to stand before the fireplace, his hands clasped behind his back.

With a foolish yet real feeling that any noise could trigger an explosion, Chris quietly pulled a chair away from the table and sat down, her knees suddenly weak. A nervous palpitation twisted her insides into knots, and Chris tightly clasped her hands together in her lap, feeling more and more apprehensive by the minute. Obviously something had been said before she came in, and whatever it was, it had David in a rage. The thought of another vile scene left her shivering. She had no insulation against the kind of cold that came with bitter recriminations.

The silence became electric. As the suspense slowly stretched to the limit of tolerance, Chris glanced at Catherine Spencer to assess how she was coping with this confrontation. The younger woman experienced a sharp jolt of alarm.

She hadn't noticed it when she'd first entered the cabin, but under closer inspection, it was apparent the boys' grandmother had aged dramatically since Chris had seen her last. Catherine was still a striking woman, but there were new lines in her face that had been etched there by months of worry, and there was a dullness in her eyes that clearly spoke of many sleepless nights. The woman was indeed perfectly groomed, but some indefinable quality about her spoke of careless neglect. Chris couldn't put her finger on it exactly, but it was there. And she felt a sudden concern. Catherine Spencer was as ill equipped to endure a nasty scene as she was. David's mother, too, had been through hell.

Chris jumped and her heartbeat faltered when David's father cleared his voice and started to speak, his voice raspy. "I think perhaps you should tell us what's been going on, David. In spite of what you obviously think, your mother and I have been extremely concerned about you."

David turned slowly, deliberately, his nostrils flaring and his eyes flashing. "If you were so damned concerned, why in hell did you come barging in here, trying to take over the whole show? What you said was unforgivable, dad." The barely contained fury in his voice cut like a knife.

As they stood there glaring at each other, their tempers flaring, it struck Chris again how very much alike they were. Only twice before had she ever witnessed a head-on battle between David and Matthew Spencer, and she would never forget either one of those showdowns. One man was as strong, as unyielding as the other, and they both could be ruthless in achieving their individual goals. Watching them square off was like watching flint strike against flint.

What unsettled Chris more than anything was what could have possibly happened in the short space of time before she came into the cabin. The three of them had been alone only a few moments, and David was furious, Matthew was battling to hang on to his temper, and Catherine looked utterly distraught.

The question had barely gelled in Chris's mind when Matthew swung his gaze to her, the muscle in his cheek twitching spasmodically. "It seems that David had taken offense because I said that seeing we'd found out about his being here, Catherine could stay here with David and the boys, since I'm sure it's been an inconvenience for you. I think what you did was commendable, Christine, but I'm sure your staying here is very . . . distasteful for you."

Chris could tell by the twisted derisive smile on David's face that wasn't exactly what Matthew had said, and the horrible truth hit her that they were, in fact, fighting over her.

David stared out the window, battling to hang on to his temper. If only she hadn't come in, if only he could have dealt with this without involving her in a showdown with his parents. If only. But he had no options. When she had turned to go, he had a very unpleasant suspicion that if he'd let her leave the cabin, she would have kept on going. As much as he didn't want her in here now, he knew he didn't dare let her out of his sight. His fury gathered new momentum when, for that brief moment he'd faced her, he saw her fragile sense of security wither before his very eyes. In a matter of seconds she'd looked as tormented, as haunted by guilt as she had when he first came back—and all in a space of time that could be measured in heartbeats.

The contemptuous sneer was still ingrained on David's face as he turned to look at his father, his jaws locked together against the fury that was building in him. But he never had a chance to speak.

Chris met his father's cool stare with a steady gaze, and there was a quiet stoicism about her when she said, "If David wants me to leave, I will. But until he tells me to go, I've no intention of leaving him."

A taut silence followed, and when Matthew finally spoke, his voice was calm but edged with bitterness. "That sounds very noble, my dear, but let me point out to you if it hadn't been for your leaving David, he'd have never been in Central America in the first place. Neither Catherine nor I can ever forget or forgive you for ripping our family apart."

Chris blanched, her dark pain-filled eyes dominating her ashen face. Matthew Spencer had just hurt her more than he would ever know. Once, long ago, he had totally doted on Chris; now he felt nothing but a seething animosity toward her. Yet she couldn't blame him. What he said was the truth. If it hadn't been for her. . . .

"That's enough," snapped David, his voice dangerously quiet. He moved toward his father, his catlike grace as menacing as an open threat. "There will be no blame laid by you or anyone else, nor is this any of your damned business." He spoke softly, distinctly, his narrowed eyes as cold as ice.

Father and son faced each other squarely. David's fury was barely contained and his father knew it. In an effort to avert an all-out battle with his eldest son, Matthew changed his tactics. "You're right, David. What's between you and Christine is none of my business, but I do have some concern for my grandsons." The older man stuck his hands in his pockets and stared at the floor for a moment. When he lifted his head, he met his son's icy stare with solemnity. "I'm asking you to consider their welfare. They've had a very difficult year, and Christine's being here with you is going to make it just that much harder on them when you and she go your separate ways."

David was staring at his father, his jaw clenched and his hands on his hips. "And what makes you think we're going our separate ways?" he asked tautly.

Matthew and Catherine exchanged an alarmed glance, then Matthew sighed wearily. He avoided looking at Chris as he said, "You can never go back to what once was, son. She's no longer your wife."

There was a brittle pause before David responded, his voice as cold as his eyes, "But she is my wife."

The shocked silence could have been sliced with a knife, and the senior Spencers stared at each other in stunned disbelief.

But David was oblivious to their reaction. There was a dramatic softening of his expression as he went to Chris and crouched down before her, gently separating her clenched hands and holding them securely in his. His chilling hardness evaporated as he looked at her with all-encompassing love, his voice husky and caressing as he said, "And she's going to continue being my wife."

Tears welled up in Chris's eyes and her mouth began to tremble, but she held his gaze with an intensity that touched him deeply. With his fingertips he wiped away the teardrops that caught on her lashes, and for a brief space of time the two of them were locked within their own sphere of intimacy. Then, with a reluctant sigh, he stroked her cheek and stood up beside her, but he maintained a physical link. Slipping his hand around her neck, he gently drew her head against him so the side of her face was resting against his hip.

His proprietary hold on Chris was not lost on his parents, and they exchanged another confused questioning look before Catherine said, "But the divorce...?"

David swung his attention to his mother. His tone was distantly civil when he answered her unfinished question. "There was never a divorce. A legal separation, yes—but no divorce."

Chris shot a startled look up at him. It was only then she realized how very little his parents knew, how little anyone knew. He had made no comment to anyone about their broken marriage; he had talked to no one about the pain the separation from his children must have caused, or about the hostility he must have felt because of her decision. He had kept it all bottled up inside him. Suddenly the guilt was back, sitting like a stone in the pit of her stomach.

David sensed her dismay and he pressed her head tighter against him, his fingers softly caressing her neck in a silent attempt to reassure her. But he could feel tension building in her body, and he experienced a burst of angry frustration at his parents' unwanted intrusion. Why couldn't they have just left Chris and him alone for a little while longer? Why did they have to butt in? His thoughts were torn by a perturbing question: how had they found out he was there? Not from Peter. He'd bet his life on Peter.

His voice was flat. "Just out of curiosity, how did you find out I was here?"

Matthew stared at David for a moment before he looked away. "Ellis came over to see your mother this morning. She felt we should at least be told you were safe."

David's frustration and anger had pushed his restraint to the limit, and for a split second he came within a hairsbreadth of exploding. But he gritted his teeth and tried to smother the heat of his rage. He inhaled deeply, the pulse in his temple throbbing rapidly as he clenched and unclenched his jaw, then slowly released his breath. "What all did she tell you?"

David's father went to stand before the windows, his arms folded across his chest. There was an air of weary disillusionment about him when he said, "Not much. I don't think she knows anything more than the fact that you're here. I take it Peter didn't enlighten her."

"Did she tell you about her visit?"

"Yes. She was pretty torn up about what had happened."

"I'm sure," snorted David in disgust.

His father turned to face him and dismissed his comment with a shrug. "Who knows with Ellis," he said. He frowned, apparently disturbed by some private thought.

Catherine Spencer's voice was unnaturally modulated, but her rigid discipline couldn't quite filter out her distress. "Why didn't you want us to know you were back, David?"

Chris didn't give him a chance to answer. Being a mother herself, she instinctively knew how hurt Catherine must be, and she wanted so badly to make her understand that it was not a deliberate decision on David's part. "It wasn't that he didn't want you to know, Catherine," she said, her voice unsteady. "He was extremely ill when we first brought him back, and getting him well was our first priority. And there were...adjustments for all of us. It was more a case of working through one situation at a time.''

There was a heavy tremor in Catherine's voice when she said, "We don't even know how you managed to get him back, Christine.... We've been so worried about him.''

Chris couldn't bear the anguish she heard in her mother-in-law's voice and she gently pulled away from David. Her eyes dark with compassion, she crossed the room and knelt in front of the older woman and grasped her cold hands. "There isn't much to tell, Catherine,'' she said quietly.

Catherine was fighting vainly to maintain her poise and her voice wavered badly as she whispered, "But I need to know.''

Suddenly the anger and the tension evaporated. Now was not the time for past differences. Now was the time to put them aside.

CHAPTER NINE

THE ROOM WAS VERY QUIET. In a sometimes halting and muted voice, Chris had just finished telling the senior Spencers the details concerning David's arranged rescue. No one looked at anyone else during the strained silence that ensued, and no one was quite sure how to break it.

David was sitting on the sofa by his mother, his shoulders hunched over, his head lowered and his hands clasped between his knees. Finally he lifted his head and looked at his wife, who was seated in one of the big easy chairs across from him. Her face was expressionless, but with Chris the lack of expression said more than most people realized. Delivering her chronicle about the mission had obviously been an ordeal for her. Listening to it hadn't been easy for David, either.

It was, he realized as her narration unfolded, the first time he'd heard the complete story. He probably wouldn't have heard it then if it hadn't been for his father's uncanny ability to ferret out specific details. And as he learned about all that had transpired in the insane campaign to bring him home, David felt more and more indebted to Chris.

There was no question about it. The rescue had been a monumental undertaking. Even without all the problems and snags and delays they had encountered, she and Peter still had to contend with the day-to-day worries of exposure and the fear that something would happen to him before the commando team arrived. It must have been a nightmare for her. If he had had any remaining doubts about her, they would have been swept away. Her action had been an exercise of devotion motivated by the very deepest kind of caring, and he was moved beyond words.

Finally Chris lifted her eyes. They were filled with pain. As if by some mental link, he knew she was not thinking about how she had effected his rescue but about why he had left Canada in the first place. David rose and crossed the room. Crouching down by the side of her chair, he slipped his arms around her. As she turned her face against his neck he felt her shudder, and even though the wide arm was wedged between them, he held her close. If David's parents had any remaining doubts about what the situation was between their son and Chris, they too were answered.

David held her for a few moments, silently comforting her, then he gently grasped her face and eased her away from him. "Are you okay?" he asked, his voice concerned.

Imperceptibly she nodded and forced a smile. She

was still very pale, but her expression was no longer clouded by tragic memories. He gave her shoulder a quick squeeze and made an attempt to ease her desolate mood. "It's stacking up to be one of those days when we should have stayed in bed, isn't it?" he murmured with a touch of perversity.

Her solemn expression slowly changed as an effervescent amusement brightened her eyes. Responding in a voice just loud enough for him to hear, she said, "And since when did you need any justification for staying in bed?"

He grinned at her. "I just thought I'd mention it. It's been a long time since breakfast," he whispered.

Deliberately misreading his meaning, she gave him an engaging half smile. "Then I suppose I'd better fix a snack for everyone."

"That's not what I meant, Christine," he said pointedly.

She patted his cheek firmly and stood up, her voice vibrant with laughter as she tormented, "But that's what you're going to get, David."

She fixed a light lunch, and as the others ate she tried to maintain as low a profile as possible. It was David they were interested in, not her. As soon as she could remove herself without appearing to be rude, she made an excuse about taking a snack to the boys, who were still at the fort. She was nearly across the clearing when Catherine called her.

Turning around, Chris watched with a certain

amount of trepidation as her mother-in-law came down the steps of the deck and walked quickly toward her. She didn't know if she was able to handle a one-on-one meeting with the older woman, especially when she knew that neither Catherine nor Matthew was exactly delighted she was back in David's life.

But Catherine was smiling as she approached. "David and his father were beginning to drift into a dreary conversation about the business, so I thought I'd come with you to see the boys."

Determined to keep the mood as amicable as possible, Chris followed her mother-in-law's lead. "They're so wrapped up in this fort of theirs they don't even want to take time to eat, if you can believe it."

Catherine laughed as she ducked to miss a low-hanging branch. "I can believe it. Timmy can be particularly single-minded when he gets a bee in his bonnet." She stooped to pick up an enormous pinecone that was lying on the ground, her face intent as she brushed off the dry grass clinging to it. "They must have been absolutely thrilled when they found David was back."

Her voice was neutral, almost totally without inflection, and Chris cast a quick glance at her, uneasy about the drift of the conversation. Her voice was subdued when she said, "They were. They didn't know he was back until they got out here."

They continued in silence for a space, then Catherine stopped walking and caught Chris's arm. Chris looked at her, and her facade of aloof politeness wavered when she saw tears in the older woman's eyes.

Catherine opened her mouth to speak, but looked away sharply as the tears spilled over. She wiped them away before she faced her daughter-in-law. "During the past hour I've come to realize how badly and how wrongly I've judged you, Christine."

Chris felt completely taken aback by this unexpected confession, and she whispered unevenly, "Why don't we just forget—"

"No!" The sharpness of her voice seemed to surprise even Catherine, and she softened her parry with a twisted smile. "No, Christine. This isn't something I'm prepared to let you sweep under the rug because it would be less awkward for me. Matthew and I are deeply indebted to you. You acted— perhaps a little rashly—but nevertheless you did *something,* while we spent months dithering with international diplomacy and bureaucracy and endless negotiating and God knows what else." She was visibly disturbed, her agitation making her voice somewhat strident. "You're always a mother, Christine, no matter how old your children are. And quite frankly, I really couldn't have given a damn if that entire republic fell into the sea, as long as we got David out first."

Chris was stunned. Catherine Spencer was a lady who had always faced any crisis with polished composure and calm logic, and her vehemence was, quite simply, out of character.

Shock clearly registered on Chris's face as she stared at David's mother. The older woman's chin was raised at an imperious angle and her eyes were flashing as she met her daughter-in-law's bemused gaze. For an instant the anger still sparked, then she smiled somewhat sheepishly, her haughty manner relaxing. "Forgive me, my dear. No matter how placid the animal, threaten a female's cub and you have the wrath of God on your hands."

Chris snapped her sagging mouth shut and smiled broadly. "You *do* surprise me, Catherine."

Catherine shrugged as she started walking through the stand of timber, the crunch of dried twigs and pinecones snapping and crackling beneath her feet. "I think I surprised myself. Matthew and I had some bitter battles over this." She glanced at Chris, her eyes slightly narrowed in contemplation. "But what you did doesn't surprise me at all. I always felt you had a good deal more backbone than we gave you credit for."

Chris's arms tightened around the plastic container in which she carried the boys' lunch and she bowed her head, her eyes filled with self-condemnation. "It's too bad the same couldn't be said for my common sense."

Her mother-in-law made no comment as she

stooped to pick up another large pinecone, and with her usual tact she changed the subject. "David seems to be recovering from his ordeal very well. Quite frankly I was mentally prepared to find him in much worse condition."

"He *was* in much worse condition," Chris responded, her voice strained by the horrible memory of David the first time she saw him. "You can't believe how bad he was when Peter first brought him back."

The older woman's tone was equally strained when she said, "If you don't mind, Christine, I think I'd rather not hear about it." They looked at each other, and suddenly there was an element of understanding between them that had never been there before.

The boys' voices were becoming louder as they wound their way around a tangle of fallen trees just beyond the clearing. Moments before they broke from cover, Catherine stopped and turned, her face etched with worry. "Christine, there's something I have to say to you, and I hope you'll forgive me for being rather blunt about it, but unfortunately there doesn't seem to be a subtle way of putting it."

Chris stared at the woman, unconsciously bracing herself for some form of confrontation. "What is it, Catherine?" she asked, her voice taut.

The older woman looked fragile right then—like one of the rare orchids she raised, with delicate blossoms that were so easily bruised. Yet there was strength in her, a pliancy. She might have to bend, but she would never break.

Catherine hesitated, then sighed heavily. "Matthew was very...disturbed when you and David separated, and I'm afraid we both judged you rather harshly." She shifted her gaze and looked down, fingering the numerous strands of silver chains that glittered against the purple silk of her blouse. "You see, I'm afraid it may take him a while to...adjust to David's and your reconciliation." She lifted her eyes and looked at Chris with a silent entreaty. There was a dignity in her humility, a touch of Catherine's undeniable class, when she said, "I'm asking you not to judge him as harshly as we did you. He was very fond of you, Christine, and I know he'll eventually forget what happened in the past, if you can only give him time."

Chris gave her mother-in-law a joyless smile that was warped by self-reproach. "I can at least do that, especially after all the trouble I've caused."

Catherine laid her hand on Chris's shoulder in a gentle gesture. "Don't *you* judge yourself too harshly, either, my dear."

"Hey, grandma, whatcha doing here?" called Mark as he came toward them.

David's mother turned to give her grandson a warm smile. "Well, darling, I thought I'd better come and see what you need for a housewarming present for your fort."

Chris pursed her lips and shook her head. Only

grandma could come up with such an excuse to lavish them with heaven only knew what.

Timmy watched them approach with apparent wariness, far more cautious than his brother in accepting things at face value. Chris could tell by the expression on his face that he was uneasy about the state of affairs between the two women, and undoubtedly his little stomach was tied up in knots for fear there would be another scene. Letting Catherine and Mark outdistance her, Chris let him know with a reassuring nod that everything was fine. He studied her a moment longer, then smiled. It was only after his mother's silent assurance that he went to meet his grandmother.

"Hi, grandma. How do you like our fort?" he asked, wiping his sweaty grubby hands on his equally grubby T-shirt. He was, without a doubt, a perfect candidate for a laundry commercial.

"Well, Timothy, it's a marvelous fort," his grandmother said as she handed him the two pinecones she'd picked up. "I thought perhaps you could use these . . . they're such nice big fat ones."

"Hey! Neato! We'll put 'em on top of two stakes by our door." He grinned up at her, "Thanks, grandma."

"You're very welcome. Now, are you going to give me a tour?"

Chris set the packed lunch down on a stump and stretched beneath a tree. Leaning back against the trunk, she felt the rough bark bite into her skin. At last the boys had a chance to show off their project. A knowing smile tugged at her mouth. An indulging doting grandma—every kid should have one, she thought as she watched her two boys with their only remaining grandmother.

Resting her head against the trunk, Chris became reflective. There was a certain amount of truth in that slightly cynical thought, she realized. Catherine might spoil them rotten, her discipline might be practically nonexistent, and she had a tendency to stretch rules, but she truly did love them. And the boys knew it. They were very lucky to have those extended family ties. Nowadays not many kids did.

As she sat there watching them, a new insight unfolded for her. She realized that until now she had offhandedly taken the Spencers' devotion to the boys for granted. Had they chosen to do so, Catherine and Matthew could have opted out of their grandparental roles, and her boys would have missed out on something special. Yes, there had been times in the past when Grandma and Grandpa Spencer had nearly driven her nuts, but in all honesty, their pandering to the boys' whims had been more an inconvenience than a complication. It was certainly food for thought.

The tour was obviously over, and Mark came and flopped on the ground by his mother. Chris took one look at his face and hands and ruefully shook her head. He looked as though he hadn't seen soap and water for at least a week.

He wiped his hands on his jeans and ripped off the lid of the container. "What did you bring us, mom?"

She grinned at him. "Liver-and-spinach sandwiches."

He shot her a look that told her he was *not* amused, and lifted out a package of sandwiches. "Hey, peanut butter and jelly," he said, as if that was the biggest surprise of the century. Mark would live on peanut butter-and-jelly sandwiches, given the opportunity. To him, they were the most important staple in any kid's diet—next to chocolate-chip cookies.

Catherine and Timmy joined them, and without any fuss, grandma sat on the ground with the rest of them, acting for all the world as if her raw-silk slacks and blouse were nothing more than a faded pair of blue jeans.

"Want a sandwich, grandma?" asked Timmy as he carefully passed her the sandwiches on the lid of the container. Chris knew very well that Catherine loathed peanut butter-and-jelly sandwiches, but she also knew she would eat one if for no other reason than to acknowledge Timmy's politeness and consideration.

"Why, thank you, darling," she said, and by the way she said it, you would have thought Timmy had just done the most marvelous thing.

Chris had to bite her lip to keep from laughing. It had been a very long time since she'd seen grandma in action with the boys, but the tactics hadn't changed. Catherine might be an abysmal failure at discipline, but she could have the boys turning handsprings to please her because she always made them feel as though they had done something extraordinary. But then, she'd had years of practice; she'd handled her husband and four sons much the same way.

Try as she might, Chris could not completely smother her amusement, and her eyes had a wicked sparkle in them as she watched her mother-in-law diligently choke down a bite. Catherine looked at her, her own eyes revealing a glimmer of wry humor as she shrugged her shoulders and swallowed again.

Chris grinned and pointed to the thermos by the tree. "Is there any lemonade left in that, Mark? Grandma might like a drink." The boy jumped to his feet and dug through a box that Chris strongly suspected was used for garbage. He came up with a paper cup that was less than clean, but at least it was whole.

Chris clamped her teeth together to keep from bossing and watched the whole operation with baited breath. The thermos was large and had a spigot at the bottom, but obviously the container was nearly empty. Mark managed to get enough in the glass to rinse it out, but then he had to wedge the thermos between his knees and tip it to try to fill the cup. He was not at all successful. Finally he placed the cup between his feet to hold it steady, and with a great deal of fumbling and heavy breathing he managed to fill the glass, as well as spill lemonade all over his running shoes. It had been an endurance test to watch him, but he had done it on his own. Catherine was relentlessly studying her carefully manicured fingernails, but Chris knew it had cost her dearly to sit there and not to go to Mark's aid. It was such a small thing, yet such an enormous step.

BACK IN THE CABIN, the two Spencer men were seated at the table. Matthew's open briefcase was sitting to one side, and the remaining surface of the table was cluttered with business papers. They had been hashing out what possible moves they could make to secure safety for their employees as well as the mines, and David realized that whatever he did, it was going to have to be discreet and carefully considered. The lives of the remaining hostages were at stake, and unfortunately many Canadian employees were still living in the country. Before any strategy could be planned, the political temperature of the republic's existing military regime had to be taken.

Several critical decisions stared David in the face, but the most critical one in his mind concerned Maria's release. He had not told his father about her, nor did he have any intention of doing so—especially after he realized how much bitterness his father and mother felt toward Chris. The knowledge of Maria could be a dangerous weapon in the hands of someone who harbored a grievance. And there was a grievance.

For the fifth time in as many minutes, David glanced at the clock on the back of the kitchen stove. He hadn't been happy when his mother had followed Chris out of the cabin, and as the time stretched by he was becoming more and more anxious. He had a nasty suspicion that something was going on behind the scenes that he didn't know anything about, and if either of his parents did or said anything to upset her or hurt her. . . . His hands gripped the empty beer glass in front of him, and concern chiseled tense lines into his face. Where in hell was she?

His uneasiness left him feeling like a caged cat, and abruptly he stood up and went to the back door. His edginess abated somewhat when he saw that both cars were still parked in the clearing, but he was apprehensive. He could hear the boys' voices at the front of the cabin and he turned to meet them; if Chris wasn't with them, he was damned well going to look for her.

But she was. She came through the patio door carrying a container and one of the boys' jean jackets, her eyes bright. He felt nearly sick with relief.

She set down the stuff she was carrying on the end of the cupboard and looked up at him and smiled. "Hi. You missed out on a picnic." Her smiled faded sharply into an expression of alarm when she saw the look on his face. "What's the matter?"

David shook his head as he caught her hand and laced his fingers through hers, his grip almost painful. He was overcome with a sudden need to hold her, to reassure himself that she was all right. Taking a quick glance at the others, he opened the back door and drew her outside onto the deck.

With a muttered oath, he pulled her against him in a powerful embrace. Chris's arms slipped around his chest, and she held him with surprising strength. "What is it, David? What's wrong?"

He probably would have made some smart comeback to cover up his real feelings if it hadn't been for the hint of panic he'd heard in her voice. Drawing her even more tightly against him, he murmured roughly, "For one awful moment I had the feeling you'd gone...and it scared the hell out of me, Christie."

She eased away from his body and looked up at him, her eyes solemn. "I won't ever do that, David. Ever." She slipped her arms around his neck, and he enfolded her in a secure embrace. He would give anything he owned to be able to have a few days with her, just the two of them alone with no interruptions, no responsibilities, no intrusions. He didn't think he could ever get enough of holding her. She seemed to be able to insulate him from everything—all the problems, all the worries—and nothing else mattered except that she was in his arms.

He had no idea how long he held her like that, and he didn't care. If he'd had his way, it would be forever.

Finally she stirred in his arms and looked up at him with regret. "We ought to go in, David. They'll be wondering where we are."

He gave her a reluctant smile. "I guess we'd better."

He didn't release her though, and for a time they remained wrapped in each other's arms. At last he gazed down at her, his eyes serious. Bracketing her face with his hands, he kissed her with supreme gentleness. "Don't stay away from me tonight, Christie. I'm going to need to touch you now and then."

He felt her breath catch, and not daring to look at her, he ushered her toward the door.

THE COASTLINE WAS CAUGHT in that mysterious half light that came between dusk and dark, bringing with it a peculiar crystal-clear stillness that seemed to carry the slightest sound for miles. Nightfall was creeping in with sinister stealth, bringing with it dark shadows and shapes of towering silhouettes that were starkly outlined against the fading light. Eventually the silver sphere of the moon would be towed up into the blackness, sending its glimmering gossamer trail across the sea, and the stars would begin to twinkle in the ebony sky. Then the night would have a beauty of its own. But now was the time of the uneasy crossing from light to dark, a time of ominous transition.

David leaned against the railing of the sun deck and stared out to sea, his expression grim. Time was running out. Maybe he would have gone on stalling indefinitely if his parents hadn't shown up. But they had, and that changed everything. By tomorrow morning, senior government officials in Central America would know of his escape, and political wheels would be set in motion. Unless some miracle happened he would be going back, and going back very soon. Those were the hard cold facts.

That left him with a formidable decision. What, exactly, was he going to tell Chris? She was still so fragile emotionally, and the thought of what it would do to her if he told her about Maria was more than he could handle. Yet if he didn't tell her, he was taking a big gamble. There was always the chance she would find out by some fluke, just as she had about the horror of his confinement. Much as he hated the thought of telling her, he hated the thought of her finding out that way even more. She was going to be hurt enough as it was when he told her he was going back. The muscles in his face tightened. There was really no decision to be made. There was no way he could tell her about the other woman in his life. He had no choice. He'd have to take that gamble.

He sensed her nearness and he turned to watch her come to him through the deepening twilight.

Her face was shadowed by concern as she looked up at him. "What's the matter, David? You've been so quiet all evening."

Feeling suddenly defeated, David straightened and slipped his arms around her slight form. "Nothing's wrong, Chris. It's just that the rest of the world is moving in on us, and I'm not quite ready for that yet." He rested his head against hers, his voice tinged with resignation. "I'd hoped we'd have a few more days alone before we had to start contending with a bunch of problems."

"Are you referring to your mom and dad?"

His eyes were bleak as he stared out over her head. "Yeah, among other things."

She didn't say anything for a while, but finally she looked up at him, her eyes solemn. "Will you promise me one thing?"

He gazed at her steadily. "If I can." By the way she looked at him, David knew Chris hadn't missed the realistic bluntness of his response, nor the sober meaning behind it. One thing he could not do to her was provide her with false reassurance by promising something he couldn't deliver. He wasn't going to play those kinds of games with her.

His extreme seriousness sent a sudden chill creeping up Chris's spine. Her voice was uneven when she said, "Will you promise me you won't make any decisions without talking them over with your dad?"

The unexpectedness of her request caught him off

guard, and it took him a split second to respond. "That I can promise," he answered quietly. A troubled frown creased his brow and he absently brushed his thumb along her shoulder blade, his thoughts preoccupied by another concern. Chris would be left on her own to deal with his family if he returned to Central America, and he had deep misgivings about that. His mother had surprised the hell out of him with her readiness to let bygones be bygones. His father, however, was a different ball of wax. Matthew admired Chris's courage, he was grateful for what she had done, but it would be a long time before he'd forgive her for leaving his son in the first place, and David wasn't sure how his father would treat Chris when he wasn't around.

He was jarred out of his sober reverie when he felt Chris shiver in his arms, and he drew her closer against him. "Are you cold?" She shook her head and pressed her face against his chest. With a gentle pressure, he tipped her head back and gazed down at her. "What is it, Chris?"

She didn't answer him, but that haunted look was back, and David sensed she was closing up on him. He tightened his hold on her face and lifted her chin a fraction, his low voice carrying a quiet warning. "Don't clam up on me, Christie."

She stared up at him with dark eyes, her voice unsteady when she answered, "I'm not clamming up, David." He saw her swallow hard, and he could sense the depth of her misery as she whispered, "I feel like our sanctuary has been violated and we aren't safe here anymore.''

His voice lost its edge as he gently prodded her to go on. "And...?"

"And I feel...exposed."

He swore softly under his breath and tightened his arms around her, trying to insulate her against the uncertainty that seemed to hover on the edge of the encroaching darkness. Finally he let her go and caught her hand in his. "Come on," he murmured as he drew her toward the patio door that led to the bedroom.

She didn't resist, and her fingers curled firmly around his. "The boys aren't in bed yet," she cautioned. "They're reading comics in front of the fire."

"I know." He shut the screen on the sliding door and led her across the darkened room to the massive bed. Tossing the covers back, he pulled her down beside him and nestled her against him in a secure embrace. "I'm going to hold you, and we're going to talk," he said.

An eerie disjointed panic assailed Chris, and every nerve in her body seemed to start trembling. *Just don't tell me about her now,* she pleaded silently. *If you tell me, I'm going to have to finally acknowledge her existence, and I'm not ready to cope with that yet. She'll become a wedge between us, and I couldn't bear it. Not now. Don't tell me now.*

A small body was suddenly outlined against the

light spilling in through the bedroom door. "Dad, are you guys in here?"

David sighed in exasperation. "Yes, we're in here."

"Can me and Tim have the thing of caramel popcorn in the cupboard?"

"Yes."

"Can we eat it all?"

"Even the container," David retorted with such tartness that he dragged a smile out of Chris.

"Is mom asleep?"

"Yes."

"Oh." Mark thought about that for a minute and obviously decided now was a good time to push his luck. "Can we have—"

"No."

"Aw, dad, you never even let me finish before you said no."

"You were going to ask if you could have the two cans of pop in the fridge, right?"

"Yeah."

"No, you can't. The popcorn's enough."

Mark came closer to the bed to plead his case. "Aw, come on, dad. Why not?" he wheedled in a hoarse whisper. "We won't spill—"

"Mark Andrew Spencer," stated David in quiet distinct tones, "if you keep at it, you're going to find that you've talked yourself out of the popcorn." Even Mark wouldn't argue with that tone of voice, and he turned to leave.

"Would you close the door behind you, please," added his father.

"Yes, sir," mumbled Mark woefully as he pulled the door shut behind him.

It was so ordinary. So unthreatening and so ordinary. Maybe it was the everydayness of that typical exchange that quelled Chris's anxiety, but whatever it was, her dark mood faded.

"Grouch," she whispered.

She felt David grin against her forehead. "You keep out of this, lady. I did my duty and got rid of the walking stomach. And besides, you're supposed to be asleep."

Chris laughed softly, and he snuggled her closer and tucked her knee between his. With long soothing strokes he began to caress her back. "Now I want you to tell me what's bothering you, love," he said.

Chris closed her eyes, absorbing the comforting warmth of his body and wishing she could postpone this conversation. She didn't want to think about the future, much less talk about it, and right now she did *not* want to know what it held in store for them. At least not yet.

David drew his own conclusions about the reason for her silence and misinterpreted her reluctance to answer. "You said you felt like our sanctuary had been violated. You were referring to my parents, weren't you?"

Relieved to have skirted other more-sensitive

issues, Chris was quite prepared to discuss this one. For a moment she stared into the heavy dusk of the room, processing her thoughts. Her voice was subdued when she finally spoke. "In a way, but not because I resented them being here, David." She hesitated, her expression growing more pensive. "It's just that so much has happened, and I need time to absorb it, to really believe it's true."

He nestled her closer and kissed her temple. "I know, love. I feel much the same way myself." He continued to rub her back with long slow strokes, his own face growing thoughtful as he stared at the ceiling. Tightening his hold on her, he voiced something that had been weighing heavily on his mind. "I'm sorry you had to be subjected to dad's outburst, Chris. I would have given anything if you had been spared that." His voice hardened to a steely edge as he added, "I can assure you it won't happen again."

Chris raised up on one elbow and gazed down at him, his face nearly obscured by the deepening dusk. "Don't make an issue of it," she implored softly. "Just let it go, David. Please."

"He had no right to say what he did."

"But he did—that's how he feels, and we have no right to judge how other people feel."

David's eyes narrowed suspiciously as he stared up at her. "Just exactly what did mother have to say to you? Did she try to lay a guilt trip on you?"

Chris sighed and shook her head. "No, she didn't. In fact she shocked me a little."

"How do you mean?"

She told him everything Catherine had said while they were outside, and as he mulled it over in his mind, she watched him intently. "Please, David. Don't say anything to him. Just give him some time."

He looked at her, and even in the darkening gloom she could feel his eyes drilling through her. "He deliberately snubbed you at dinner, and I don't like that."

"I can live with being snubbed. At least I know where I stand with him." She touched his face, her voice husky with her entreaty. "Don't say anything, David. Please, just let it sort itself out."

David scrutinized her face. "Is that what you really want?"

"Yes, that's what I really want." Their eyes locked together, and when hers didn't waver, David sighed and slid his hand up her back. "Okay, I'll let it go—for now." Smoothing away a lock of hair that was clinging to her neck, he slipped his fingers up the back of her head and pressed her head down. His lips were moist and pliant as they moved against hers, evoking a heady breathlessness in her. With his hand David probed the upsweep of her hair until he located the two wooden pins that held it. Tossing them aside, he slowly combed out her hair, his fingers sensually caressing her scalp. As he unbound the mass of curls a light fragrance drifted free, and David dragged his mouth away from hers and held her tightly against him, burying his face in the silky tumble. "Did I ever tell you why I came back for you twelve years ago?" he asked.

Slipping her hand under his shirt, Chris caressed his chest. She smiled in the dark. "I thought it had something to do with your...virility."

David laughed softly and gave her a quick hug. Shifting slightly, he stretched out his arm and switched on the small bedside lamp. Still smiling, Chris squinted against the muted light as he pressed her back against the bed and clasped her face in his hands. "Well, that had something to do with it, but—" he tapped her on the chin "—there was more to it than that."

She gave him a skeptical look. "Is this one of your awful stories?"

He shook his head, the gleam in his eyes mellowing. "We had the company plane, and we had to wait a day and a half in San Diego for a shipment of electronic equipment. I was fed up with hanging around the airport, so I went to a movie to try to take my mind off you. I was sitting in the theater, and all of a sudden I caught a whiff of fragrance, and I felt like I'd been hit by a cement truck."

He ran his fingers through her silky curls and smiled down at her. "It was the same scent you've always used in your hair, and it was right then I knew there was no damned way I could endure ten or twelve months without you."

A warm glow shone in Chris's eyes as she lightly caressed his rugged face. "And so you came back for me, even though you thought I was too young."

David's smile deepened and he caught her hand and held it against his mouth. "Even though I thought you were too young," he murmured, his lips brushing against her sensitive palm.

Her face grew sober as she gazed at him. "Was I, David?"

He shook his head. "No, love. Believe me, that was never a problem." He leaned over her and gave her a gentle fleeting kiss. "I guess I felt like I was taking advantage of you. I didn't even let you finish your first year of university. I didn't give you any time to think about anything. I just showed up on your doorstep and said we were getting married in three days, and that I was taking you with me come hell or high water."

Chris smiled as she traced the lines of his brow. "Personally, I loved it. I thought it was all very romantic."

His expression became intent. "Did you ever regret it, Chris?"

Her gaze grew luminous with tenderness as she touched his face. "There was never anything to regret during that time in our lives, David," she whispered tremulously. "That was always so special."

He brushed the back of his hand against her cheek, his touch hypnotizing her, and he slowly lowered his head. His mouth was intoxicating as it covered hers in a kiss that sent her senses spinning, and Chris felt herself sinking into a weightless dimension—a dimension free from the nameless unknown.

She realized they couldn't hide from the realities of the world forever. All she wanted was a little more time. Neither of them was healed enough to be fully secure in this fragile new happiness of theirs, and they needed time to let their confidence mature. But she knew they weren't going to get it. There was that shadow pushing—no, driving—them toward the uncertain future, and suddenly her passion was fueled by fear.

CHAPTER TEN

CHRIS CAST A QUICK look at David as she turned off the highway onto the long paved drive that led to his parents' estate. He had his arm propped on the open window, and the back of his hand rested against his mouth as he stared unseeingly at the road in front of them. Ever since Peter had delivered the letter that morning, David had been withdrawn and moody, and his reaction filled her with uneasiness. She had known the letter did not carry good news the minute he took the envelope from Peter. The look they'd exchanged said it all.

Sighing softly, Chris tried to push the troubling thoughts out of her mind. She glanced in the rearview mirror and smiled. As always, both boys had fallen asleep almost as soon as the car started moving. Timmy had dropped off with a comic draped across his chest, and Mark was out cold in the other corner, his baseball cap twisted to one side and his body scrunched up against the door.

Easing her foot off the accelerator, she looked at her husband again. Her uneasiness would not be subdued, and the suspense was beginning to wear away at her nerves. "I wish you'd tell me what's wrong, David," she implored quietly.

He met her gaze with a veiled look and glanced away. "I don't know if anything is wrong. I'll know more once I talk to dad." For one reason or another he was purposely shutting her out, but she sensed that he was, in his own way, trying to protect her. She wasn't sure if she liked that.

A panoramic view of the Juan de Fuca Strait and the hazy American coastline came into sight as they crested a hill. Knowing it was a favorite view of David's, Chris pulled over onto the gravel shoulder of the road and parked the car. She hated it when he looked like that, as if his face was hacked out of granite. It made him seem so remote, so unfamiliar, and her apprehension grew.

Resting her arms across the top of the wheel, she turned to look at him, concern showing on her face. "Are you still annoyed at not being able to drive?"

The sun was washing brightly across his face, and she could see worry lines around his eyes. Inhaling slowly, he raked his hand through his hair and undid his seat belt. As he straightened up, he shifted his position so his back was braced against the door and his head rested against the frame. "That was just the final straw in a long list of frustrations," he said, his words laced with weariness. "It was a stupid thing to explode over, but I was feeling so damned hemmed in by circumstances, and that just added to it." Leaning forward slightly, he caught her wrist and pulled her arm off the wheel. His touch was caressing as he turned her hand and wound his fingers through hers. "I'm sorry I blew up like that. It had nothing to do with you."

The compassion she felt for him made it hard for her to speak, and her voice was huskier than usual. "It wasn't stupid, David. You were speaking of a lack of identity, and that's no small matter. I don't blame you for exploding." She honestly didn't. She only wished she had realized before how much the lack of identification and his enforced confinement at the cabin were affecting him.

They had been getting in the car to leave the cabin when Peter, who was leaning against the front fender, voiced a warning as David opened the driver's door. "You shouldn't be driving, David. You don't have a driver's license, and if something should happen and you get stopped, all hell could break loose."

David had glared at his friend for a moment, then slammed the door and strode around to the other side of the car. "God," he snarled, "I'm as much a prisoner here as I was back there. I've had to stay shut up so no one knows I'm back. I couldn't cash a check—if I had one to cash—anywhere on this damned island because I don't have any identification. I can't drive because I don't have a driver's license. I don't even have a watch or my own goddamned clothes."

Knowing David the way she did, Chris had said

nothing, and she gave her head a little shake as Peter shot her a worried look. Just then the boys had come barreling out of the cabin with the comics they'd wanted to take. To camouflage the tense silence, Chris had given them some unnecessary instructions about doing up their seat belts as she slid behind the wheel. Even though it was the first time he'd been away from the cabin since his return, he had remained distant and uncommunicative for the entire drive.

His grasp on her hand tightened and his face showed signs of severe strain as he said, "Chris, I want you to understand something." He hesitated, and she saw the muscle in his jaw flex. For a moment he seemed absorbed by some distant object, but finally he met her gaze, his eyes revealing his raw emotions. "I want you to know these few weeks with you have been the most vital, the most treasured time of my life. I love you, and I'm going to need you to believe in me." His voice broke and he hurriedly looked away.

Chris's own throat ached with the pressure of unshed tears. She knew the source of his anguish, but she also knew Maria was a subject she didn't dare introduce. When he looked back at her, his expression was disciplined and guarded, but his voice was still unsteady. "I'm going to have to ask you for your blind trust, Christie. And the only thing I can give you in return is my solemn word that I love you more than you'll ever know."

Chris couldn't answer him. Her vision blurred as she unlocked her seat belt, and whispering his name, she slid across the seat into the viselike hold of his embrace.

David held her for a long time, trying to draw all the comfort he could from the warmth of her body. He was all too aware that the real world could not be eluded any longer, and his dread grew, knowing the strength of their new relationship was soon to be tested.

"Why are we stopping here?" came a sleepy voice from the back seat.

With obvious reluctance Chris eased out of David's arms, her eyes shadowed by distress. They exchanged a charged look as she softly caressed his face, then with a deep shaky breath she turned to face the back seat. "This is a favorite view of your dad's so we just stopped for a while."

Mark squinted at her and sat up, his face marked by sleep. "Are we just about at grandma's? I have to go to the bathroom."

"We'll be there in a few minutes," Chris answered, somehow managing to keep her voice steady. Slipping behind the wheel, she glanced at David. He was sitting in the same position he had adopted before, but now his hand was doubled into a white-knuckled fist. With a heaviness of heart settling on her, she put the car into gear and pulled back onto the road.

The Spencers' silver limo was parked on the long

sweeping drive that curved in front of the house, and she pulled in behind it. Mark wakened Tim, and with some sleepy grumbling the two of them scrambled out of the car as Catherine appeared at the front entryway.

Chris was suddenly dreading this visit more than she could logically explain. As she automatically took the keys out of the ignition, she caught herself silently wishing she had asked Peter to bring David over instead.

Reluctantly she climbed out and shut her door. David was waiting for her at the front of the vehicle, and he cast a searching look at her as she moved toward him. For a moment their gazes met and held, and with a hint of a smile, he slipped his arm around her shoulder and drew her beside him, the weight of his embrace giving her a fleeting sense of security.

The boys had already entered the house, but Catherine was waiting for David and Chris, and as they neared, Chris could tell by the movements of her mother-in-law's hands that she was not at ease. Chris's own apprehension grew.

"You must have hated to leave the cabin on a day like today," Catherine said, forcing a tight smile on her face. "It's so bright and sunny." She closed the door behind them as they stepped into the dim foyer, and she motioned to the hall on the right. "Your father is in the study, David, so you can join him there."

David slowly withdrew his arm from around Chris, but before he released her completely, he caught her hand and gave it a squeeze. He smiled at her, but it was a smile that did not reach his eyes.

Catherine lightly rested her hand on Chris's arm, gently but firmly guiding her in the opposite direction. "We may as well go through to the conservatory, Christine. I have some new orchids in bloom that I'd like to show you." A smooth and polished hostess, but also a nervous one.

Chris didn't absorb one word Catherine said as she watched David go down the hallway, knock on the study door and open it. She heard the sound of voices, and she caught a whiff of cigar smoke. Her stomach contracted and she turned cold. Neither David nor his father smoked. Ever.

The remainder of the afternoon was a marathon of waiting for Chris. Half a dozen times she started to ask Catherine who was cloistered in the study with David and his father, but for some reason the compressed set of Catherine's mouth kept her from posing the question. The two women played their game of pretending nothing was amiss, but Chris was feeling segregated and alone.

Everyone appeared to know what was going on except her, and try as she might, she couldn't override the hurt she felt at being deliberately excluded. She shouldn't have come. No one wanted her there, and she should have had enough foresight to realize that right from the beginning. She was forced to suffer through this endurance test of nerves, and it was obvious her presence was putting a terrible strain on Catherine.

It became increasingly apparent to Chris that dinner would be unbearable with this kind of tension hanging over everyone, and she wondered if she had the equanimity to get through it. She began to experience that same smothering sensation she remembered from years ago, and as it intensified, she had an overwhelming urge to disappear. It was so stupid, but suddenly she missed her father very much.

Making the excuse that she was going to check on the boys, she slipped out through the French doors that led to the stone terrace at the back of the house. The light ocean breeze caught her, billowing the skirt of her green voile dress and whipping at her hair as she went down the granite steps toward the fabulous gardens surrounding the estate. There was an air of quiet desolation about her as she slipped her hands into her pockets and started walking across the grass, her head bent as she became lost in the sobering thoughts of her solitary world.

David sat in the study in front of the paneled windows, his concentration fractured by her appearance outside. She looked so alone, so delicate and easily bruised. He could tell by the way she walked and the angle of her head that something was troubling her deeply. Yet even from so far away, she could weave a spell like some elusive sorceress from an old legend. There was something mystical about the way she looked. She had on a light green dress that blended in with the serene beautiful surroundings, and the style emphasized her uniqueness. The off-the-shoulders neckline was very bold, but long full sleeves added a dramatic innocence to the simple design.

She seemed to drift like thistledown before the wind as she crossed the old stone bridge that spanned the series of man-made ponds. A dull ache constricted his chest as he watched her, a solitary figure with no one to give her comfort, and he had to force himself to disregard the powerful impulse to go to her. He dragged his eyes away and made himself concentrate on what was being said by the large swarthy man who was seated in the easy chair across from him, the smoke from his cigar curling up in a blue swirl through the dusk of the shaded room.

General Sanjuro Rafael Gilberto was the real power within the tiny republic, and his arrival in Canada had been unexpected and shrouded in secrecy. He had come because he did not want to see the newly developed economic base in his impoverished country collapse—which was a real possibility. Now that David Spencer was safely out of the country, LaFontaine could decide to close down its Central American operations, and his government could not afford to let that happen. A company with LaFontaine's international reputation for excellence in efficient management and productivity was simply too valuable an asset to his country's development.

But the general had also come because he needed David Spencer's help. He had come to trust the man's intelligence and integrity, and after numerous dealings with him he knew for certain that the man's loyalty could not be purchased. In a country where assassination was a very real threat, that was no small compliment.

In faultless English that bore only a slight accent, he concluded his explanation. "So you see, whoever organized your rescue did our government a very big favor. By having it appear that the splinter organization captured you, it has created an open hostility between the two groups, and the rebel movement is rapidly losing credibility and momentum."

He paused and frowned slightly as he slowly rolled the ash from his cigar along the edge of a heavy crystal ashtray, then he looked at David with a steady troubled gaze. "I know you too well to be less than honest with you. We cannot afford to lose LaFontaine and the enormous employment market your company provides. Our standard of living has steadily improved since you opened your operations." He gave an expressive shrug and smiled somewhat wryly. "You have become an important, if unwilling, player in our game of chess, my friend."

David gave him a mirthless smile and leaned back

in his chair. Annoyance flashed through him when he realized that Colonel Carlos Hernandez, Gilberto's right-hand man, was standing at the French doors at the opposite end of the room and watching Chris with uncommon interest.

It took considerable discipline to drag his attention back to the general. "You feel certain our mining operations will be able to operate without threat of sabotage now that the conflict between the rebel leadership and the splinter fraction has become more hostile?" he asked, watching the general's face through hooded eyes, his fingers loosely intertwined across his chest.

David appeared relaxed, almost disinterested, but something about the set of his jaw revealed his inner tension. Matthew Spencer watched his son, a glint of amusement in his eyes. He knew that look. Now was not the time to tangle with David, nor was it the time to be anything less than completely honest with him.

The general raised his hands and shrugged again in a very Latin gesture. He gave David a half-hearted grin. "I can promise you no absolutes, my friend. I *can* promise you that our government will give you every cooperation to assure a safe operation for your mines and safe conduct for your employees. That is all I can guarantee."

David stared at him for a moment. "No one can ask for more than that." Picking up his drink, he slowly swirled the amber contents in the glass, and his face became even more inflexible. Finally he looked up. His eyes were devoid of all expression, but there was a tensed watchfulness about him as he said, "Have you located the rebel encampment yet?"

General Gilberto's gaze bore into David with hawk-eyed sharpness, and there was an electric pause before he shook his head. "We had hopes that you could be of some assistance to us in that matter."

"I have some information that might be useful."

Butting his cigar, the general lifted his glass and gazed across the rim at David. "Don Fernando Hervas had an audience with me a brief time ago also concerning the rebel encampment. You do remember him, do you not?"

David had been waiting for the bomb to drop all afternoon, and now that it had, the first image that flashed into his mind was one of Chris the day she told him about her father's death. He would never forget the hollow look of contained grief he'd seen in her eyes that gray dismal afternoon, and deep in his gut he knew he was going to inflict that kind of pain on her again. A sickening feeling of self-disgust set him on edge as he stared at Gilberto. "Yes, I remember him."

Matthew folded his arms across his chest. "Who is Don Fernando Hervas?"

Colonel Hernandez turned from the doors and faced the other three men. "He is a coffee plantation owner—very wealthy and has considerable influence in our country. He has a granddaughter who is being detained by the guerrillas, but we do not know why she is being held. We have received no demands or requests for ransom, and neither has the family. Very curious.''

''How old is she?''

Hernandez shrugged. ''In her late twenties, I would think. Her husband was killed in an automobile crash some years ago.''

David closed his eyes as an extreme weariness claimed him, draining him of all energy. The conversation turned into an indistinguishable drone as he became lost in his grim thoughts. So now he knew. Maria was still being held. He felt hopelessly embedded in a situation he had little or no control over, and no matter what he did, he was going to be forced to hurt somebody he desperately did not want to hurt.

During the four years he and Chris had been apart, he had never seriously considered the possibility of a reconciliation. All the times he had been tormented by memories of her, David had never let himself think there was a shred of a chance that they might get back together. If he had, there would be no damned way he would be in the jam he was in right now.

He opened his eyes, an irrational anger flaring in him when he realized Hernandez was watching Chris again as she came across the grounds with an armful of freshly picked flowers. The room seemed to shrink to claustrophobic proportions, and David knew he had to get out before he lost his temper over something as adolescent as another man watching his wife.

His comment was not directed to anyone in particular as he thrust himself out of the deep easy chair and headed toward the doors. "If you'll excuse me, I need some air before dinner."

Matthew watched him as he went down the stairs and headed toward Christine. Something was going on he knew nothing about, and he had every intention of finding out what it was, one way or another.

"Who is the charming young lady in the green dress?" asked Hernandez, his tone of voice revealing considerable interest.

Matthew cast him a perturbed look. "That's David's wife." He shifted in his chair and fixed his eyes on General Gilberto. "General, there are a few questions I'd like to ask, if you don't mind."

CHRIS'S HEARTBEAT was centered in her throat as she watched David come across the expanse of green velvet lawn toward her. She could tell by the way he was walking that he was incensed about something, and that left her feeling even more isolated than before. It all seemed like an unpleasant replay—once again they couldn't talk about the nameless problems that were pressing in on them, and that realization was disturbing.

As he neared, she shifted the flowers she was holding into one arm and turned slightly so the wind wasn't blowing her hair across her face. He paused in front of her, and the look on his face softened as he silently studied her through eyes squinted against the sun. Reaching out to tuck a loose curl behind her ear, he slowly caressed the side of her neck. The intensity in his eyes left her feeling slightly disoriented, and for a moment she thought he was going to kiss her, but then he glanced up at the study windows. There was an angry set to his jaw as he clasped her hand and started leading her toward the house.

"What's the matter, David?" she asked as she gazed up at his profile.

He didn't answer her, and as they walked across the lush grass, the rhythmic chatter of the water sprinklers was interwoven with the silence. Finally he looked down at her, a strange defeated expression on his face. "How long until dinner?"

"About an hour. Why?"

Again he didn't answer her. "Where are the boys?"

"They're with Samuel at the goldfish ponds." Samuel was the Spencers' gardener, and the boys adored him.

David tightened his grip on her hand. "Come down to the gazebo with me."

Chris gazed at him with perplexity but she didn't ask him why. She could see by the solemn look in his eyes that it was important. "Let me take the flowers in to Mrs. Bradley—"

"Never mind about the flowers." It wasn't a command but a plea. "Just come with me now, Christie."

Chris nodded and wordlessly followed him as they started back the way they had come.

The gazebo was in a secluded area of the grounds hidden from the main house by a natural stand of trees. The quaint little structure sported a wrought-iron weather vane on the cupola. Ivy climbed up its latticework and created a shaded bower within, yet the front of it was left open to a spectacular view of Juan de Fuca Strait. Since it was a favorite sanctuary of Catherine's, it was fully outfitted with luxurious lawn furniture.

Just outside the gazebo was a jardiniere partially filled with rain water. Taking the flowers from Chris, David placed them in the urn. He avoided looking at her as he led her inside, but the minute they were secluded within the dim shadows, he pulled her against him. The rustle of leaves infiltrated the quietness, and Chris closed her eyes, savoring the feel of his strong arms around her and the solidness of his body pressed against hers.

But as much as she longed to, she could not shut out the real world. She wished she could block out the uncertainties that faced her, but they kept cropping up with nagging persistence. Finally she could stand it no longer and she looked up at him. "I think it's time you leveled with me, David. You can't keep me in the dark forever.''

He stared at her for a moment, his face schooled into an unreadable expression. As he released her and turned toward the door, she saw a nerve twitch in his cheek.

David stuck his hands into his pockets and stood staring out as he sorted through his thoughts, looking for the kindest way of telling her what he had known for days. He was going back, and he was going back very soon. But he couldn't tell her that—not yet. But he had to tell her something.

"Who were you and Matthew meeting with today?"

He turned abruptly, the unexpected accuracy of her question catching him off guard. "How did you know there was anyone there?"

Chris was sitting on the chaise longue, her arms resting across her knees. The delicate green gossamer of her dress draped softly around her slender form, making her appear even more delicate than ever. Her shoulders were bare and her hair was loosely caught up in a knot on top of her head, exposing the graceful curve of her neck. She looked so damned beautiful—and so wary. There was a guarded tenseness about her as she sat staring up at him, a hurt accusing look in her eyes that made him feel like a traitor.

There was an unnatural tautness to her mouth when she answered him. "I smelled cigar smoke when we first went in, and your mother was obviously very edgy.''

With a sigh of resignation David sat down beside her, and placing his hand against her cheek, he gently turned her face toward him. ''And you've been roaming around all afternoon, wondering what in hell's going on.''

Her mouth began to tremble and her unshed tears seemed to change the color of her eyes to an emerald green. ''Don't shut me out, David.''

''I didn't intend on shutting you out, Christie,'' he said. ''I didn't want you worrying, so I thought it was better if you didn't know.''

Chris turned her head, struggling to hang on to her composure. She wanted to avoid facing the starkness of the truth, but something inside her wouldn't let her evade it any longer. ''You're going back to Central America, aren't you?''

He stared at her for a moment, then looked away. ''Very likely, yes.''

Chris could feel the first tentacles of fear uncoil inside her, and she struggled to master them. She must not react. Not now. She had known when she brought him home that he would feel compelled to go back once he was physically able. This was no surprise. But she was terrified, realizing the danger he'd be in the minute he reentered the country. She didn't know how she could endure it again, or how she could withstand the endless days of not knowing if he was dead or alive.

And what about Maria? Chris had refused to think about Maria, but the time had finally come when she could no longer eliminate her from her thoughts. Chris didn't play games with herself; she fully grasped the implications behind the facts. This faceless person, this unknown woman, had a powerful claim on David, perhaps even more than he realized. David possessed a deep sense of responsibility and he was carrying a heavy burden of guilt. Chris knew him; it would be impossible for him to turn his back on Maria, and knowing that threatened Chris more than anything else ever could. If the cards were down, who would win? Chris or Maria? She felt defenseless against this woman, as if she was contending with a ghost.

Her lips seemed numb when she finally whispered, "You're going to be leaving soon, aren't you?"

He didn't try to avoid her eyes, nor did he evade her question. His voice was solemn when he answered, "Yes, I am."

Chris turned her head and started to rise, but David caught her arm and held her down, feeling like a bastard for hurting her yet again. How could he explain to her that what he *had* to do was completely divorced from what he wanted to do, especially when his obligation was to another woman? He knew she wouldn't plead with him or try to make him feel more guilty than he already did. She would simply close up like a clam, and that would be fatal to their relationship.

He caught her by the shoulder and forced her to meet his eyes—eyes that revealed a depth of anguish that came from his very soul. Remorse weighed heavily upon him. "I hate doing this to you, Christie." His voice broke, and he looked away as he tried to clear his throat of the constriction, but the raggedness was still there when he continued. "You asked me a few minutes ago not to shut you out." His words were spoken with a gut-wrenching intensity as he whispered hoarsely, "I'm asking you to do the same for me."

Chris stared at him, her body stiff in resistance. He tenderly caressed her face, his eyes pleading with her and his voice barely audible when he said, "Please, Chris. Don't shut me out again."

Closing her eyes, she turned toward him, and slipping her arms around him, she buried her face against the soft skin of his neck. David swallowed hard, a deep ache encasing his lungs. He held her until he felt her relax, then, cradling her closer to him, he shifted her weight so they were lying against the reclining back of the longue. His fingers thrust into the upsweep of her hair as he stared blindly at the ceiling of the gazebo. He loved her so much, and he didn't know how he was ever going to leave her.

Chris huddled in the warmth of his arms, that awful empty feeling of dread unfolding inside her. She had known that sooner or later she would have to face her nemesis, and sooner or later she would have to give him the opportunity to tell her the real reason he was going back. At this moment she fervently wished Peter had never told her; it would have been so much easier if she'd been kept in the dark. Easier for her. She winced inwardly—she was turning into such a coward.

Collecting her courage, she eased her head back so she could see his face. "Will you tell me why you have to go back?"

It was as if shutters closed across his eyes, and there was a remoteness about him when he said, "There are company matters that have to be dealt with." He fell silent, obviously preoccupied by some private and unpleasant thoughts. Then he sighed and looked at her with unnerving steadiness. "But that's not the entire reason. Gilberto said they haven't located the rebel stronghold yet."

Fear left a cold hollowness in Chris as the impact of what he'd told her hit home. She felt anesthetized as she forced herself to speak. "And you know where it is."

"I have a damned good idea."

She was grasping at straws and she knew it, but her sense of survival pushed her into asking, "Why can't they send the army in?"

David's expression was grimly serious. "The rebels are dug into the side of a mountain. A large force would be detected before they got within five miles of the place, and the guards have instructions to shoot all the prisoners if it looks like there's going to be an attack."

Chris was feeling more ill by the moment and she could feel her color slowly draining away, but some perverse curiosity drove her on. She had to ask, she had to know. "Do you think the remaining hostages will still be alive?"

He stared at her for a second, and she could read in his eyes his grave doubts, the sense of helplessness and desperation he was experiencing. "It's hard to say," he said, his voice so low she could barely hear him. "Some of them were in fairly good shape, considering, but a month can make a big difference." He looked away, a harsh set to his mouth. "The ones I feel sorry for are the poor bastards they've captured who are in the government forces. They'll have been to hell and back—if they've survived."

"You mean the prisoners of war?"

He gave a derisive snort. "If you want to call them that. Guinea pigs for the newest techniques of torture would be a more apt description. Most of them are officers in the regular army, and you can rest assured that the rebels will wring every bit of information out of them they possibly can."

Deeply troubled, Chris watched him, longing to protect him from the horror of the memories she knew were running through his mind. The thought of him going back into that brutal hostile environment was too grim to even contemplate, but she did understand why he was driven to do it. Maybe that's why she loved him as much as she did—because he had such strong values, values he was committed to.

She turned his head gently toward her, and she felt like weeping when she saw the agony in his eyes. Fighting to keep her emotions under control, she tried to smooth away the lines of tension around his mouth, and from some inner resource she found the strength to ask the crucial question. "How soon will you be leaving?"

He stared at her bleakly for a moment, then drew in a deep breath. "I'll go as soon as arrangements can be made...probably within two weeks." He closed his eyes and there was a formidable set to his jaw, as though he was trying to contain his pain. When he finally looked at her, his pupils had dilated so much his eyes were nearly black. "Don't ask me not to go, Christie."

Her voice was so weak and grief stricken it was barely audible when she whispered, "The thought of you going back there terrifies me, David. You'll be taking such a dangerous risk."

Resting his hand on her cheek, he nestled her head on his shoulder and softly kissed her forehead. "I know you might not understand this, but if I could ignore my responsibilities, I wouldn't go." His voice was heavy with regret. "It's going to be like ripping myself in half to leave you, but I *have* to go back."

He could almost feel her collecting her strength to face this new ordeal, and after a moment's silence, she turned on one shoulder so she could look down at him, her hand resting on his chest. "I do understand that, David," she whispered solemnly. "That's one of the reasons I love you as much as I do." She looked away, her voice breaking as she said, "I wish you'd quit trying to protect me, though. I hate it—not knowing what's going on."

The tinge of resentment he heard in her voice made him realize he hadn't been fair to her; in his attempt to shield her from the unpleasantness, he had only hurt her more. Exhaling slowly, he said quietly, "What do you want to know?"

She met his gaze, her eyes heavily clouded. "Who's here, and why? And how does it involve you?"

Covering her hand with his own, David met her solemn stare. "After dad and mom were out to the cabin, dad got in touch with a man by the name of Luis Illas to notify him I was no longer a hostage."

"Why Illas?"

"We've had extensive dealings with him in the past, and he's a senior elected official within the coalition government—and we trusted him."

Chris frowned slightly. "Is he here?"

David shook his head. "No. He notified General Gilberto. The general and his senior aide flew in as soon as the Canadian government could arrange for adequate security for them. They arrived here just before we did."

"Why is he here?"

'It's mostly a fence-mending mission. He wants to be certain LaFontaine doesn't close down its operations. Those mines are crucial to the country's economy, especially when they don't have the advanced technology or expertise to develop their own natural resources."

Chris propped her head on her hand and her frown deepened. "Aren't they afraid the rebels will gain control of the mines?"

David shook his head. "Not really. The mining operations have never been in any real danger— they're in too remote an area—and besides, the rebels would never get to them without being detected by the military. Our concern has always been the safety of the workers. Gilberto has assured me the government will give its fullest cooperation in protecting them."

"Do you think the existing government is strong enough to maintain control, or is there going to be one coup after another?"

David shrugged his shoulders in a gesture that spoke of cautious acceptance. "Gilberto thinks the momentum of the rebel forces has been arrested, and if that's the case, I think the political situation will soon stabilize, especially with the turnaround in the economy." He tucked his hand beneath his head, idly stroking Chris's back with the other hand as he stared past her. His eyes filled with consternation as he recollected the appalling conditions.

"You've no idea what the poverty was like when I first went down there, Chris. God, it was awful. At least now the workers in the mines have a good income and decent living accommodations."

Chris was well aware why the workers had decent homes, but she said nothing. David had personally developed and directed an extensive community improvement program that had received international recognition for its effectiveness, but he seldom talked about it. If David had a motto, it would be Put Your Money Where Your Mouth Is.

She brushed a mosquito off his neck and looked at him intently. "Why were you so annoyed when you came out of the house?"

The laugh lines around his eyes crinkled engagingly as he smiled, a wicked sparkle growing in the blue depths. "If I told you, you'd flounce off in a huff."

Instead of discouraging her, his answer intrigued her, and she pressed for an explanation, her own eyes narrowed with suspicion. "You'd better damned well tell me, David Spencer."

He wrapped his arms around her and gave her a lazy grin. "Colonel Hernandez has a reputation for being a real womanizer, and he happened to be standing at the French doors in the study, watching you with far too much interest as far as I was concerned. I wanted to punch him in the mouth."

Chris stared at him with mistrust, and David met her look with unblinking frankness, almost as though he was daring her to disagree. She cast a dubious look down at him. "You're kidding."

"Like hell I am."

She stared at him for a moment longer then burst out laughing. "David, you're impossible. That's how eighteen-year-olds react."

He gave her a significant look. "Don't kid yourself, lady."

She gazed down at him, a soft smile playing around her mouth. "I think I like you being all silly and possessive," she murmured pensively as she slowly caressed his bottom lip with her finger.

David caught her hand and pressed her palm to his mouth, and there was laughter in his eyes. "You'd better remember that at dinner."

They were both caught up in a heady spell, and they gazed at each other, temporarily lost in their own private world. Suddenly the expression in her eyes altered, and she closed them against the shaft of pain that shot through her when she visualized saying goodbye to him. She shivered against the sudden chill that slithered up her back. The thought of him going filled her with desolation, and her eyes were tormented when she finally opened them.

David was watching her, his face set in rigid lines. She was at a loss for words, and the silence between them became strained as he continued to stare at her with inscrutable eyes. He held her chin so she couldn't move her head, his grip unyielding as he said, "Tell me what's wrong, Christine."

For one brief fleeting moment, she considered asking him about Maria, but she rejected the idea almost instantly. It was simply too big a risk. Once her existence was out in the open, it could change everything between them. Besides, they had a few more days before that unsettling reality would dominate their lives, and she wouldn't let anything—absolutely nothing—taint their dwindling time together.

She touched his mouth with her fingertips, and David was instantly aware of how badly her hand was trembling. "You said I wasn't to ask you not to go...." Her control faltered, and her voice was strained when she finally whispered, "I won't ask you not to go as lóng as you promise me you're coming back."

"Chris—God, love," he groaned as he enfolded her in an embrace that fused her against him, his own voice breaking under the pressure building in him. "I'm coming back to you just as fast as I can, and I'm coming back if I have to crawl on my hands and knees." He ran his hand along her back, and he felt her yield, willingly molding herself against him until her breasts were flattened against his chest.

Her skin had the texture and fragrance of rose petals, and he left a trail of lingering kisses on her soft shoulder. As he moved his mouth along her neck, he felt her shiver and knowing that her fear left her defenseless, he held her with tenderness, trying to shelter her from anguish. When she pulled away and gazed down at him, her eyes were mesmerizing.

David felt his heart begin to thunder against his ribs as she moistened her lips and slowly lowered her head. He tried to brace himself for the shock waves when she covered his mouth with a scorching kiss. She was trying to incinerate her fear with passion and he knew it, and that realization made him want to protect her all the more. His mind was fighting for supremacy, but his body responded to the fever of hers, and he locked her against him, famished for the feel of her. Pulling his mouth away, David tried to fill his laboring lungs.

"Love me, David," she murmured tremulously against his ear. "Please love me."

He silenced her with a gentle kiss. "We can't, Christie. Not here." His sensual eyes seemed to be absorbing her as he touched her swollen mouth with his finger and murmured huskily, "You know Samuel wanders down here for a smoke, and the kids could turn up here any time."

Chris had to break the heady spell of his warm gaze. She buried her face against his sweat-dampened neck and tried to steady her erratic breathing.

David smoothed the hair from her flushed face and kissed the curve of her neck as she slipped her arms around him. They lay together in silence until the far-off voices of the boys perforated the solitude. With reluctance David loosened his hold on her and stood up, lifting her to her feet.

His expression was intent and controlled as he encircled her waist with his arms, then bent to kiss the sensitive hollow behind her ear. When he lifted his head and looked at her, his eyes were smoking, and she could tell by the rise and fall of his chest that desire was burning beneath the surface of his rigid veneer. He touched her face with a restrained longing, and she caught his hand and pressed it to her lips. "Let's go home, David," she whispered as she gazed up at him.

"I can't, love," he said. "I have to get a few things settled with Gilberto before he leaves." He brushed the back of his hand against her face and gazed at her with regret. "I'm sorry, Chris."

She took his face in her hands and kissed him, letting her mouth linger against the moistness of his for as long as she dared. "Then make it quick," she murmured against his lips.

David gave a soft laugh and hugged her hard. "I'll do that." He pressed her more tightly to him and let out a long sigh. "We've been gone quite a while, Christine. We'd better go back." Releasing her, he picked up her sandals from beside the chaise longue and handed them to her with a lazy look that made her knees go weak. "If Samuel hadn't been wandering around out here, I can damn well tell you your shoes wouldn't be the only article of clothing lying on the floor."

Chris gave him an eloquent look, but David only laughed when he saw the faint hint of a blush coloring her face. She narrowed her eyes at him, but there was no mistaking the fact that she intended on giving him measure for measure when she leaned against him, deliberately tormenting him with an intimate caress.

"Talk is cheap, David Spencer," she said huskily. There was a spark of laughter in his eyes, and a flare of rekindled desire that left her breathless.

"Witch," he said through clenched teeth as he caught her hand and nearly dragged her out of the gazebo. Samuel was coming through the trees toward them, and David muttered with amused vehemence, "Damn you and your filthy habit, Samuel."

She laughed and looked up at him, her expressive eyes luminous with love. That familiar feeling of protectiveness rose up in David, and he encircled her shoulders with his arm and drew her against his side. Slipping her arm around his waist, Chris rested her head against him, and they idly strolled back toward the house, their bodies linked together.

Colonel Hernandez was standing at the French doors of the study, an aperitif in his hand as he watched Chris and David cross the stone bridge. General Gilberto came to stand beside him, waiting for Matthew to return with his sherry. He, too, stared out at the couple, his hands clasped behind his back.

"Señor Spencer is a lucky man to have such a lovely wife waiting for him," Hernandez said, as though thinking aloud.

General Gilberto's brow creased in a worried frown, and he slowly nodded his head. "It would be very tragic if such a young woman was made a widow, my friend."

Hernandez cast him a sharp puzzled look. "What are you insinuating, general?"

"I insinuate nothing, Carlos," he said with a mixture of weariness and concern. "I must request a favor of our Canadian friend, and I have reason to believe Señor Spencer will say yes. Unless I have misjudged the man, he will be leading a patrol to the guerrilla fortress. There will be considerable danger for him, and if Felipe Sanchez has the opportunity, he will make certain that David Spencer has a slow and horrible death." Shaking his head, Gilberto turned away from the window. "I spoke before about the upheaval in our country being similar to chess. David plays a dangerous match against Sanchez, but he employs the fundamental strategies of the game, I think. Perhaps he makes a hazardous and daring move to protect his queen."

CHAPTER ELEVEN

DAVID QUIETLY SLIPPED into his jeans and picked up his T-shirt from the chair. Pausing by the bed, he drew the sheet up over Chris, then soundlessly moved through the murky shadows to the door. He hesitated, his hand on the knob, making certain he hadn't wakened her, then softly closed the door behind him.

Drawing the shirt over his head, he put it on and went to the windows. It was not yet dawn, but the blackness of night was fading into the indigo shades that heralded first light. Even the sea looked oppressive and bleak.

His expression was fixed as he went into the kitchen and turned on the small light in the overhead fan above the stove, then opened the fridge and took out the pitcher of orange juice. He poured himself a glassful, replaced the pitcher and went into the living room and sat in one of the easy chairs. Closing his eyes, he stretched his legs and leaned his head back. Everything seemed to be caving in around him, and there wasn't a damned thing he could do to stop it.

It felt like three years instead of three days since

his final meeting with General Gilberto. David fixed his gaze unseeingly on the mantel of the fireplace and mentally went back over his private exchange with the president of the tiny, war-torn republic.

After dinner that night, only he and the general had retired to the study to discuss the situation concerning the hostages and the possibility of a rescue mission. It was during this conversation that the subject of Maria's grandfather's visit was once again brought up by Gilberto, and David found out more information.

Discussing Maria with Gilberto had been an ordeal for him, but it could have been ten times worse. The general did not know the whole story. All he knew, or all Maria's family knew, for that matter, was that she had been determined to negotiate David's release. She had disappeared six months ago and no one had heard from her since. The entire conversation with the president had been matter-of-fact, but David had the uncomfortable feeling that the general knew, or suspected, far more than he let on.

It was no secret that David had had a brief affair with the woman, nor was it secret that the liaison had been over for nearly a year before the hostage-taking incident. There had been a great deal of speculation within the wealthy business community as to what had happened between Maria and David, especially when they remained friends after the split. But David hadn't realized how closely observed his association with Maria had been until General Gilberto made a very astute observation.

The two men had been discussing David's rescue and how extensively Chris had been involved. The general had been studying David with the watchfulness of a hawk, and he steepled his fingers across his chest and tilted his head to one side as he said, "Your wife is most lovely, David. There is something about the way she moves, the way she holds her head that reminds me of a gazelle." He had slowly nodded his head, a reflective look on his face. "She would not be an easy woman to forget, even with one as beautiful as Don Fernando Hervas's granddaughter."

David had shot him a wary look, but the general's face had been bland as he snipped the end off a cigar. He lit it and for a moment studied the red-hot ash at the end. "How long were you separated from her?"

Reluctant to discuss his personal affairs, David had been drawn by some strange compunction to answer, "A little over four years."

The general's eyebrows had shot up and a wry smile appeared on his face. "You are a lucky man, my friend, to instill such loyalty in your women."

The sound of a strong gust of wind against the exterior shutters aroused David from the sober introspection, and draining his glass, he set it on the table by his chair.

His time with Chris was running out. Gilberto

and Hernandez had returned to Central America immediately after their meeting with him, and David would be following just as soon as they could make quiet diplomatic arrangements to get him out of Canada without alerting the international press. Secrecy was an absolute priority; both David and the general had agreed it was critical that no one find out he was to lead the small, hand-picked group of soldiers who would make up the patrol.

Under different circumstances he wouldn't feel compelled to return to the steamy rotting jungles, but as it was, his conscience gave him no choice. Locating the encampment for the existing government was only one of the reasons that impelled him to go. Another was his strong sense of responsibility to the other hostages. They had been through hell together, and through the blood, sweat and pain of their existence, a bond had been forged. He had to do whatever he could to assure their safety.

And then there was Maria. He felt sick every time he thought about her and the perverted abuses she'd probably endured because of him. Gilberto had been right. He was a lucky man to have the un-swerving loyalty of such courageous women, but he found no comfort in it. He sure as hell didn't deserve it. And he sure as hell didn't deserve Chris.

There was a tautness around his mouth and his face became more drawn as he thought about her. She had become so quiet and solemn since his meeting with the two military men. He'd tried to break through her silence, but he was feeling so guilty and so damned miserable that he was unable to give her much comfort. He realized what a dangerous risk he was taking, and he also realized there was a very real possibility that he would not be coming back. How in hell could he ever explain to her, how could he ever say all he wanted to say, knowing these might be the final days of their time together? And how was he ever going to deal with that last goodbye? His bleak thoughts filled him with an agony of emptiness.

He could make certain she and the boys were well provided for, and he could arrange for the best financial advisers in the country to look after her investments, but what she needed most was something he couldn't arrange. He'd never forget what an unpleasant awakening it had been when Timmy said his mother had never had anyone to hold her when she was hurting inside. It was true. She had no one to turn to for comfort, and he was going to have to leave her knowing he was subjecting her to her own private hell, and knowing she would endure it alone in stoic silence. He would do anything, absolutely anything, to protect her from any more anguish.

"Why don't you come back to bed, David."

Her voice was so soft it was almost inaudible, and David opened his eyes. She was standing beside his chair, her housecoat wrapped tightly around her as if she was cold. He didn't answer her but caught her hand and drew her down onto his lap and wrapped his arms around her.

He found that she was shivering. Nestling her more firmly against him to ward off the chill, he murmured against her hair, "You're cold, love. I should have covered you up with the quilt when I got up."

Her arm slipped around his back and she rested her head on his shoulder. "I just need you to hold me," she said very quietly.

Some subtle nuance in her voice touched David deeply, and he tightened his arms around her, trying to encompass her with his warmth. Neither of them spoke, and the silence seemed to become part of the shadowy darkness that infused the cabin. The weight of her against him helped dispel the bleak mood that had settled upon him, but he was still tormented by oppressive thoughts. Closing his eyes, he submerged his face in the tangle of her hair, trying to block out the disturbing images that kept flitting through his mind.

Chris stirred in his arms and suddenly he wanted to hold her, to feel the warmth and softness of her against his entire body. Shifting his hold on her, he stood up, bringing her with him as he straightened. As he lifted her up in his arms, he pressed a soft kiss against her temple and carried her into the bedroom.

He laid her amid the tumbled bedding, and without looking at her he straightened up and peeled off his T-shirt. He had intended to leave his blue jeans on, but she raised up on one elbow and touched the fastening at his waist, an unspoken entreaty in her eyes. A familiar heat started pumping through his body as he removed the rest of his clothing and sat down on the edge of the bed.

He carefully slipped the housecoat from her shoulders, the feel of her velvety skin too tempting to resist. His pulse accelerating, he gently molded his hands around one of her breasts, cradling the fullness of it as though it was some exquisite sculpture. He felt Chris's breath catch as he stroked her soft flesh with his thumbs, and a thick rush of anticipation surged in his veins as he slipped one arm around her and drew her down beside him.

No words could describe how mind-blowing it was the moment her body pressed against his. He felt as if he'd been struck by a thunderbolt, and he had to grit his teeth together to remain silent. His flesh was welded against hers, and his arms were locked so rigidly around her he couldn't have let her go if he'd wanted to. Closing his eyes, David was overpowered by the fever she aroused in him, a fever that had every nerve in his body responding to the current of sexual electricity that sizzled through him.

He felt the cool draft from the open patio door feather across her naked back, and holding her securely in one arm, he reached across her and grasped the light quilt. Drawing it over her, he gently smoothed her hair back from her face and let his hand lie along her jaw, his fingers resting against the sensitive hollow behind her ear. He drew his thumb across her moist mouth, the light pressure of the caress parting her lips. His heart began pounding erratically against his ribs, and he covered her mouth with his own.

It was one of those sweet searching kisses that drained his strength and wrung the breath out of him. She was surrendering all, provoking a hunger in him that was escalating out of control. But through the sensual fire storm that was scorching through him, he somehow sensed that her response was for his pleasure alone.

He didn't want that. He wanted the blinding climax of their lovemaking to be the culmination of their shared passion. Chris was prepared to let him use her body for carnal gratification, but he loved her far too much to use her that way, even wanting her as much as he did. Fighting to suppress the storm she had aroused in him, he pulled his mouth away and clasped her tighter against him as he waited for the frenzy of desire to ease.

Sensing his restraint, Chris moved against him, the warmth of her body tormenting him as she slowly ran her hand up his back. Her voice was as soft as a caress. "What's wrong, David?"

David hauled in a ragged breath, then eased his hold on her so he could see her face. "You don't need this kind of involvement right now, love," he murmured as he slowly combed his fingers through her hair. "I don't want to take what you're offering unless I can give back in return."

"David, I—"

He pressed his thumb against her mouth as he gazed down at her. She evoked a tenderness in him that he could never express in words, but the depth, the intensity of his feelings was expressed by his sensual eyes. "I love you, Christie," he said with quiet sincerity. "And above all else, I want to give you the kind of loving you need. I don't want you to feel it's your duty to provide a means for my pleasure."

Her eyes were brimming with tears. "I don't feel it's my duty," she whispered unevenly. "I just want to give you whatever measure of happiness I can."

David tightened his arms around her in a nearly brutal embrace. "God, Chris, what you've given me can never be measured."

He could taste her tears on her mouth as she cradled the back of his head in her hand and kissed him. Her other hand was resting on his shoulder, and with a light pressure she silently urged him onto his back. "Let me lie on top of you," she whispered as she leaned over him, her breasts resting against his chest.

He knew what she was going to do, but there was no way he could deny her husky entreaty, and his gaze was locked on hers as she straddled his body. Her lips parted and her eyes darkened as she raised up on her knees and gently guided him into her.

Slowly, so slowly she lowered her body, impaling herself on the throbbing hardness of his erection, and David sucked in his breath through clenched teeth. She was kindling a fire in him that was more than flesh and blood could endure.

She began to move against him, and the erotic sensation of the warm moistness of her body slowly gently stroking him drove him into a fever pitch. He was hovering on the brink of release, but he fought to hold back, to sustain the wild hunger she was arousing in him as she sensuously rotated her hips against his.

Sensing his battle to prolong the agony of excitement, she ceased her tormenting movements and leaned over and kissed him deeply, her tongue languidly exploring his mouth, and David, his mind reeling from an explosion of desire, sunk into a dimension of indescribable sensations. Her touch sent pulsations of ice and fire shuddering through his body as she brushed her full breasts across his chest, caressing his flesh. His hold on her hips tightened convulsively as the kiss became more searching, more thirsty; then she moved, slowly drawing her body away from his.

David felt as if she was pulling his body inside out, and he groaned against her mouth as she began to rhythmically stroke him, her body tight and liquid around his. The pressure was building up in him, mounting until it finally became unbearable, and he thrust upward against her, his need demanding relief until it crested in an explosion of volcanic proportions. Deep throaty sounds were wrenched from him, and he crushed her against him as pulse after pulse was wrung from him with devastating force.

Through the daze of the galvanizing aftermath, he was aware of a dampness against his neck, and he knew Chris was crying. In the backwash of exhausted emotions, he was filled with a desolation, a sorrow so bottomless, so intense, he could barely endure it.

IT WAS AN ANGRY SEA. It crashed against the craggy shore below the cabin, lashing out in fury against the rocky face as the tide thundered in. David stood at the windows watching the battering force of nature, his arms folded across his chest, his drawn face etched with tension.

At least the suspense was over. They had just finished dinner that evening when his father arrived, and David knew the minute he entered the cabin the waiting was over. Matthew had brought a report on the travel arrangements, and in four days David would be on his way to Central America. Four days. Now he was going to have to tell Chris. He didn't know where he was going to get the courage, or the composure, to tell her. The last few days had been an endurance test of nerves, and the growing tension had tainted their remaining time together.

They had managed to maintain a facade of normalcy for the boys' benefit, but that had only added to the strain. When they were alone they barely spoke to each other. They didn't dare. Their silence was a protection against exposing raw nerves to more stress, or worse yet, revealing how close they both were to coming apart. David understood that, but the knowledge didn't ease the stark emptiness that kept churning inside him.

More than anything, he loathed what the pressure was doing to Chris. She'd lost weight, and she was so pale and lifeless he felt a real concern for her. The only telltale manifestation of her anxiety was how tightly she'd hang on to his hand whenever she had the chance, and every time she clasped her fingers around his, loneliness would nearly suffocate him, and he'd feel like the lowest bastard on earth. There was so much he'd wanted to tell her, to share with her, but now they had only four days left. So little time and so much to say.

Shifting his stance, David sighed and leaned one shoulder against the window frame as he thought about how to break the news to Chris.

He dreaded facing her. As soon as his father arrived, he could see her withdrawing even more into her shell of silence, but he could do nothing to prevent it. She had left them alone with the excuse that she had to put the boys to bed, and David was forced to admit he'd been relieved. He wanted to be the one to tell her what was going on, but it had bothered him that she had made a point of staying

away from the two men to avoid Matthew's obvious
aloofness. He'd give anything if the situation between Chris and his father could be resolved before
he left, but he knew it was an impossibility. That,
too, needed time.

He heard Chris come out of the bedroom and he
turned to face her. She'd donned a deep green
velour robe that intensified the green of her eyes,
and she looked delicate and so very beautiful. He
sensed her hesitancy as she came toward him, and
he stretched out his hand toward her, trying to ease
the strain. She swallowed hard and slipped her hand
into his, her fingers closing around his in a tight
grip. He could feel her fear.

His solemn face was marked by both concern and
intense regret, his dread weighing heavily upon him.
"I think maybe we'd better have a talk—"

"No, David." Her voice was unsteady. "Don't
tell me yet." She appealed to him with a beseeching
look, and longing to shield her, David gathered her
against him. She began to tremble, and he tried to
encompass her with his warmth as she whispered
brokenly against his neck, "I need you to hold me
for a while before you tell me."

As the anguish in her voice inundated him, he
wanted to strike out at the world in angry frustration, and a wave of self-reproach washed over
him. Why in hell did she have to suffer because of
his mistake? It was so damned unjust—and so inescapable. There was absolutely nothing he could

do to change what had already happened. Nothing.

"What's the matter, dad?"

He looked up to find Tim standing at the banister of the loft, his arms draped over the railing, a solemn questioning look on his face. David tried to keep his voice level when he answered, "Nothing's the matter, son."

Tim's chin thrust out at a stubborn angle, and his eyes squinted. "Why is mom crying then?"

He felt Chris take a tremulous breath, and David was caught off guard when she unobtrusively wiped away her tears with her fingertips. He hadn't even realized she was.

She lifted her head and looked at her son, her voice wavering slightly as she said, "I'm just really tired, Tim. That's all."

The boy stared at her, his jaw still set at a tenacious angle. "Dad's going away again, isn't he?"

Reluctantly Chris pulled out of David's arms and turned to squarely face Tim. Her expression was grave as she answered him. "Yes, he is."

"Why?" There was defiance and anger and so much hurt in his blunt question that David felt as if Tim had struck him.

Folding her arms across the front of her, Chris rubbed them with an absent gesture, as though she was cold. But there was a calm reassurance about her as she explained, "Some of the hostages that were captured with your father are still being held.

He knows where they are, and he's going back to help get them out."

David started to go to Tim, but Chris caught his arm. When he shot her a questioning look, she gave her head an imperceptible shake, and he realized she was giving Tim the space to deal with this in his own way.

Timmy swung his unflinching stare to his father, his small white face schooled by a rigid discipline that went far beyond his years. "Are you coming back this time?"

The question nearly did David in, and his voice was pained when he answered, "Yes, I'm coming back."

He could visibly see the stiffness go out of the small boy's body and his chin begin to quiver. Tim turned his head away and dragged his pyjama sleeve across his eyes. "How soon are you going?"

How soon. David had never felt more impotent than he did right then. There was nothing he could do or say that would protect them from the grim reality of the truth, and he felt as if he was betraying them both. He glanced at Chris, and it was a subtle kind of torture to watch what little color she had drain from her face. He could not tell her—not like this.

There was an air of indomitability about her when she asked in a stiff voice, "How soon, David?"

He turned away, unable to look at her. "Four days."

The room was cloaked in a silence that seemed to drag on and on, and the soundlessness was nearly suffocating. It was finally broken when Timmy whispered in a tear-riddled voice, "It's all right for boys to miss people, isn't it, mom?"

It was like a blow. David was aware that Chris had gone to Tim, but he was incapable of giving either of them any kind of glib assurances. He was too torn apart inside to be of any comfort to anyone. His face haggard and lined by exhaustion, he went into the bedroom and closed the door.

After she comforted Tim and had him settled back in bed, Chris knelt by his cot and slowly rubbed his back, trying to soothe him back to sleep, her mind numbed by David's news.

Four days. They had so little time left. Yet short as it was, she didn't know how she was going to get through it without coming apart. She didn't know where she was going to find the courage to let him go, especially now that she seriously suspected she had a reason to keep him from leaving.

Resting her free arm on the edge of the bed, she laid her head on her forearm as she methodically massaged her son's back, overcome with a weariness that drained her energy and distorted her thinking. She tried to block out the flurry of disturbing thoughts by making herself concentrate fully on what she was doing.

Tim was lying on his stomach, his face turned toward her, his long thick lashes fanning out across his tanned cheeks. He looked so much like David, and he seemed so little and defenseless as he lay there, hovering on the verge of sleep. She could distinctly feel the structure of his rib cage as she moved her hand over his back, and she marveled at the resilience and durability of the human body. His bones felt so frail, so small, but someday he would be as big as his father.

Her expression became more pensive as she thought about what Tim would be like as an adult. She hoped he would have more than his father's looks. She hoped he would have the qualities that made David the man he was: his sense of responsibility and his commitment to his beliefs, and the courage to fulfill his obligations.

Closing her eyes, Chris felt a cold weight settle in her stomach as a bleak realization came to her. She'd been hoping that if she ignored the existence of Maria, she could also ignore the prime reason David was going back, and if she was able to shut all that out, she wouldn't have to deal with the unsettling feelings that went along with it. It was the easiest way out for her, but in the meantime David was being torn apart by guilt and regret, and that shadow would always be there between them unless she quit hiding from the truth.

Startling realizations began to take shape in her mind, leaving Chris a little dazed. She felt lightheaded as she began to look at the situation from a different point of view, a whole new perspective.

She knew, she *really* knew, that even if Maria had played a major role in the breakup of their marriage, she still would have wanted David back. But Maria hadn't played a part. That had been Chris's fault, and he had turned to another woman *after* she had walked out on him.

Then there was the jealousy she felt toward Maria. That, too, was unfair. If she was truly honest with herself, she would have to admit that this woman deserved her gratitude rather than her resentment. If it hadn't been for her, David might have died of starvation several months ago—along with the seven who had. Maria had made a supreme sacrifice to keep him alive, and Chris owed her for that.

A peculiar kind of nervous energy fluttered in her as she eased her hand away from Timmy and stood up. If only David would level with her, if only he would hear her out, they could openly face this thing between them. With that one thought uppermost in her mind, she quietly left the loft.

Anxiety had her nerves vibrating and her pulse racing by the time she reached the bedroom. She didn't have a clue how David would react. He might explode, he might withdraw into a cold silence, he might react a dozen different ways, and the uncertainty filled her with apprehension. Resting her forehead against the closed door, she shut her eyes and took a steadying breath. She was so scared. She wiped her clammy hands on her housecoat, groping for some semblance of composure, and with her heart in her throat she turned the knob.

The room was in total darkness, but light spilled in from the open door, illuminating the room with a faint glow. Very softly, Chris moved across the room and stood looking down at David. He was lying on his side, and he appeared to be asleep. But she knew he wasn't. An overpowering wave of compassion brought tears to her eyes as she gazed at him, her thin veil of composure torn to shreds by the knowledge of what an awful price he was paying to protect her. But what hurt her the most were the lines of suffering carved around his mouth.

Kneeling beside the bed, she curved her hand along the rigid line of his jaw, and struggling to master her own overwhelming feelings, she bent over and kissed him softly on the mouth. She felt him clench his teeth, and she knew he was fighting an inner battle that was tearing him apart, but he refused to look at her. Choking back a sob, she lifted her head and gazed at him. She saw his mouth harden as he tried to swallow, but she was not prepared for the excruciating ache that gripped her when she saw moisture gather along his lashes.

Her throat was so constricted she could barely speak, but somehow she managed a shaky whisper. "I do love you, David." Her face was streaked with tears as she smoothed back his hair, and then with infinite tenderness she drew her thumb across his damp eyelashes. She felt a violent tremor shudder through him, and his response pushed her to the verge of her own breaking point, but somehow she managed to force herself to say what had to be said. "Why don't you tell me about her."

She nearly cried out as he caught her wrist in a brutal hold. But it was his eyes—the agony, the frantic torment in his eyes—that finally brought her down. Her body shook with stifled sobs, and it was impossible for her to speak. Slipping her arms around his shoulders, she held him with all the strength she possessed. He seemed to be trying to absorb her with his body as he hauled her beside him in a savage grip, his arms welding her against him.

It was a violent purge, all emotional restraints and inhibitions blown away by the breaking storm. They no longer had any barriers left to hide behind, and all the fear, all the guilt, all the pain came pouring out. It was a tempest that was a long time passing.

But like a squall at sea, the storm finally exhausted itself, and Chris was emptied of all the tormenting feelings she had kept bottled up inside. Taking a shuddering breath, she pressed David's head closer to her and felt him wipe his face against the material draped across her breast. She transferred her weight onto her arm, and leaning over him, took his face in her hand and kissed him. He raised his hand to her head and held her immobile as his mouth moved against hers with a thirsty insistence.

Another tremor rocked through his body as he tore his mouth away and crushed her against him. "God, Christie," he whispered hoarsely, "I love you so damned much it scares me."

She was again threatened by tears, and in an attempt to regain some shred of self-control, she hid her face against the soft skin of his neck. As soon as the aching tightness eased in her throat, she raised her head and gazed down at him, the intensity of her feelings reflected in her eyes.

"No matter what happens," she said, "I could never stop loving you, David. I need you in my life." Her eyes began to blur, and she looked away until she felt she could speak without choking up. "I felt as though my life was a living death for so long, and now that I have you back, nothing else matters." Her voice started to break beneath the pressure, and she whispered, "Nothing could be worse than that."

"Christie—" She saw the muscles in his throat work as he, too, struggled to maintain self-control. Seemingly engrossed in what he was doing, he stroked her cheek with his knuckles, but his unsteady hand betrayed his inner turmoil. Finally he met her eyes. "How did you find out?"

Catching his hand, she pressed a kiss against his palm, and she felt his chest expand sharply. "Peter told me the day he brought me back."

"And you still came."

There was a tone of quiet wonder in his voice that

drove home how unsure he'd been of her, and Chris longed to erase that shadow of doubt from his mind for all time. Her voice carried the strength of her sureness when she said, "Because that's where I wanted to be."

Her response shook him badly and he closed his eyes and pressed her against him in a fierce embrace. This was going to be an ordeal for both of them, especially with both of them so raw, but Chris was determined to see it through. It would eliminate the remaining ghosts, and after the last few weeks she had learned that secrets, even if maintained for the most noble of reasons, only drove a wedge between them.

Please don't let me be jealous. Please give me the strength and the wisdom to cope with this, she silently prayed. *Let how much I love him get me through this without coming apart.*

She stroked his head as she struggled to control the roiling nervousness inside her. Mentally gathering her resolve, she took a controlled breath and whispered, "I want you to tell me about her, David."

His body stiffened as though she'd stabbed him, and it was several moments before he spoke. When he did, his voice was hoarse. "I can't do that to you, Christine."

Chris eased out of his nearly bruising embrace, and propping her weight on her elbows, she took his ravaged face in her hands. Never in her life had she seen such agony, such pain imprinted on a human face, and compassion for him gave her new strength. She didn't try to hide the tears that filled her eyes as she said intently, "We have so much in common, Maria and I. We both love you, David, and that's a very special sisterhood." A weakness of relief flooded through Chris, and she rested her head against David's chin, waiting for the strange paralysis to pass.

It was true. What she said was true. If she could look at Maria's involvement in their life from that point of view, she could face anything he told her. If she could see Maria as an ally rather than a rival, it would change everything. It was going to work out. She felt giddy with the heady feeling of deliverance, and her eyes were steady as she lifted her head and looked at him. "Don't be afraid for me, David. No matter what you tell me, it isn't going to diminish how I feel about you."

It sounded melodramatic and artificial, but right then David would have walked through a river of boiling oil for her. His love for her overwhelmed him and he closed his eyes, fighting to contain his feelings, but they overpowered him. He locked his arms around her, pinning her against him. She was so vital to him, so damned vital, he was afraid to let her go.

The vehement onslaught eventually eased and he was able to relax his embrace. "I love you, baby," he whispered, his voice hoarse.

She raised her head and looked at him with an unwavering gaze that was so open, so unguarded, it was like looking into her very soul. "I know you do," she said.

A kind of inexpressible peace soothed the pain in him as he finally comprehended she was prepared to stick by him, no matter what. A solidness, a new strength had been forged by their agony, and they were both more secure because of it. They had, however, paid a heavy price to achieve this unbreachable confidence. A very heavy price.

He inhaled slowly as he reached up and wiped away the last of her tears. "I wanted to tell you about her, Chris, but I didn't know how without hurting you."

Her eyes were soft as she rubbed her face against his hand. "I know that. And I was so unsure of myself that I was afraid to tell you I already knew. I guess I felt if I ignored her existence, she'd cease to be."

"What made you change your mind?"

Resting her arm on his rib cage, she propped her head up with her hand, and her mood became thoughtful. "It hit me when I was upstairs with Tim how much I owed her." She glanced at him, a grave sincerity in her eyes. "I do, you know."

His voice lacked strength as he said, "We both do." He waited for the ache in his throat to ease, then he deliberately changed the subject. "How's Tim?"

Chris gave him a lopsided smile that conveyed a wealth of understanding. "He's fine. Once you can get him talking about whatever's troubling him, he handles it very well." There was a certain wryness to her tone as she said, "The trick is to get him talking."

There was a knowing look in David's eyes as he retorted pointedly, "Very much like someone else I know."

She gave him a rueful look. "Well, he could have inherited your temper instead."

An hour before David felt as if he would never laugh again, but he did, and he hugged her hard. "Maybe there's something to be said for genetic engineering after all."

She smiled and leaned over and gave him a light kiss. David caught the back of her head and held her lips against his. Her mouth was moist and pliant, and the intoxicating potency of her kiss sapped what little strength he had.

With a reluctant sigh she raised her head and gazed down at him, her eyes soft and misty. "Do you know you're better than warm brandy."

David laughed. "Nothing is better than warm brandy."

They exchanged a look that seemed to stretch on forever. Finally Chris broke the spell when she lowered her head and gave him a fleeting kiss. There was a gleam in her eyes as she said, "Since you think there's nothing better, I guess I'm wasting my time, aren't I?"

He gave her a slow intriguing smile. "Are you?"

Tipping her head back as she laughed, Chris exposed the long slim column of her neck, and David wanted to pull her back against him and savor the taste and texture of the soft skin along her throat. But he didn't move.

Chris patted him on the cheek as she slipped out of his arms and stood up. "Maybe I'd better fix you a drink, and then take it from there," she said, her voice tinged with amusement.

He caught her hand and looked up at her. "That sounds like a hell of an idea." His eyes grew smoky as he pressed her hand against his mouth and said softly, "Don't be long."

He heard her breath catch as she answered, "I won't."

By the time Chris returned, David had undressed and was in bed, the pillows piled behind his back. The small lamp on the night table filled the room with a golden glow. Taking the snifter of warmed brandy she handed him, he caught her wrist and gently pulled her down. She curled up beside him in the protective curve of his arm, her head resting on his shoulder, and for a moment neither of them spoke.

It was Chris who broke the silence. "How did you meet her?"

David lifted up her chin until he could see her face. "I don't want to talk about her if it's going to be hard for you, Chris," he said quietly.

She met his troubled gaze, and her tone was certain. "It won't bother me."

"You're sure?"

"Very sure."

He downed half the brandy and began to swirl the remaining contents in the glass, deliberately avoiding her watchful eyes. "I met her at an embassy party."

"What's she like?" she asked softly.

David still wouldn't look at her, but she saw a muscle twitch in his jaw, and his voice had dropped in pitch when he answered her. "She's very much like you—that's what attracted me to her in the first place."

His unexpected admission left Chris feeling stunned and strangely disconnected, and it took her a while to collect her fractured thoughts. Steeling herself, she asked the toughest question of all. "How long did you live with her?"

"I never lived with her." He tossed back the rest of the brandy, then finally met Chris's gaze. She was staggered by the burden of guilt she saw in his eyes. "I didn't live with her because I was too damned self-centered. I was trying to put my life back together after you—" He looked away. "I was using her to fill up that goddamned awful emptiness."

His frankness touched her, and she struggled to suppress her emotions. Even after what she'd done to him, he'd still missed her. She gazed at his rigid profile, confusion muddling her thoughts. For some reason she sensed that his guilt evolved from something more than the reasons he'd given. That intuitive feeling left her feeling slightly off-balance. What was going on in his mind?

In a flash of insight she suddenly understood. Setting her glass down on the table, she placed her hand on the side of his face and forced him to meet her gaze. He looked so emotionally battered. Longing to erase his pain, she caressed the hard line of his mouth, her voice softened by compassion. "You feel like a heel because she was worthy of loving, and you couldn't. You feel you've shortchanged her. That's what's really tearing you apart, isn't it?"

He twisted his head out of her grasp, and she felt him shudder as he looked away. She pulled the glass out of his hand and set it beside hers. Her chest was aching as she put her arms around him and tried to pull his stiff body against hers. "I can understand those feelings, David."

Yanking her arms away, David reacted with a violent flash of anger, and Chris stared at him with wide eyes. "How the hell can you sit there and say that?" he seethed through gritted teeth. "If it had been you who'd been involved with someone else, I'd bloody well want to kill somebody. I couldn't stand knowing. I damned well couldn't stand it. How can you possibly accept something like this?"

Her face had gone ashen but her composure

didn't falter. "I can accept it because I'm very different from you." She knew how to completely defuse David's temper. It was an underhanded move, but she couldn't let him go on feeling this way, especially when they had so little time left together. She lifted her chin and met his furious gaze dead on. "And maybe I can accept what happened because I love you a damned sight more than you love me."

It stopped him cold, and he stared at her for a long time before he found his voice. "God, Christie, don't say that—don't even think it."

She took his hand and gently unclenched his fist before she wove her fingers through his. She lifted her face, her eyes brimming with tears. "Then don't be stupid, David Spencer," she admonished softly, her lips trembling.

For a moment there was a silent standoff, but David finally relented and pulled her into his arms. "I don't deserve you, you know," he said, and he kissed her tenderly, lifting her up against him until she was cradled across his chest.

Tucking her arm around his back, she kissed him lightly on the neck and said, "Do you want to talk about it, or do you want to drop it?"

He didn't say anything, then, drawing up one knee, he tightened his hold on her. "I'd like to talk."

The hands of the clock moved from one day to the next, and the first hint of dawn touched the

eastern sky before one lazy silence stretched out for a
long time. David glanced down and smiled fondly.
Chris had fallen asleep in his arms, her face turned
toward him and one hand resting on his chest. Carefully he took the pins out of her hair, then gently
tightened his hold on her and dropped a soft kiss on
her forehead. For a moment her breathing altered,
but her lips parted and she settled again. He studied
her face with solemn intensity for several moments,
then reached out and shut off the light. Closing his
eyes, he savored the weight of her against him. But
he didn't sleep. These moments with her were measured—maybe forever—and he wasn't going to sacrifice a single one.

CHAPTER TWELVE

CHRIS STOOD BY the French door in the conservatory, which overlooked the back terrace of the Spencer mansion, solemnly watching the two boys, her arms folded beneath her breasts. They were squatting in front of a huge ornate urn filled with flowers, putting together a game their grandmother had bought for them. They were at odds with each other over some aspect of the directions, and she could hear their voices becoming more and more shrill. She knew they would both end up in indignant tears, tears that had little to do with what they were doing.

It had been a bad day right from the beginning. They had closed down the cabin early that morning, and that had cast a long shadow over the rest of the day. It had been all Chris could do to maintain a composed appearance as they drove down the winding trail for the last time.

The narrow, twisting lane was hedged with clumps of spruce and fir, their stately grandeur reminding her of haughty dowagers. Sprinkled between the massive rough-barked trunks was the

fresh adolescent growth of evergreens, and wild
bushes crowded to the edge of the trail like small in-
quisitive children.

She loved that lane. There was something almost
surreal about the setting that always struck her
fancy. And she loved the cabin. But most of all she
treasured the host of beautiful memories that had
been gathered there during the last few short
weeks, and leaving it all was akin to ripping out
her heart—especially when she knew this was the
last day, the final hours. David was to leave the
following morning, and that cast an even deeper
longer shadow.

She had briefly toyed with the idea of going back
to the cabin after David left, but he was opposed to
it. He was worried about her being on her own in
such an isolated spot, and she secretly doubted if
she could stand the loneliness after he was gone. Besides, the boys would be going back to school in a
few days, and she would eventually have to move
back to town anyway. She decided it would be
easier for everyone if they did it this way. Easier...
it couldn't have been much harder.

Strident voices pierced through her sober reverie
and she returned her attention to the boys just in
time to see Mark send the base of the game flying
and then shove Tim against the urn.

Her eyes flashing and her face set in a tight-lipped
expression, she yanked open the glass-paneled
door, and squinting against the blinding sunlight,

she stepped onto the terrace. "What was that all about, Mark?" she asked sternly.

He cast her a mutinous sullen look and started to stalk away, his small stiff body made ungainly by anger. Catching his arm, she hauled him up short and turned him around. "I asked you a question, Mark Spencer," she said in a tone of voice that meant business, "and I expect the courtesy of an answer." He wouldn't meet her gaze, but she could see his chin start to quiver as he bent his head and scuffed his toe against the stonework beneath their feet. The light breeze ruffled through his hair as she waited for him to respond.

Chris glanced at Timmy as he spoke up for his brother, a contrite expression on his face. "It was my fault, mom. I was bugging him."

She released her hold on Mark's arm, and shaking her head in exasperation, she stared at her eldest son, a tight look around her mouth. "Honestly, Tim, why do you take so much pleasure in aggravating him?"

Tim shrugged and dropped his head. Chris stared at him for a moment longer, then turned toward Mark. He was headed for the French doors that led from the terrace into the study, and she sprinted after him and again caught him by the arm. "I told you and Tim that you can't bother your dad," she said in a more lenient tone. "He and grandpa have to go over some papers with the lawyers before he leaves, so you mustn't interrupt."

His face was white and his lips were colorless as he tried to pull free of her grasp. "I'm going to see dad."

She could feel the throb of his escalated pulse beneath her fingers, and she recognized the undertone of panic in his voice. Her expression became more solemn. Kneeling before him, she brushed back his windblown hair with a maternal gesture and grasped him by the shoulders. "He shouldn't be much longer, Mark," she said. "And once the lawyers leave, you can go in."

"I'm going to see dad," he repeated stubbornly, and he tried to twist away from her, his face growing paler and more tragic by the minute.

Timmy came to stand beside him, his expression revealing compassion for his younger brother. "He's feeling bad about dad going," he explained in an unsteady voice.

Chris fervently wished she could come up with the right words to comfort them, but there was no pat formula to magically erase their unhappiness. Trying to swallow the sudden lump in her throat, she ran her hand up and down Mark's deeply tanned arm and tried to soothe him. "We're all feeling bad about dad going, honey. But he's going to be coming back just as soon as he can."

His staunch determination seemed on the verge of crumbling as Mark pulled free of his mother and backed away from her, his eyes wide and glassy. "I'm going to see my dad," he choked out through stiff lips.

Chris could feel her own resolve start to crumble and she was swamped by pity for her son. He was too small to hurt so much. She reached toward him but he let out a single racking sob and darted by her.

Coming out of the shadows toward them, David crouched down and caught the boy as he flung himself into his arms. "It's okay, Mark," David said in a rough whisper. "We'll talk about it, okay?"

Chris drew her eyes away from the two of them and stood up. She inhaled deeply and fix her face into an unreadable expression. This was going to be the longest toughest test she'd ever faced.

Tim was hanging back, watching his father and brother. Chris walked across the terrace to where he was standing. She gave him a little push of encouragement as she said, "Go on, Tim. Your dad will want to talk to you, too."

Timmy shook his head and turned away. "I don't want to."

Chris frowned, not understanding what was going on in his mind. "Why not?"

He didn't answer her for a moment, then bent his head and mumbled, "Because I don't want to cry."

"There's nothing wrong with crying," she admonished gently.

He shrugged his shoulders in a gesture that indicated he didn't quite agree with her. "Yeah, but when we cry it makes dad feel awful bad." He glanced up at her, then looked down and started kicking his foot against an urn of flowers. "Besides, we had a talk already."

Just by the way he was ignoring her, Chris suspected he was leading up to something, and she watched his face with speculation. Finally he looked up. "I told dad not to worry about us when he's gone."

Any other time, she probably would have been amused at his reach for maturity, but now she was caught off guard by how adult he seemed, and his quiet confidence touched her even more as he slipped his hand into hers. "Don't be scared, mom. Everything's going to be okay. You'll see."

She remained silent but tightened her grasp on his hand. If only she had a tenth of his confidence. If only.

About half an hour later Mark came into the conservatory, his usual sunny disposition obviously restored. She laid down the magazine she'd been idly leafing through as he leaned against the wing of her arm chair.

"Hi, mom. Whatcha doing?"

She held up the magazine so he could see the cover. "I was reading one of grandma's books on orchids."

"Where's grandma?"

"She's gone to the kitchen to talk to Mrs. Bradley about what we're having for dinner." Chris gave the tail end of his shirt a tug. "Do you think you could put yourself back together and tuck in your shirt?'' she said with a touch of dryness. "It *would* be a nice change.''

He grinned and started haphazardly stuffing wads of fabric into the waist of his jeans. "Dad wants you to go down to grandpa's study, okay?''

Closing the periodical and laying it on the table, she stood up. "Will you go tell grandma where I've gone? She was going to have Mrs. Bradley bring coffee for us.''

"Sure.'' His eyes brightened with a satisfied and impish gleam. "I'll go down to the kitchen and tell her *right* now.''

"And no doubt con Mrs. Bradley and grandma out of a handful of cookies while you're there,'' she retorted with maternal astuteness.

He gave her an ear-to-ear grin. "Well, maybe.''

Bending slightly, she caught his chin and smiled, then her expression grew serious and she chastised him quietly. "Before you go, though, you have to tidy up the mess you made on the terrace. And I think you owe your brother an apology.''

Mark quirked his mouth in a sheepish grimace and nodded reluctantly. She ruffled his hair and dropped a kiss on his forehead, then straightened.

"Ah, mom,'' he moaned in disgust, scrubbing away the kiss.

"Ah, mom,'' she teased as she walked past him.

David was standing by the oak desk with his back to the door, a sheaf of papers in his hand and a look of intense concentration furrowing his brow. As the door clicked shut, he turned to face her. The room seemed shrouded in one of those churchlike silences that somehow defied noise, and her voice was hushed when she said, "Mark said you wanted to see me."

He gave her an expressionless stare that drilled right through her, and the stern set to his mouth left her feeling uneasy. She felt a strange sinking sensation as he turned away. "While the lawyers were here, I did some shuffling of my personal business," he said in a clipped tone, "and there's a few things I want to go over with you before I leave."

Chris's knees didn't want to function, and she sat down abruptly on the leather sofa adjacent to the desk. David picked up a document, placed it at the bottom of the ones he was holding, and came over to her, his face still set with that inflexible look. He refused to meet her gaze as he sat down beside her, and she felt a chill of foreboding, knowing that she was facing another ordeal.

"First of all, I've cleared the deeds on both properties you mortgaged...." He left the sentence hanging on an odd inflection, and she knew exactly what he was going to say before he decided it was wiser to say nothing. The thought of having to raise that kind of money again, of having to get him out a second time, unsettled her.

Her face grew paler and her hands curled into fists as he explained that he had arranged for her to have his general power of attorney, and she knew, with a sick empty dread that she did not want to hear what he was about to say. He was putting all his affairs within her control.

With uncanny clarity, she also knew what the bottom document was. Like a blindfolded man at the firing wall, she sat with her body tensed, waiting for the inevitable pain. The awful suspense seemed to stretch out into an infinity, and finally the blow struck. She was right.

It was his last will and testament.

MORNING CAME. Dismal. Gray. Heavy with mist. David stood before the windows in the study, a mug of steaming coffee in his hand, his face etched by fatigue. The final minutes, and he didn't know how he was going to get through them. Last night had been bad enough. The dark hours had marched relentlessly on, but there had been no escape into sleep for him. Memories, regrets, a terrible loneliness—all had tormented him and he had lain awake long after Chris had fallen asleep, his mind caught on a ceaseless treadmill. And as that treadmill turned, it kept tossing up images to haunt him.

There had been one special memory, and it was so clear, so real in his mind that it seemed as though he had been transported back in time. It was of Chris walking along the beach in white shorts and a yellow top, her long tanned legs covered with dried sand and a smudge of dirt along her jaw. The sun was caught in the silken strands of her hair as the wind whipped it across her face, her bewitching eyes casting their spell as she laughed up at him. And he knew it was impossible for him to leave her.

But that beautiful memory was intruded on by another—one of a dark-haired woman looking back over her shoulder, helplessness in her black eyes as a swarthy man with a cruel and ruthless face shoved her toward a crude shack. And David knew he had to go.

There was no peace for him, and he was finally driven from his bed by restless energy and the instinct of self-preservation. He had gone downstairs to the study with every intention of drinking himself numb, but his solitary brooding had been interrupted by the appearance of Matthew Spencer.

David took a sip of coffee and rested his shoulder against the window frame, his expression steeled by grim thoughts. Maybe it was an act of desperation, maybe it was his way of grasping at straws, but he had tried to talk to his father about Chris during those barren hours of early morning. It was like talking to a wall. David wasn't sure exactly what had motivated him, whether it had been because he wanted Matthew to soften his attitude toward his wife, or because he was in the habit of hashing problems out with his dad, but whatever the reason, he found himself telling his father about Maria. Now he was wondering if it had been a wise move.

The sound of the door opening jarred him out of his sober introspection, and David turned.

It was Matthew. "I just had word from the hangar that there's bad weather rolling in, David."

David rubbed his neck in an attempt to ease the tense muscles. The company helicopter was to fly him to the mainland airport, where the jet was stationed. Fog could completely shroud the island in a matter of minutes.

"How bad?" he asked tautly.

Matthew looked haggard and his voice was tinged by weariness as he said, "The pilot wants to leave immediately. He said he'd be here in fifteen minutes."

Fifteen minutes. He drained his cup and set it on the desk. "My gear's by the door. I have to see Chris—"

"She and the boys just came down. I asked them to wait in the library."

David had never dreaded anything more. Never.

If he'd had his choice, he would have left without seeing anyone. He hated goodbyes at the best of times, but this goodbye was going to be hell.

He entered the oak-paneled library, his expression rigidly fixed. Without question, this was the worst ordeal he'd ever faced in his life.

Chris was standing in front of the windows, watching the mist roll in, and she turned to face him as he came into the room. She had on the same green dress she had worn the day in the gazebo, and David had a sudden crystal-clear recollection of the softness, the fragrance of her as she lay in his arms, her body cradled against his. The memory nearly ripped him in two.

Chris's gaze was riveted on him, and her face drained of all color as she witnessed the flash of pain across his face. The space that separated them seemed like an invisible barrier holding them apart, and neither of them moved. For an immobilizing moment their eyes locked, and it was as though a telepathic line of communication suddenly opened between them, and mind was speaking to mind, a surging tide of immeasurable love and longing ebbing and flowing between them. All was revealed: every emotion, every thought, every feeling. But beneath the onslaught was a single overwhelming affirmation, and that was the awareness, the unquestionable knowledge that they were indivisible, that one was essential to the other.

The boys came flying in from the terrace, their voices high-pitched with excitement. "We can hear the helicopter coming, dad."

It took every shred of discipline he had to turn toward his sons, and he was rocked by what he saw on their young faces. He had expected Timmy to be the one who would have the most difficulty handling his departure, but he had been dead wrong. This was no child who faced him. His ten-year-old son was watching him with a calmness, an unshrinking courage that seemed far too old for his youth.

That was bad enough, but when Mark's mouth began to tremble and his eyes suddenly brimmed with tears, David felt as though he was coming apart. He could not handle the agony of all this. He could not.

As if sensing the emotional turmoil he was trying to cope with, Chris interceded. Kneeling down in front of Mark, she took his face in her hands, and somehow she managed to keep her voice composed and reassuring as she said quietly, "Your dad is flying to Vancouver, and he's going to spend some time with grandpa at the office. Then he's going to fly all night to El Cayos, where the mines are." She smiled at him as she tidied his hair with her fingers. "You've gone down there lots of times to visit dad, Mark. Remember all the pictures you brought back?"

David understood what she was doing. She was giving the boy familiar places to identify with, places he'd been, and by doing that she was taking the mystery, and the fear, out of his father's departure. Strangely enough, it helped to ease David's anguish.

The clatter of the helicopter was directly overhead, heralding the final countdown. Mark forgot about his tears and darted outside to watch the aircraft land on the concrete pad beyond the rock garden, and Timmy followed, leaving their parents alone.

Now came the hardest part of all. What could he say to her, how could he give her some comfort, and how was he going to say goodbye to this woman who meant everything to him? For an unbearable few seconds they stared across the empty space that separated them, their eyes tormented by their common pain, then, unable to speak, David reached out his arms.

Clenching his teeth together as she came to him, David crushed her against him, his face twisted by grief. In absolute silence they clung to each other, hanging on to each fleeing second, and David felt as if a part of him was dying with each departing moment. He didn't know how he was ever going to let her go.

"I'm sorry, David, but we're going to have to leave." David motioned with one hand, silently acknowledging his father's solemn warning. For a few more treasured seconds he held her, an unbearable ache in his chest. Then, feeling as though he was severing a vital part of himself, he slowly withdrew his arms. He couldn't look at her. He'd come apart if he did.

With that special gentleness that was so much a part of her, she wiped the dampness from his face with her fingertips, her touch sending a violent tremor shuddering through him. Closing his eyes, he caught her hand and pressed her palm against his mouth, but he drew away when he heard her breath catch on a strangled sob.

Their eyes met and held, and then David lowered his head and kissed her once: tenderly, softly, and with all the love he had to give her. Then, without speaking, he turned and left the room.

The rest was a blur. Saying goodbye to the boys, his mother hugging him and telling him to take care, the walk to the helicopter, the strap of his kit bag cutting into his shoulder. He felt completely numb and disconnected from it all as he waited for his father to climb into the machine before he tossed his gear into the back storage area. Climbing into the seat beside the pilot, he mechanically went through the motions of closing the door and doing up his safety harness.

The pitch of the motor changed, and the nose dropped as the helicopter lifted off the pad, the violent downdraft from the blades sending up a flurry. Through the machine-made dust storm he could see her standing on the terrace, her slight figure diminishing in size as the aircraft climbed. His vision blurred and the green of her dress became indistinct. It struck him then that they had not exchanged a single word. But there had been no need. They had said all they needed to say.

NIGHTS WERE THE WORST. Nights were unbearable. No matter how hard she tried, there was no way Chris could block out the agony of thoughts that tormented her, and she found little solace in the haunting memories. Recollections of the intimate moments they had shared during their brief time together only magnified her loneliness, and the thoughts of the unknown horror he could be enduring magnified her fear. Three weeks. He'd been gone three weeks, but it seemed like a lifetime.

She lay in her bed listening to the midnight
sounds that infiltrated the darkness of her room.
The soft hum of the electric clock on the table by
her bed, the ruffle of the drapes billowing in the
breeze that whispered in through the open window,
the indistinct murmur of one of the boys talking in
his sleep. They were sounds that should have been
familiar, reassuring, but they seemed oddly incom-
plete without the deep even breathing of David beside her, and that feeling of incompleteness only
intensified her loneliness and fear.

After David's departure, Chris had returned
home, returned to the small brick house she had
shared with her father after she'd left David four
years ago. Once back in the security of her child-
hood home, she had deliberately isolated herself
from the rest of the world. It seemed to be the only
way she could survive. She left the house only when
she absolutely had to, and the only people she saw
were Peter and Catherine. Neither of them had any
idea how reclusive she'd become, and she was grateful for that—it would only add to the stress if they
started pressuring her to do things with them. She
wanted nothing more than to be left alone.

But she could no longer indulge herself with solitary isolation. Now there was a new worry. Now
there was the health of her unborn baby to consider. The doctor had made no bones about it. With
her medical history of extremely unstable pregnan-
cies plus a previous miscarriage, he was expecting

problems, and until the pregnancy advanced and her condition stabilized, Chris knew she was going to have to have help. As much as she hated the thought of having her privacy invaded, there was no other choice. Not only did her welfare and the baby's depend on it, but so did that of the boys. It was impossible for her to look after all their needs without jeopardizing the tiny life that was implanted within her. And she desperately wanted this baby.

Along with his concern over her pregnancy, the doctor had been disturbed by her obvious exhaustion. Chris couldn't argue with that. Ever since David left, her nights had been tormented with dark thoughts that left her sleepless with anxiety. Between that and morning sickness, she was constantly tired, and she was beginning to feel guilty about the lack of care Tim and Mark were receiving. Added to all that was the constant worry that one of the boys would forget and make a slip about their father, and the strain was leaving its mark.

Turning onto her side, Chris rested her head on her arm and stared solemnly into the darkness. Her decision not to tell David that she suspected she was pregnant had been an extremely hard one for her to make. Knowing that she was carrying his child would have made it ten times harder for him to do what he had to do. As much as she didn't want him to go, she didn't want to use this as the means to make him stay.

It had been bad enough as it was. If he'd known about the baby, he would have been weighed down with even more guilt, and she couldn't do that to him. Yet she knew if something happened to him on the trip, and if he died not knowing, she would never be able to forgive herself for remaining silent. Never.

She wiped away the tears that were slipping down her face, and rolled onto her back. Somehow she had to quit thinking such disturbing thoughts. Somehow.

"Are you sleeping, mom?" came an uncertain whisper from her doorway.

She raised her head, and trying to relax the tight muscles in her throat, she said, "No, honey. I'm awake."

The outline of Tim appeared by her bed. He was dragging his comforter behind him. "Do you want to talk, maybe?"

She moved over and patted the space beside her. "I think that might be a good idea. Why don't you crawl up here?"

Wrapping his blanket around him, Tim climbed up on the bed and sat cross-legged beside her. She could feel him fidgeting with the cuffs on his pyjamas.

"What's the matter, Tim?" she asked quietly as she reached out and took his small hand in hers.

He hesitated for a minute, and she heard him take a deep breath before he spoke. "Are you really worried about dad?"

Worried. Worried didn't even come close to defining what she was feeling. Frantic, maybe. But she managed to keep her voice calm as she answered. "I don't like it when he's gone, Tim. And yes, I do worry a little. He's a long way from home."

"He's going to come back, though." He said it with such confidence that it forced a small smile out of his mother. The boy hesitated, then his hand tightened around hers as he said, "I don't want to go to grandma and grandpa's anymore."

"Why?"

"Because I don't like leaving you here by yourself."

Chris rested her arm across her forehead as a heavy weariness pressed down on her. "Grandma invites me to go, Tim. It's just that I'd rather stay here, that's all."

Tim let go of her hand, and turning slightly he switched on the lamp by her bed. He looked very much like his father as he stared down at her with unwavering eyes. "Are you sick or something, mom?"

This boy saw far too much for a ten-year-old, and Chris looked away. "I've been feeling a little off, but it isn't anything serious."

He remained silent for so long that she finally looked up at him. He was still watching her with that same steady stare, and there was a stubborn set to his chin. "I told dad I'd look after you, you know."

Chris shifted her arm so he wouldn't see the tears that suddenly blurred her vision. She could hear him saying it in that quiet determined voice of his. *Don't worry, dad. I'll look after mom when you're gone.*

Several moments passed before she dared answer him, but finally, tucking her hand behind her head, she met his worried gaze. "I may have to get a housekeeper for a while—until I'm feeling better."

"Like Mrs. Bradley?"

"Well, maybe not *exactly* like Mrs. Bradley."

Timmy grinned at her as he pulled his blanket around him. "There's nobody *exactly* like Mrs. Bradley."

Chris laughed softly and reached up to ruffle his hair. "You're right. There's nobody like her." She smoothed his hair and let her hand rest on his shoulder. "I think you'd better hustle back to bed, Tim. You have school tomorrow."

With a deep sigh of reluctance he slid off the bed and started toward the door, but then he turned around to face her. "Don't worry, okay?"

She tried to make the tightness in her throat relax before she smiled at him and answered, "Okay."

He hiked up the dragging comforter. "Good night, mom."

She wanted to say, *God bless you, Tim, for being the special child you are,* but instead she said, "Good night, love."

It was not a good night for Chris, and the morning was even worse. The lack of sleep left her light-headed, and the minute she raised her head off the pillow she was hit with a wave of morning sickness. By the time she called the boys and crawled back into bed, she was covered in a cold sweat, and she closed her eyes, willing the dizziness to pass.

"You look awful white, mom."

Not daring to move her head to look at him, Chris murmured unsteadily, "Do you think you and Mark could fix your own breakfast this morning?"

Timmy was standing in the doorway, his hair tousled by sleep. He stared at her for a moment before he answered, "Sure." He turned to go, then hesitated, "Do you want any juice or anything?"

Chris swallowed hard and said weakly, "No thanks."

He opened his mouth as if to speak, but changed his mind and walked away, an oddly resolute look on his face.

Remaining very still so her queasiness wouldn't be further agitated, Chris heard him say something to Mark, then she heard both of them going down the stairs to have their breakfast.

It was some time later that she heard footsteps coming back up the stairs, but even when she sensed a presence at her door, she didn't open her eyes. If they had brought her something to eat, she'd be sick for certain.

"Well, Christine, Timmy tells me you've been ill for several days."

If anything could have instantly neutralized her churning nausea, the shock of hearing the voice of Matthew Spencer in her bedroom was it. But the respite was only temporary. The moment she sat up, dizziness washed over her, and she had to rest her head on her upraised knees and wait for the room to quit spinning.

Slowly lifting her head, Chris took a measured breath and reached for the housecoat that was lying on the foot of her bed. She slipped it on over the cotton nightie she wore, each movement unsettling her even more. Her face was ashen when she finally looked at her father-in-law.

Timmy and Mark were standing beside him, and there was a slightly defiant look on her eldest son's face as he said, "Dad said if we were ever worried about you, we were to call grandpa or Uncle Peter."

Chris's shoulders slumped wearily as she stared at him in silent reproach. "Timmy...."

"Why don't you boys finish getting ready for school?" interjected their grandfather smoothly as he smiled down at the two boys. "I'd like to talk to your mother for a minute."

"Okay, grandpa." The two of them disappeared, and with a thoughtful air about him, Matthew closed the door behind them. He went over to the window and stood staring out, his arms folded across his chest, a preoccupied frown on his face. Raking her hair back from her face with trembling hands, Chris sank against the pillows. She was feeling quite uneasy about her father-in-law's unexpected presence.

Finally Matthew turned and looked at her, scrutinizing her with a penetrating stare. "I was just about to leave for the office when Timothy phoned this morning." The head offices for LaFontaine Minerals International were located in Vancouver, and Matthew usually commuted two or three times a week by helicopter.

Timmy must have made her illness sound urgent for his grandfather to postpone his departure, and Chris's chagrin was apparent. "I'm sorry, Matthew. He's exaggerated the situation, I'm afraid—"

"Don't try to dodge the issue, Christine," he broke in sternly. "I have eyes in my head. You are *not* well, and don't try to pretend you are." He leaned back against the wide, old-fashioned windowsill, his arms still folded across his chest. "Have you been to the doctor?"

Chris met his piercing gaze and looked away. "Yes," she answered with resignation. "I went to the doctor's."

"And?"

Chris pleated the hem on the floral-patterned sheet, her expression becoming more strained. It took considerable will to make herself look at him. "I'm seven weeks pregnant."

Not one flicker of reaction showed on his face, but she sensed a new tension in him. "Is the doctor expecting difficulties again?"

An ache started to unfold in Chris's chest. She couldn't bring herself to say *abortion,* and the strain left her voice barely audible when she finally spoke. "He recommended that the pregnancy be terminated."

Matthew's eyes fastened on her, and the lines that sixty-seven years of living had etched on his face were suddenly carved deeper. "What was your decision?"

She tried to swallow but couldn't, and her words caught as she whispered, "I told him no."

"Does David know?"

The pressure expanding within her was nearly unbearable, and she felt as if she was being slowly suffocated. Unable to answer him, Chris looked away, her eyes brimming with tears as she shook her head.

David's not knowing was bad enough, but the visit to the doctor had been even worse. Dr. Grant knew that David and Chris had been separated, and because of the secrecy surrounding David's return, she couldn't tell him any differently. Thinking she'd been caught in an unwanted pregnancy, the physician had leaned on her quite hard, deeply concerned about the risk she was taking.

"Did you go back to Dr. Grant?"

"Yes."

Matthew narrowed his eyes and continued to stare at her. "I take it that he doesn't know the baby is David's."

Chris avoided looking at him. "No."

"What exactly did he say when you said no to an abortion?"

Chris heaved a sigh, finally meeting his eyes. "The same as before. Plenty of rest. No lifting, no strenuous activities, no long walks, no alcohol. He said there was a very real possibility that I might abort spontaneously again, but if I get through the next nine weeks, the danger should be over."

There was a brief silence, and Matthew cleared his throat. "Well, that settles it, Christine. You simply cannot continue to stay here by yourself." He stared at her for a moment, as though he was contemplating something, then sticking his hands in his pockets, he went back over to the window and stood looking out. "You obviously aren't well, and Catherine has nothing else to do but worry herself sick over David." He turned to look at her, his face solemn. "The obvious solution is to move you and the boys in with us."

Matthew Spencer was not a man who made impulsive decisions, and his suggestion left Chris more shaken than she would have imagined. For a moment she simply stared at him, her mind numbed by his solution. Then, collecting her wits, she stammered, "But the boys have school...."

He nodded his head in acknowledgment of her

concern. "Davis spends a good deal of time with his feet propped up, reading mystery novels. He certainly can spare a few moments, I'm sure, to drive the boys back and forth," he answered with a touch of humor. Davis was the Spencers' driver, and no one could suggest he even came remotely close to being overworked. "And we can arrange to have someone look after the house while you're gone."

There was a strained silence as Matthew waited for her to offer further reasons why she couldn't go. But Chris didn't have any—except one. And it was uppermost in her mind. "What if David phones? What if he tries to call and there's no one here?" she said unevenly.

Matthew came over to the bed and looked down at her, an unreadable look on his face. "I'll have one of those electronic answering devices installed today," he said, his tone brusque. "You can leave a message saying that you can be reached at our number." He was about to say something else but shook his head and turned away. "Your coming to stay with us will be best for everyone, Christine," he said sternly, as if he expected further objections from her.

Chris leaned her head back and wearily closed her eyes as dizziness started to rotate sickeningly through her senses. Maybe it was knowing Matthew was there to take charge, or maybe it was plain simple exhaustion, but she no longer had the strength or the will to face what was before her—at least not alone. She didn't want to face it alone.

CHAPTER THIRTEEN

MATTHEW HAD BEEN RIGHT. The move to the Spencer estate was best for everyone—especially for Chris. Knowing the boys were being well looked after took an enormous weight off her shoulders, and for the first time since David left, she found she was able to relax. Catherine insisted Chris remain in bed until she started feeling stronger, so for the first few days Chris did little else but eat and sleep. It wasn't long before her improved health began to show. She started to gain back some of the weight she'd lost, and the dark smudges beneath her eyes disappeared.

But something else was happening that she'd never expected. Day by day, she and Catherine were growing closer. Their deep concern for David's welfare was a common link, and the constant gnawing worry was something they shared, something each of them understood, and Chris began to realize how much she'd missed by losing her own mother at the age she had.

There was only one drawback to her being at the Spencers', and that was Matthew's continued remoteness. She had expected him to make a point of avoiding her, and at first he did. But as the days wore on and Chris spent less time in her room, he made less of an effort to remove himself from her presence. Even though he no longer totally ignored her, he still treated her with a polite aloofness that somehow seemed to discount her existence. She tried not to let it bother her, but it did. Catherine had said to give him time, and Chris kept reminding herself of that advice, but she had the sinking feeling that time would change nothing.

Knowing that there was little she could do to make amends made the estrangement harder for her to bear, and the sense of sorrow she experienced because of it became another silent companion—a companion that continued to haunt her.

It was one of those bleak and rainy nights that seemed to amplify the hollow rattle of the rain against the windows and the low moan of the wind. It was such a lonely sound. Unable to sleep, Chris found herself thinking about the situation with her father-in-law, her wakefulness triggered by a heavy melancholy. She would give anything to erase whatever bitterness Matthew harbored, but that was wishing for the impossible. She stared into the darkness, her sadness leaving her vulnerable.

She turned onto her side and looked at the luminous dial of the clock on her bedside table. One o'clock. Hours to go before morning—hours to endure before the light of day sheltered her from the grim thoughts that tormented her at night. Thrusting her hands into her hair, she roughly drew it back from her face in a gesture of quiet desperation. If there was only some way she could switch off her thoughts.

With a sigh she raised herself up on one arm and turned on the light by her bed. She knew from experience that it was useless to lie there and try to will her mind into blankness. Too many memories kept creeping in. She had to snap out of this despondent mood or she'd end up so miserable she'd never be able to go to sleep.

Swinging her legs over the edge of the bed, she picked up her housecoat and put it on. She'd go downstairs and have a dish of yogurt. A sharp recollection flashed into her mind of Mark standing before her and David, his face screwed up into an expression of distaste. *Ambrosia! That sounds like some yukky awful health food—like yogurt.* A wave of unbearable loneliness hit her as she clearly recalled the strength of David's arms around her that morning and the warmth of his body against her. A stifling ache filled her. Maybe she'd make herself a cup of hot chocolate instead.

The kitchen seemed oddly vacant without Mrs. Bradley bustling about, and Chris felt as if she was encroaching on the housekeeper's private domain as she prepared a carafe of hot chocolate. The uneasy sensation that she was illegally trespassing exaggerated the silence, and she found herself moving stealthily around the room, the hush setting her nerves on edge.

"Aren't you feeling well?"

Chris jumped, nearly dropping the carafe of hot liquid as her heart contracted in fright. Her pulse was throbbing wildly in her throat and a sudden loss of strength left her trembling as she turned to face Matthew. "I'm fine," she said weakly. Her hand was unsteady as she set down the jug she was holding. "I was having trouble sleeping so I thought I'd make myself some hot chocolate."

Her father-in-law stared at her austerely for a moment, then said gruffly, "I'm sorry. I didn't mean to startle you."

Feeling ill at ease, Chris didn't know quite how to respond, and an awkward silence stretched between them. Giving her another intense look, Matthew turned to leave. He was wearing slacks and an old golfing sweater, and from the papers he was holding in his hand it was evident he'd been in the study, working late. Chris felt a surge of compassion and concern. He looked old and very tired.

"There's plenty of hot chocolate, Matthew," she said hesitantly. "Would you like a cup?"

He paused at the doorway, his back to her as he considered her offer. Finally he turned to face her. "Yes, thank you," he said stiffly. "That would be nice."

Christine unhooked two mugs from the cup rack and filled them, her thoughts in a nervous muddle.

It was the first time since she'd come to stay with the Spencers that she'd been alone with her father-in-law, and maybe now was the best time to say some things that had to be said.

If only she could scrape up enough courage to be honest with him. She handed him the steaming mug of cocoa, and without looking at her, he started to turn away.

"Matthew...." Her voice trailed off as her nerve faded, and she was left with an awful ball of tension in the pit of her stomach.

He glanced at her, his expression fixed. "Yes?"

Her knuckles were white as she grasped the mug, and taking a deep unsteady breath, she spoke, her voice breaking treacherously. "I want to thank you for doing what you did for the boys and me." Forcing herself to meet his steely stare, she felt oddly intimidated and found it hard to maintain eye contact with him. "It was very generous of you to do what you did, especially under the circumstances."

She half expected him to say something cutting, such as he didn't do it for her, he did it for the boys. Nothing had prepared her for the jolt she received when he said, "Why did you never once contact Catherine and me after you left David?"

Feeling suddenly weak, Chris went to the table and sat down abruptly, her face drawn. She wrapped her hands around the hot mug, trying to absorb the heat, completely staggered by his unexpected question. Finally she lifted her eyes to meet his, her voice barely audible as she said, "I didn't think you'd want to talk to me—and I was afraid to face you."

"Catherine and I were very upset, Christine," he said curtly. "We weren't totally insensitive to the situation between you and David. It was obvious he was married to his career and that you and the boys were suffering because of it. It was also very obvious that you simply didn't belong with the empty-headed crowd that seemed to hang around the yacht club. We really did see the problems, but when you left without a single word to us, we didn't know what to think."

Chris stared at him, so dumbfounded she was un-affected by his vexation. It had taken her months to sort it all out, and he'd seen it all the time. Trying to collect her thoughts, she looked down at the table. "I didn't even know what the problems were when I left, Matthew," she said, her voice strained. "I just had the awful feeling that if I was going to survive, I *had* to leave."

"I can understand you feeling that way, but I don't see what that had to do with Catherine and me."

"David is your son. I thought you wouldn't want to see me after I hurt him the way I did."

"You mean you thought we'd take his side."

"Well, it seemed obvious that you would."

"Did you think us so shallow, Christine? We'd looked upon you as a daughter, not as some... someone imposed on us through marriage."

Matthew was very agitated and his face was turning red, the veins in his neck pumping heavily. Chris could tell that his blood pressure was climbing. This confrontation was far too much for him, and it hurt her to see him so upset. Yet she knew she couldn't let it drop, she had to give him an explanation.

"I was so confused and so hurt, I just wanted to hide. And I honestly thought you and Catherine wouldn't want to have anything to do with me after David and I separated. It would have been so... awkward."

"That was very unfair of you."

She looked at him, her face pale. "I can see that now, but at the time I couldn't see beyond my own misery."

There was a tense silence, and Chris felt on the brink of tears. She hadn't honestly realized until now how much her leaving David had affected Matthew and Catherine. She hadn't been fair, and she was more sorry than she could ever express in words. She had never meant to hurt them. She cleared her throat and spoke, her voice choked. "I'm so sorry, Matthew. I reacted blindly, and I was so upset I couldn't see what I was doing to everyone."

"You could have talked to us. We would have understood," he said defensively.

Chris raised her head, her eyes dark with distress as she gave him a mirthless smile. "In the shape I was in, I couldn't talk to anyone." She twisted her mug around on the table, her expression reflective as she stared at her hands. Suddenly she was very conscious of her aloneness, and sadness engulfed her. It must have shown on her face, because Matthew reached across the table and grasped her hands, stilling their restless movements.

His voice had lost its harshness when he spoke. "You see, Christine, we had hoped you felt close enough to come to us, and it hurt us badly when you didn't."

She glanced up at him, her eyes revealing how much she was hurting inside. "It never entered my head that you and Catherine would feel that way. I thought you wouldn't want to see me."

He patted her hand with a fatherly gesture and said gruffly, "Well, my dear, you were very wrong."

It was the first time he'd called her "my dear," and his use of that endearment meant more to Chris than anything else he could have said. Tears filled her eyes, and she bent her head so he couldn't see, knowing that her display of emotion would embarrass him.

Placing his hands flat on the table, he cleared his throat and said brusquely, "I think under the circumstances, we must let bygones be bygones, Christine. It would make Catherine happy."

She quickly brushed away her tears before she lifted her head and looked at him, her sincerity showing in her eyes. Her voice wavered as she said, "It would make me happy, too, Matthew."

He avoided looking at her and picked up his cup and took a drink. His own voice was oddly choked when, after an uncomfortable silence, he said, "It's good to have you home, my dear."

Chris wanted to put her head on the table and weep, but instead she said tremulously, "I'm glad to be here."

That was the turning point. From then on, Matthew's attitude toward her began to slowly change, and it wasn't long before he was treating her in the same fatherly way he had before she and David separated. In many ways it was like coming home.

And it was home. Chris didn't know how she would have survived without Catherine and Matthew. With each passing day, the waiting, the wondering became harder and harder to bear. David had left the island the last week in August, and for four weeks Chris received frequent letters from him. Those letters were her lifeline, her one remaining link with him. But October arrived, and the letters stopped coming. Week after week dragged by, and no word. Nothing. The fear started mounting.

October slipped away. And November. Chris became more and more withdrawn. She felt as if she was dying by degrees. If it hadn't been for that inner glow, that deep sense of fulfillment she experienced because of the baby, she was sure she would have slid into a severe depression. Yet her concern for her unborn child was a constant strain.

On a day when Chris felt her ability to cope was

about to collapse, the age-old miracle of life renewed her strength. One crisp morning early in December, at completion of her fourth month, she felt the first tiny flutter of movement inside her, and out of sheer relief she had shut herself in her room and wept. Her spirits brightened noticeably after that, and she was able to share the boys' growing anticipation of Christmas.

It was going to be a hectic Christmas. For the first time in several years the entire Spencer family was going to be home for the holidays. David's three younger brothers were scattered around the world, all of them involved with LaFontaine mining operations. Kevin, the youngest, was in Australia, Dirk was in Africa and Jerry was stationed in South America with his family. Each of the brothers had phoned home in August, just before David left for Central America, and it was then the enthusiastic plans for a reunion at Christmas had been made. But as the days slipped by and there was still no word from David, it became a grim possibility that one brother might be missing. It was not an easy thing for any of them to face.

David's parents, Chris and the boys all made an effort to immerse their anxiety in activity as they made the necessary preparations. Lengthy shopping expeditions were out of the question for Chris, but Catherine was an inveterate shopper, and between her and the boys, Matthew claimed he was kept on the fringes of poverty. Chris was kept busy wrapping gifts. Decorations were hauled out and checked, elaborate menus planned and rooms prepared. A magnificent tree was delivered—and the anticipation grew.

There was, however, a solemn side to the festive preparations. It was a season for giving, and the Spencer family had always given generously to various programs for the needy. But it was Matthew who exposed the boys to a deeper and very sobering definition of the word *gift*.

One Saturday he took them to the warehouse that held the supplies that were being airlifted to several orphanages David had personally sponsored while he was in Central America. The boys helped load the company plane with bags of rice, crates of foodstuffs, medical supplies, bales of blankets and clothing. In reality Tim and Mark were probably more of a handicap than a help, but they actively participated in an act of giving that really meant something to them, and it meant even more knowing that they were acting on behalf of their father. But the understanding of what it was all about went deeper than any of the adults realized.

They were all gathered in the library later that evening, and Timmy was sitting on the floor, his arms locked around his knees as he stared into the dancing flames of the fire.

Chris watched him for a moment, her brow creased with a worried frown, instinctively aware that something was bothering him. "What's the matter, Tim?"

He shrugged his shoulders, refusing to meet her gaze.

Chris glanced questioningly at Matthew, her eyes troubled. He nodded his head slightly, as though he was silently advising her to press the issue. She stared at her father-in-law a moment and then looked back at her son. "Are you worried about your dad?" she asked quietly.

He jerked his head in a negative gesture and for several minutes said nothing. But when he turned to face her, there was an intensity about him that caught her by surprise. He stared at her for a second, then he spoke, his voice fierce with emotion and his eyes ablaze with pride. "I'm so proud of my dad. He cares about the kids who don't have moms and dads. He *really* cares."

There was a tremor of deep feeling in her voice as Chris responded quietly, "Yes, he really does."

"Grandpa says that's what Christmas is all about," piped up Mark.

Chris looked at her father-in-law. *God bless you, Matthew, for teaching them a lesson they'll never forget,* she thought fervently. *God bless you.*

THE DAYS EDGED ON, bringing them closer and closer to the holidays, and as the red *X*'s on the boys' calendar multiplied, Chris became more and more anxious. She would wake up at night in a cold sweat, her fear pressing down on her like a tangible weight. If only they would hear something of David. Anything. But still there was no word. Nothing. She had a strong hunch that Matthew maintained daily contact with General Gilberto, but she stopped asking him weeks ago if there was any news. It was so hard on him to have to tell her there was no word from the expedition.

There were only ten days remaining until Christmas. Chris stood at the library window, watching the early dusk of winter creep across the grounds. It was so quiet. So morbidly quiet. Catherine had left to pick the boys up from school, and Matthew had spent the day in Vancouver at LaFontaine. The emptiness of the house seemed to spread through her, and Chris wrapped her arms around herself, feeling so hollow, so alone. She couldn't stand being by herself anymore. Frightening thoughts would seep into her consciousness, awakening a panic that was terrifying in itself. What would she do if David never came home? How would she survive?

The sound of the helicopter landing on the concrete pad behind the house cut through her grim musings, and she turned from the window. Not wanting Matthew to find her brooding, she busied herself rearranging some of the decorations on the enormous Christmas tree, which stood in all its tinseled splendor in the corner by the fireplace. Only a few moments passed before she heard him cross the tiled foyer, and she tried to dredge up a genuine smile, but for some reason she found herself suddenly fighting tears. She didn't dare face him until she got a grip on herself, and she kept her back to the door when he entered the room.

There was a brief silence, and a voice quietly said, "Well, at least you could say hello."

Chris's heart convulsed painfully, then started hammering wildly against her ribs, and for a split second she was paralyzed with terror, scared to death it wasn't real, that it was only her imagination. She couldn't seem to breathe and her legs felt as though they were about to collapse beneath her as she slowly turned.

He was standing in the doorway, his shoulder braced against the oak frame, his hands rammed in the back pockets of his jeans, his deeply tanned face animated with elation. But one look at her stark white face and his expression altered instantly, his eyes darkening with alarm. He crossed the room in two strides, his arms encompassing her as she reached toward him, and her knees slowly buckled beneath her.

Chris had never experienced anything like it, not that kind of absolute joy or the violent explosion of hysterical relief. All she was aware of was that he was there, and he was holding her, and she clung to him as if her life depended on it, laughing and crying at the same time.

As he held her trembling body against him, David

felt incredibly shaken. Since he'd left the airport at El Cayos, he'd been counting the hours, the minutes until he was back with Chris. He'd been unable to sleep on the flight back in the company plane, and he'd nearly driven the flight crew crazy with his restless pacing.

He'd been even worse when he landed in Vancouver. One delay after another kept cropping up, and to make matters worse, he'd been caught in a spontaneous and time-consuming celebration when he walked into his father's office unexpected and unannounced. He had little patience with the excitement his arrival caused. All he wanted was to get back to his family, and when Matthew told him of Chris's pregnancy during the helicopter flight to the island, his urgency to get home had only increased.

That bit of news really rocked him. He didn't think anything could have affected him more than that. But when he walked into the library and saw her looking like an absolute angel, framed against the backdrop of the glittering tree, he felt as if he'd been hit by a locomotive. No words could explain how desperately he'd missed her, and no words could express how grateful he was to be alive, to be able to hold her again.

The unsurpassed joy he was experiencing was tempered by his need to be careful with Chris and the tiny life she carried, and instead of crushing her against him as he longed to do, he held her with immeasurable gentleness. God, but he did love her so.

He didn't know how long they stood wrapped in each other's arms, wordlessly rejoicing in their reunion. What he did know was that he finally felt whole; he felt restored. And now, at last, the anguish was behind him.

David held her until her trembling stopped, then tenderly cradling her face in his hands, he gazed down at her. She was thinner than when he'd left, and there were tiny worry lines etched around her eyes that hadn't been there before, but an inner radiance seemed to emanate from her. Such a special radiance. Even though she knew what a risk another pregnancy was, she had elected to carry his child, and he was deeply touched by that. It was such a miracle, this gift of life, and his voice was unsteady and very gentle when he said, "Why didn't you tell me about the baby before I left? I wouldn't have ever left you, love, had I known."

Tears were still clinging to her lashes as she covered his hand with her own, and her eyes shone with love. She gave him a tremulous smile. "I couldn't do that to you, David," she whispered, her voice breaking. "I had to let you go."

"God, Chris," he murmured as he drew her against him, his cheek pressed against the top of her head. "I couldn't believe it when dad told me. Another baby— you don't know how damned pleased I am." He slowly exhaled. "I've missed you so damned much, and I have so much to tell you."

As it turned out, it was a long while before he had

a chance to tell her anything. Catherine returned with the boys and they went absolutely wild with jubilation when they found out their father was home. Their excitement infected everyone, and the whole family ended up having a celebration to end all celebrations. Chris looked as though someone had uncorked a sparkling champagne in her, and happiness shone from her with a hypnotizing vitality. David couldn't take his eyes off her.

It was getting late when Matthew, who was worrying out loud that Chris was playing herself out, gruffly ordered her to bed. Under different circumstances David would have taken heated exception to anyone bossing his wife around, but it was obvious that Matthew was once again Chris's champion. He was watching out for her, and that neutralized any ire David might have felt. It was apparent that she was back in his father's good books, and nothing could have pleased David more.

He solemnly agreed with his father, but there was a gleam of amusement in his eyes as he helped her to her feet, and with the boys as escorts, ushered her to her bedroom. He put his sons to bed and returned to her, struggling to get a grip on the sexual excitement that was burning in him. But the moment he entered the room his struggle was lost, and David fell victim to her spell.

Closing the door softly behind him, he leaned back against it and folded his arms across his chest, his eyes fixed hungrily on her. She was in bed, her naked ripening body covered only by a sheet, her golden-brown hair fanned out in a lustrous tumble against the pillow. The soft light from the bedside lamp cast a bewitching glow on her skin—skin that seemed more delicate than ever against the dark blue of the bed linen. She was so incredibly lovely, and so damned tempting. He knew he was going to have one hell of a battle to keep his hands off her.

She was watching him with those eyes that hypnotized him, and David was irresistibly drawn to her. As he crossed the room, his pulse began to beat with a heavy throb, pumping a hot weakness through his veins. Countless nights he had lain awake, wanting her so badly he could barely endure it and torturing himself with sensual thoughts of this first night home with her. Four months of that kind of hunger had created a ravenous appetite, but he would not assuage it. Not now. He would do nothing that might risk her health or that of the baby she carried. He sat down on the bed beside her, and when she reached up to caress his face, he found it almost impossible to breathe.

Her eyes were troubled as she asked softly, "What's the matter, David?"

He could sense her uncertainty, her unspoken fear, and catching her hand he pressed a passionate kiss against her palm. His voice was husky as he said, "Nothing's wrong, Christie. It's just—" He had to pause and try to haul air into his constricted lungs. He closed his eyes against her silent appeal, fighting to hang on to his rationality.

When he finally looked down at her, the fear he saw in her eyes devastated his common sense, and with a low groan he took her in his arms. It was supposed to be a tender kiss, a kiss to reassure her, but it backfired into something much, much more, and they were suddenly caught in a fire of desire. David's heart was slamming against his ribs, and he was holding her in a crushing embrace when he came to his senses. Pulling his mouth from hers, he gentled his hold on her trembling body.

A sob was wrung from her and she pressed her face against his neck. "David—God, David—"

"Easy, love," he said unevenly, pressing a lingering kiss against her temple. "I think we need to talk, Christie."

"Later...."

Trying to ignore the entreaty he heard in her throaty voice, David tipped her head back so he could see her face. His eyes were filled with tenderness as he gazed at her. "No, love. I think we'd better talk now." He caressed her face, feeling physically unable to contain all the love he felt for her. "I'm not going to make love to you, Chris," he explained softly. "Not until I have a chance to talk to the doctor. I'm not going to risk harming either you or the baby."

"Everything's fine—"

David pressed his hands across her lips and said quietly, "No, Chris. Not until I know for sure."

She stared at him for a moment, then acceded to him with a sigh. Her fingers were trembling as they outlined his lips, her voice just as unsteady as she whispered, "But you will come to bed, won't you?"

He knew as an added precaution to safeguard her he should not stay, but there was no way he could walk out of the room and leave her. He simply didn't have that kind of strength.

He kissed her lightly and smiled at her. "As long as you damned well promise to behave yourself."

She didn't say anything but watched him with a spellbinding intensity that elevated both his awareness and his pulse rate, leaving him weak. A deep aching need gripped him, and he reluctantly eased out of her embrace and stood up, his hands inept as he began to shed his clothes. He was setting himself up for an endurance test, but he had to hold her, to feel the fullness of her naked body against his. He had to have at least that.

As if drawn by an invisible bond, he went to her, his body tensing as he steeled himself against the explosion of desire that he knew would rip through him the minute he touched her. And there was an explosion. He closed his eyes and clenched his jaw against the raw emotions that fired his blood as he gathered her in his arms and she melted against him. He couldn't help himself, and he responded with a searing kiss that thrust them into the path of a storm. Reality was slipping away as passion claimed them, and David struggled to hang on to some vestige of sanity as she moved against him, tempting him beyond belief with the rhythm of her body. A few more seconds of this and he would never be able to stop.

Twisting his mouth away, he caught her head against his shoulder and held her fast, his pulse pounding frantically. "God, Chris, I'm sorry," he murmured hoarsely against her ear. "I wasn't going to let this happen."

Chris tightened her embrace, and he could feel the pulse of her erratic heartbeat against his chest as she began to caress his back. Slowly her hold on him relaxed, and David yielded to the pressure of her hand as she stroked his chest, silently urging him onto his back. He felt himself drowning in a sea of sensations as she continued to touch him, to explore his aroused body with the softest of caresses. But the intoxicating warmth that was drugging his senses was sharply dispelled as her hand closed around him and he realized what her intention was. He ground out her name as he caught her wrist and yanked her hand away, his heart pounding so wildly he could hardly breathe.

Chris turned her head so that her mouth brushed his cheek, and she whispered huskily against his skin, "Let me, David. Please let me."

It took a while for David to gain some control over his stampeding senses, but finally he released her wrist and gazed at her, his eyes smoldering. "No, love. Not like that." He sucked in a deep breath, trying to ignore the aching hunger throbbing through his body. When he spoke, his voice was low with an urgency to make her understand. "I want *you,* Christine—not sexual gratification. Without you, everything else is meaningless."

She pressed her face against his hand, her lips parting as her breath caught in a soft sob. Her eyes were dilated with desire when she finally looked at him. "I'm sure there's no risk now."

He gazed at her, his expression one of concern. "But you haven't talked to the doctor about that, have you?"

She shook her head and sighed, "No."

"We had to abstain for five months when you were pregnant with Mark, Chris," he reminded her. "I don't want to take any chances—there's too much at stake." He gathered her against him, his hunger rigidly restrained. At least he could hold her, and that alone gave him immeasurable pleasure. Relishing the scent of her hair and the velvet texture of her skin, David kissed her softly with a quiet tempered passion. "I'm so damned pleased about the baby, Christie," he said. "I couldn't believe it when dad told me."

She pulled away slightly and looked at him, a hint of laughter in her eyes. "It's a good thing you came home when you did, David. Facing Dr. Grant without a prospective father was bad enough, but I didn't know what I was going to do when my pregnancy became *really* obvious."

"Have you told the boys yet?"

"No." Her voice was strained by some painful memory as she said, "I wanted to wait. I kept hoping you'd get back before I had to tell them."

His expression altered, and he smoothed his hand over her hair. "It must have been hell for you, Christie—the waiting. I never thought I'd be gone this long."

She didn't say anything for a moment and seemed lost in thought as she absently stroked his shoulder. When she looked up at him, her face was drawn and her eyes were filled with apprehension. "I need to know what happened, David."

His smile was filled with understanding and compassion as he said, "I know you do." He loosened his hold on her, and raising up on one elbow piled the pillows behind him. He lay back against them and slipped his arm around her. "Come here," he murmured, and he gathered her to him. He dropped a light kiss on her forehead. "Where do you want me to start?"

"I want you to tell me about Maria."

David could detect a note of indecision in her words, and he suddenly realized that in spite of what she'd said before he left, Chris had been uncertain. His strong sense of responsibility for Maria's welfare had subtly undermined her sense of security, and for the first time he fully comprehended what an act of blind trust it had been for her to let him go. Altering his hold on her so he could see her face, David gazed at her intently. "You're my life, Christine. Without you, everything else is meaningless." He brushed the heel of his hand against her cheek, his fingers curving against her neck as he tried to reassure her. "There're going to be no more ghosts, love. Ever."

Tears welled in her eyes and he had an overwhelming urge to enfold her tightly in his arms, to insulate her from everything, but he held back. She was so vulnerable, and he couldn't trust himself to resist her mute appeal.

He saw her swallow with difficulty, then she asked the question he knew she dreaded asking. "How is she?"

David relaxed and smiled. "She's fine."

She was watching him intently. "Are you telling me the truth?"

"The absolute truth." He reached across her and picked up the two pillows that were lying on her side of the bed, and partially sitting up, he stuffed them behind his shoulders. "Here. Let me hold you like this, Christie. You'll be more comfortable." David nestled her closer and tucked her leg between his, keenly aware of the nakedness of her body as she curled against him.

"Is she really fine, or are you just stalling?"

There was a touch of amusement in his eyes as he gazed at her unwaveringly. "Quite frankly, I don't think she could be better."

Tipping her head back slightly, Chris looked at

him with a slight frown. "Why? What do you mean?"

David became serious. "Maria's always led a very sheltered life, Chris. Her family was extremely wealthy and she was very naive about some of the harsher realities of life."

"Are you referring to the political unrest in her own country?"

"Well, partly." He paused, his frown deepening as he considered his next words. "She knew what was happening politically, but she was so removed from the horror that she had a distorted concept about what was really going on."

Chris had raised up on one arm and was watching him with unswerving interest. "So what happened?"

"In a nutshell, she discovered starving, homeless and illiterate kids."

Chris looked mystified. "Maybe you'd better start at the beginning."

"I think the beginning was pretty rough, but she never talked about it. She seemed to have dismissed it totally from her mind."

"You mean Sanchez, don't you?"

David's expression grew grim, and a flash of loathing flared in his eyes. "Yes, that's what I mean." He took a deep breath and, as though trying to impose some self-control, released it slowly. "I guess after she'd been there about a month, they needed someone to look after the kids who'd been left homeless. So one of the top honchos overrode

Sanchez's claim on her, and she was taken to the camp where the kids were housed."

Chris's eyes widened in amazement. "You mean she wasn't even with Sanchez for all that time?"

He gave her a twisted smile. "That's what I mean. I guess that miserable bastard didn't want to lose face in front of me, so he never let on." David became sober as he absently fingered Chris's hair. "Maybe he did me a favor. I hated him with such a vengeance, and I think that hate helped to keep me going. Every day I vowed I'd live long enough to kill him with my bare hands."

"Did you?"

The quiet intentness of her question snapped David out of his dark reflections, and his eyes met hers. "No, I didn't. He was killed in the raid, but it was one of the soldiers who shot him."

"Was it bad, David?" she asked, her voice compassionate.

He sighed and frowned as he considered her question. "It's funny, Chris. It was and it wasn't. It was pretty damned grim, and the condition that the hostages were in was so revolting it was bloody hard to stomach, but they were so damned happy to see us it turned into a bizarre celebration." His voice faltered. "It's something I won't ever forget."

Chris tightened her hold on him. It had not been an easy mission for him, not by any stretch of the imagination.

For a long while they lay together, silent, each of

them locked in private thoughts. Finally Chris
stirred and looked at David. "You said that Maria
couldn't be better. What did you mean by that?"

"She's found a worthwhile mission in life,
Chris," he said solemnly. "There are countless kids
who've been orphaned, who are living in the foulest
conditions—kids who have no one." He looked at
her, his eyes distressed. "It's awful, Chris—the
poverty, the hopelessness. It had a profound impact
on her, and she's bound and determined she's going
to give these kids a chance. She's taken on a crusade
that's going to be her life." David's tone changed,
and there was a softening, a new openness about
him, as though he'd just been relieved of a heavy
burden. "She knows that for the first time in her
life, she's really needed, that somebody is depend-
ing on her, and she's really happy, Christie. Really
and truly happy, and I'm so damned glad for her."

There was no undercurrent of past jealousy when
Chris said, "She deserves to be, David. I didn't
want to see her hurt."

"I know you didn't, babe."

"Did she stay at the rebel encampment?"

"No. That's what took us so long. We had to
move the hostages and her thirty-two kids to a loca-
tion where we could airlift them out. I took Maria
and her gang to one of the orphanages that LaFontaine sponsors, and it just so happened that the airlift of supplies dad sent arrived just before we did.
That's how come I was able to catch the company

plane back." His eyes filled with an intoxicating warmth as he gazed at her. "And I couldn't get back here fast enough, Christie. You'll never know how much I've missed you."

He felt he was losing touch with reality as she gazed down at him, casting her spell, her intentness kindled by desire. Chris leaned over him and gave him a soft searching kiss, her lips warm and pliant against his.

"Christie, don't be a torment, love," he murmured hoarsely against the moistness of her mouth.

"I'm not tormenting," she whispered as she slowly slid her hand down his torso, her touch electric. "I need to love you, David, and I want you to love me back."

"Chris...God..." he ground out as she began to caress him, annihilating his restraint.

"Touch me," she pleaded, and she guided his hand between her thighs, her breathing ragged as she moved against him. "Love me, David. Please love me."

He was lost, and with immeasurable tenderness, with infinite gentleness, he loved her.

EPILOGUE

THE SOUND OF THE SURF rolled in on the warm summer breeze with a lulling rhythm, but the drone of a bee cut through the tranquilizing murmur, and Chris opened her eyes. She was lying on her stomach beneath the shade of an enormous spruce, her arms folded beneath her head. Her eyes softened as she looked at the baby sleeping on the blanket beside her. Four-month-old Cathy Lee Spencer was lying on her stomach beside her mother, her long thick lashes fanning out against her pink cheeks. She had her thumb stuck in her mouth, and her knees were drawn under her, lifting her tiny bottom in the air. Her dark hair was curling damply against her head, and Chris brushed it loose before she drew back the thin quilt she had draped across her small daughter.

"She looks like an angel, doesn't she?"

Chris raised up on her elbows and squinted against the sun as David sat down on the edge of the blanket. "You're hardly an impartial judge," she pointed out with a lazy grin.

He gave her head a playful push and stretched

out beside her. "What do you know? You're only her mother."

A smile hovered around her mouth, but Chris didn't give him the satisfaction of a retort. Folding her arms in front of her, she lay back down and closed her eyes, the heat sedating her. She could hear the far-off voices of the boys as they worked on their fort, and her smile broadened. With the new additions that were being planned, the fort could turn into a five-year project.

In fact she hoped it was a five-year project. There was nowhere on earth she would rather spend the summers, and it delighted her that David felt the same. He had taken two months off from LaFontaine, and as soon as the boys were out of school, they had headed for the seclusion of Peter's cabin. Chris was in heaven.

"Are you planning something sneaky, or are you simply amused? You make me nervous when you smile like that."

She opened her eyes and made a face at him. "Good. I like to keep you on your toes."

"Oh, you keep me on my toes, Christine," he said, and there was a throaty suggestive tone to his voice as he added, "Among other things."

Chris laughed and leaned over and gave him a swift kiss. "Let's talk about the other things."

"I think I could handle that," he said, sliding his hand under her top.

"Hey, dad, can we sleep in the fort tonight?"

Mark called out as he came running through the trees. "Can we? We've got the roof fixed so it won't leak. Can we, dad? Can we?"

Chris laughed and sat up as David made some pointed comments about small boys.

Mark grinned and ignored him. "Come on, dad. Can we?"

David narrowed his eyes into a menacing expression and said, "Yes."

"Ah, dad, why can't we—" A bewildered look crossed Mark's expressive face, and he shook his head in confusion as he stared at his father. "Did you say yes?" he queried tentatively.

David laced his hands behind his head and laughed. "Yes, I said yes."

Mark looked stunned for a minute, then let out a yell. "Yippee!" He started racing back toward the bush. "Hey, Tim, dad says we can!"

His shouting woke up the baby, and with a disgruntled grunt she started sucking her thumb. His expression a mixture of paternal pride and delight, David picked her up and laid her across his chest. "Hello, button. Did you have a good sleep?"

Cathy Lee responded with an enormous smile that flashed her dimples, and sacrificing the consolation of her thumb, she reached for his face. Her dad caught her chubby hand and blew against her palm, and she rewarded his efforts with a chuckle. Chris watched them, her eyes soft with love. He was such a fantastic father.

She reached out and brushed an insect from his arm, then looked down at him questioningly. "Did you finish drafting up the proposal for the construction of the new building?"

This was one project both of them were very involved in. Since David's final return from Central America, Maria had been given full responsibility for the operation of the orphanages LaFontaine sponsored, and on her request the company was building a larger facility to house the ever-growing number of homeless children. Both Chris and David dedicated much of their time and energy to the program, but Maria's enthusiastic letters compensated them for their efforts. Since her involvement with the project, Chris had developed a deep admiration and respect for the woman. Maria was completely dedicated to her mission.

"Yeah, I did. But the board of directors are going to howl bloody murder when they see the figures."

Chris grinned. "Let them howl. It's only money."

David laughed. "I'll tell them that when they start throwing fits."

The boys came racing up, and both flopped down on the blanket by their father. Tim caught one of the baby's hands and gave it a little shake. "Hi, Cath. Whatcha doing?"

"She's drooling all over me, is what she's doing," said David. "Hand me that dry diaper, would you, Tim, so I can wipe her face."

Timmy handed it to his father and said, "When are grandma and grandpa going to get here?"

Stretching her legs out in front of her, Chris braced her arms slightly behind her to support her weight. She and David were going to spend three or four days cruising around the island, and the senior Spencers were coming to stay with the kids. Chris was looking so forward to those few days away— just the two of them. "Grandma said she thought they'd be here sometime this afternoon." She gave both boys a stern look. "And you guys had better behave while we're gone, or so help me. . . ."

"Ah, come on, mom. We're always good for grandma," protested Mark as he rolled over onto his stomach.

"Sure you are," she responded with an utter lack of conviction.

Mark grinned at her. "We are!"

"Can we have some lunch?" interjected Tim as he lay on his back, absently watching the clouds drifting by.

"I suppose that could be arranged." Chris stood up and brushed the dried grass off her bare legs.

Timmy took his little sister from his father and held her with practiced ease. "Come on, Cath, let's go."

Mark scrambled up and they all started ambling back toward the cabin. "Where are you and dad going when you take the boat out?"

Draping his arm around her shoulder, David grinned wickedly at Chris. "In search of utopia."

Mark gave his dad a skeptical look. "Are you talking silly again? I don't know what you're talking about."

David's voice had a provocative undercurrent as he tightened his arm around his wife. "As long as your mother knows what I'm talking about...."

He left the sentence hanging, and Chris laughed up at him. "Given enough time, I think I could figure it out."

"Parents!" snorted Mark. "A guy never knows what they're talking about!"

Chris slipped her arm around David's waist and rested her head against his shoulder, totally aware of his strong body moving against hers. She looked up and met his warm gaze, and his eyes sent her a heady silent message that ignited a profound happiness within her. She didn't have to go searching for her utopia. She had it all right here.

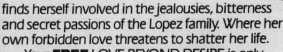